The Dead Queen

Thrones of Ruin, Book One

BRIAR KNIGHTLY

THE DEAD QUEEN

This book is a work of fiction. Names, characters, places, and incidents are the product of the author's imagination or are used fictitiously. Any resemblance to actual events, locales, or persons, living or dead, is coincidental.

Published by Fox & Thistle Press

Cover design by Damonza

eISBN: 979-8-9997857-0-1

ISBN (paperback): 979-8-9997857-1-8

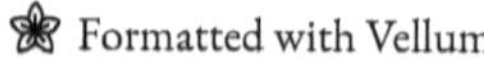

For those who believe dark tales
make the dawn burn brighter.

Part One

The Fox

CHAPTER 1

SOME DAYS, the power to heal feels more like a curse.

The soldier on the cot is young, maybe twenty, but already, he's seen more horror than any man should.

It takes all of my strength to push the saw through the thick sinew of his leg, above the point where dead tissue has taken root. Two healers hold him down while a third stands at his shoulders, whispering calming words even though he's fainted from shock.

Blood oozes like a bubbling spring around the saw. The bone resists beneath me, but it eventually gives way with a sickening crack just below the knee. I set the saw aside and wipe away the sweat dripping down my face.

But I'm not finished yet.

My hands tremble as I place them on the bleeding wound. I close my eyes, blocking everything out. The metallic scent of blood vanishes along with the dingy fabric of the medical tent.

In the quiet of my mind, I dig deep, searching for the spark of power inside my core. As I draw it out of its hiding place, the light moves through my veins like cool water. It spills out of my palms, knitting the soldier's torn muscle and severed skin back together. The power heals what's left of the leg so thoroughly it looks like there was never a limb there to begin with. But no matter how powerful a healer I may be, I can't cure dead flesh. It must be cut out. Otherwise, he'd still have the rest of his leg.

This is what it means to be the heir to the throne of Llwyn. By wielding the power to heal, I end up cutting people into pieces. Daily.

In Llwyn, anyone with noble blood can wield light and heal minor scrapes and bruises. Those with strong ability can ease physical pain or draw out infection, too. But only the royal family can perform extraordinary feats like this. Even though it isn't lost on me—nor anyone else, I'd wager—that I'm the only royal out here, dripping in our soldiers' blood.

One might accuse my family of being more like the northern kingdom of Annwyn than we'd prefer to admit. There, they embrace death, going so far as to bring people back from the grave, including their immortal queen. It's why Annwyn is known as the Kingdom of Corpses.

When I'm finished, I step back, breathless.

A healer in a blood-splattered apron nods to me out of respect. "Well done, Your Highness."

The title is jarring in this place of gore, but no matter how many times I ask the other healers to call me Sienna, they never do. They wouldn't dare.

I look down at my hands to see they're shaking. My white apron is dark and sticky with blood, but the wounded man will live another day. And with a proper prosthetic, he will fight for Llwyn another day as well. We need all the help we can get to keep Annwyn away from our northern border.

When I look around the healers' tent, it's clear that protection comes at a high cost. There are at least a dozen men and women lying on cots. They're the worst of the wounded, those for whom the other healers can do nothing. Many will die while they wait for aid.

A healer puts a hand on my shoulder. "You should go back to your quarters, Your Highness. If you exert yourself much more ..." She lets her sentence hang.

I'm risking burnout, she means. And maybe she's right. A quick glance at the clock tells me it's been nearly twenty-four hours since I last slept. If I overextend myself, my power will recede deep into my core. Then it could take days, maybe even weeks, to draw it back out. Even though the tent is overflowing with makeshift cots and bloodied rag bins, I know I can't take that risk.

And yet.

I bite down an ember of anger reserved for my father. Our ancestors possessed power far stronger than any other noble family in Llwyn. It's how we've held the throne for thousands of years. But you won't see my father, King Corsac, anywhere near this wasteland of an army camp. He wouldn't sully the hem of his lovely cloak with the blood of people who fight for our kingdom. My grandmother, Áine, did though. And so here I am, trying to make her proud of me, even after her death.

I give the healer a nod before heading out of the tent and into the cool moonlight.

It's quiet for a borderland outpost, no wounded troops returning at this hour. Nearly everyone is asleep. We've only been at this location for one week, but already the camp looks worn. I pass rows of barracks, spaced between well-trodden pathways like tidy stitches on a tapestry. Mud splatters the heavy canvas tents. Laundry lines hang from posts, each speckled with collections of socks, trousers, and underwear.

I wipe more blood off my hands as I walk toward my tent.

Guards in copper-plated armor appear out of nowhere to flank me. It frustrates me to no end that I'm shadowed like this, but no amount of begging will convince them to abandon me here on the edge of the world.

Trampled grass muffles our steps as we pass tent after tent filled with sleeping soldiers. Somewhere in the night, a man screams. A night terror, no doubt. Many soldiers are plagued by them. The undead creatures in the nearby battlefields are the stuff of nightmares, so I'm told. The Annwyn border is guarded by legions of bears, wolverines, and wolves, all brought back from the dead.

When we reach my tent, the lanterns inside are lit, even though I've been gone for an entire day and night. I give the nearest guard a questioning look, but he offers no sign that anything is wrong.

I sigh and try to push down the anxiety roiling in my gut. This could mean only one thing.

Inside the tent, a nervous-looking messenger awaits. When he spots me, he bows with as much grace as a newborn calf. He can't be over seventeen years old, likely a lower noble. He's dressed in the traditional copper livery of the Llwyn royal household. In his hands, he holds a letter sealed with crimson wax.

I'd recognize that enormous seal anywhere. It's my own, after all. A red fox, the symbol of the royal family.

The messenger's eyes grow wide as he gets a proper look at me. Perhaps it's seeing the elusive heir in the flesh. Or maybe it's the gore soaking my clothes. His face grows paler by the second. So, it's the blood, then.

"They've finally done it, haven't they?" I ask the messenger.

Before he can respond, I turn to the washbasin in the corner of my tent. It's simple and practical, no different from any other here in the borderlands. If the basin's dented metal is good enough for the soldiers, it's good enough for me.

After washing the dried blood from around my fingernails, I remove my apron to hide the worst of the gore. I tuck some of the stray strands of hair back into my braid. It's caked in sweat and filth. Still, the longer I delay, the longer I can put off the inevitable.

A deep sigh escapes me. I've always known they'd drag me home, eventually. Me, the harebrained, foolish, stubborn heir. They've called me all of it, and worse.

Just like her grandmother, Father always said, as if it's an insult.

The sting of grief is so poignant it takes my breath away. It still feels like yesterday that we lost Grandmother to Annwyn's corpse wolves. Logically, I know it's been much longer than that, but tell that to a broken heart. Tell that to the little girl who lost her best friend. Tell that to the heir who's had no answers, no explanation for twelve damnable years. A heart cannot heal from death. Even we mighty royals know that.

I splash tepid water on my face to chase away the grief.

Somewhat cleaner now, I look into the small cracked mirror above the basin. Doubtless, the messenger expected an heir of great beauty and refinement. Instead, water drips over my round cheeks, which are flushed with exhaustion. My brown eyes have purple rims, and my family's trademark auburn hair bursts from my untidy braid in a frizzy halo.

This is it. The heir of Llwyn. I can do nothing to change that.

I turn to the messenger and hold out my hand for the letter. When he passes it over, I bite back a few choice words. This man is not to blame; someone sent him here to confront the king's rebellious, backwards daughter. The one who ran away three years ago to use the royal family's birthright, our healing powers, for war. It's better than being locked up in a gilded tower to fester until my father deigns to die and give me the Fox Throne.

The messenger bows, awaiting instruction. I crack the seal and unfold the paper to find only three words from my father.

"Come back. Now."

Chapter 2

WITH MY FATHER, THE WORD "NOW" is meant to be taken literally. There's no delaying until morning. No taking my time to help one last wounded soldier, or even to sleep away the exhaustion nipping at my bones. Now means now.

By the anxious expression on the messenger's face, I know he's secretly praying that I'll leave without a fuss. Part of me wants to give him a show, something that he could tell his friends about back home.

"The heir threw her scalpel at me! She screamed and swore like a wild animal!"

But the truth is, while the stories about my rebellious nature aren't unfounded, the specifics are mostly untrue. I'd prefer to sneak out of a political meeting to read a book than cause chaos and disorder. Not that my father ever saw the difference.

I groan and look longingly at my bed.

It doesn't take long to pack my belongings. I learned to travel light, moving camp every few months, whenever the soldiers gained back lost territory. Everything fits in a satchel over my shoulder, just a few soiled dresses and my grandmother's silver knife. It's heavier than it looks, with its bronze handle and dainty moth carvings along the blade. Some might call it a frivolous weapon fit only for courtly fashion, but I take great pains to keep the blade polished and sharp. It's all I have left of my grandmother.

The last time I saw her she'd pressed it into my hands with a warning: *Keep it safe*. The next day, she travelled here, to the borderlands. She never came back. Even then, as a child, I understood she was trying to tell me something important. It's why I spent the next twelve years learning how to use the moth blade. And it's why I know, deep in my bones, that Grandmother's death was no accident.

Everything else in my tent can stay behind. I won't need any of it in Caerwen, the capital city, and home of the royal seat. They'll strip me of everything short of my dignity. I'll be primped, scrubbed, and stuffed into ridiculous gowns—all for the glory of the kingdom.

Truth be told, I won't miss the camp's endless mud and inadequate latrines. It's been nearly three years since I've had a proper bath, with warm water and lavender perfume instead of cold water from a rain barrel with lye soap. And I certainly won't miss the constant presence of death that I've grown numb to. Without me, the healers will have to rely on basic apothecary and medical skills. There aren't many nobles with healing power in the borderlands.

It won't be enough. Then again, neither was I. But at least here I was *something*, even if only a temporary plug in the hull of a sinking ship.

Still, as much as I hate the thought of returning to my father's palace in Caerwen, I know I'm ready to go home. When I was a child, no one would tell me what happened to my grandmother, Áine. This time will be different. This time, I *will* discover the truth. I'm twenty-four now. Older. Smarter. More determined.

And when I find out what happened to her, I *will* make the person responsible suffer. Just like I've suffered every day since she died.

My horse, Nell, whinnies as I strap bags of food and water to her saddle. She's a smart one. She knows we're in for a long ride. Her eyes roll warily from the messenger to the two guards he brought for protection on the road.

I lean in and whisper into her soft ear. "I'm sorry, Nell. We have no choice." I, like everyone in Llwyn, exist to serve my father.

Nell nuzzles her nose into my hand in understanding.

With one last look toward the darkened tents, I swing up onto the saddle. I won't waste time with messy goodbyes. When the other healers and the soldiers realize I'm gone, they'll know why. Frankly, I'm surprised it's taken this long.

We ride off into the night, escorted by the copper-clad guards. The messenger gallops ahead with an arm extended, using his power to light the way. A golden orb leads our path.

"We are the light in the darkness," my family always says. No matter how much we disagree on other fronts, I can't argue with *that* after what I've witnessed in the borderlands. I've seen the pain and death that darkness brings. The Dead Queen must be stopped from taking more territory from Llwyn.

Only light can heal what darkness fades, and we must protect ourselves in any way we can.

My hand reaches toward my thigh where the silver blade hides beneath my skirts.

The guards, messenger, and I ride through the trampled fields at the edge of Llwyn territory and into the dark forest. The road here is empty of troops on their way to and from camp. I've ridden it many times, but never at night.

My eyes strain toward the trees, searching for signs of fae. It's silly, I know. The fae were killed off over five hundred years ago. Now they're nothing more than bedtime stories to be told to mischievous children. Still, I listen for signs of them—faint music in the night, tiny flickers of light, footprints left along the path. There's nothing.

The messenger's light casts an eerie glow on the gnarled trees as we pass. Small creatures scurry further into the darkness, spooked by our horses' stomping hooves. But not all the creatures run away. The prickle on the back of my neck tells me something watches us from the shadows where our light can't reach.

Far ahead, something quick as lightning dashes across the path. It's too fast to make out, but the horses notice it and they snort in protest. Nell tries to stop, to turn around, but that's the worst thing to do with a potential predator in the woods. The quick prey is the prey that survives.

I pat her neck and whisper in her ear, promising treats once we're out of the woods. She settles somewhat, but I can still feel her heart beating through her sweating skin. The messenger keeps looking behind us, his eyes wide, and the guards' hands grip their reins tighter.

With a click of his tongue, the messenger urges us to move faster. I can't help but agree. The sooner we're out of the forest, the sooner we'll be safe.

Branches rustle behind us, loud enough to be heard above pounding hooves. I glance back just in time to glimpse a massive, gray animal darting back into the safety of the darkened trees.

My heart ricochets through my chest. It can't be. There are no wolves in the forests of Llwyn. We pushed them beyond the border generations ago, hunted them near to extinction. I tell myself it's just my mind playing tricks on me. No one else seems to have seen it. Their eyes remain fixed on the road ahead and the darkness just beyond our orb of light.

While my eyes scan the shadows and trees whirring past,

Nell pulls to a stop so suddenly I nearly topple off her. I quickly pull myself back up and see she's not the only frantic horse. All four buck in alarm, each of the riders scrambling to gain control. Nell lifts her front hooves and kicks as if at an invisible enemy.

My heart races with fear. I don't know what to do other than hold on. I use all of my strength to stay seated, but it's not enough. I tumble to the ground, landing on my shoulder with a sickening pop.

Light flashes behind my eyes. The pain in my shoulder is nauseating, but even if I *could* heal myself, there's no time.

Everywhere I look, hooves kick and stomp. I roll just in time to avoid being trampled by a guard's horse. The animal is wild with fear. The whites of his eyes are showing, his breathing unnaturally fast, and he's starting to foam at the mouth.

My eyes scan the forest's edge, trying to find what's frightened them so badly, but I don't see anything. Shadows dance from the messenger's light as he tries to regain control of his horse. I hold up my hand, igniting my own golden glow, but there's nothing. Just darkened trees and brush along an empty dirt road.

Ignoring the pain in my shoulder, I scramble to my feet. I attempt to grab Nell's reins, to get her under control, but I'm next to useless with an injured arm. She snorts, kicks, and eventually turns to run back toward camp.

"Nell!" I try to call her back, but she won't listen to me.

She speeds away, back toward the camp. Then, quick as a flash, something large and black pounces from the forest, tackling her into the trees on the other side of the road.

My heartbeat thumps in my ears as panic rises in me like a building storm. Nothing in Llwyn is big or powerful enough to tackle a full-grown horse like that. Nothing natural, that is.

"No," I whisper. It can't be. They don't dare travel into Llwyn territory.

"Run!" I yell to the three men.

Their heads turn toward me in alarm. Their horses are still bucking, fear-crazed and panicked.

"Corpse wolves!" I scream.

I only pause for a moment to pull my grandmother's knife out from under my skirts. It won't do much to protect me from the giant undead creatures hunting us, but it's better than nothing. I bolt as fast as I can in the opposite direction from where I hear Nell screaming in pain in the distant trees. There is nothing I can do to save her.

The guards have gained some control of their horses, but the young messenger is still struggling to stay in his saddle. His horse bucks and kicks, snorting in panic.

The corpse wolf emerges from the woods where it just feasted on Nell. In the dim light, I see its luminescent white eyes and muzzle covered in blood. I force down a wave of grief and nausea at the sight. The creature's teeth poke through rotting holes in its face. It's larger than any living wolf should be, as if reanimation stretched its knobby joints beyond their former capacity. Fur hangs from its emaciated ribs, exposing cracked bones and black muscle. It has no use for food. When this creature hunts, it's just to kill.

We lock eyes for one long moment before it leaps forward, running at full speed. I brace myself for death, but I only feel the whoosh of wind as it leaps past me.

In the span of a second, it jumps at the messenger, knocking him from the back of his horse. The messenger barely has time to scream before the corpse wolf grabs his face with its gnarled teeth and tears it clean off. Then, the creature goes for his chest. The messenger lies still, blood pooling in the dirt road.

I run.

When I near the two guards on horseback, I reach for them with my good arm. One stretches a hand toward me. In a single, swift motion, he pulls me up behind his saddle. I wrap my arms around his waist, desperate to hang on, ignoring the pain in my shoulder. The guard pushes the horse forward as I turn my head to watch the carnage in the road.

When the corpse wolf is barely visible through the stretch of my light, it looks up. Its white eyes watch me as we round a bend in the road.

I face forward, trying to banish the memory of the messenger's gruesome death, far worse than anything I've ever encountered in the camp hospital. This is what those poor soldiers have been fighting in the borderlands. This is what we're up against.

And it's only *one* of the Dead Queen's beasts. There are so many more to fear.

The guard I'm holding is mumbling to himself. "This isn't right. They aren't supposed to be here!" His voice is high-pitched, hysterical.

It's *not* right. Corpse beasts *aren't* supposed to pass beyond the Annwyn border, but they obviously have. This fight isn't about protecting our border from the Kingdom of Death anymore. Now, it's about getting the Dead Queen's rabid corpses out of Llwyn.

Chapter 3

We stop at the first town we find after our run-in with the corpse wolves. The locals watch us warily from behind shuttered windows. There aren't any healers here, so one guard mercifully helps pop my dislocated shoulder back into place. The pain and bruising will go away with time.

We don't stay long. After a fretful sleep and a bowl of lukewarm porridge, we purchase another horse and ride off before the townspeople grow brave enough to ask questions. Like why I'm covered in mud and nursing a sore shoulder. Or why a twenty-four-year-old woman is being escorted through the kingdom by armored guards.

The news of the corpse wolves will have to stay quiet until I can tell Father myself.

It takes three hot, miserable weeks to reach the capital city of Caerwen using the main roads. Not long enough. Not when the destination is home.

The grand, copper-plated gate shimmers like a mirage in the late-summer heat. As we draw nearer, it looms impossibly tall over the dusty road. It's an entrance worthy of the kingdom's wealthiest citizens, protecting them and their riches from the outside world.

As we pass through Caerwen's famous market, vendors call for our attention. They buzz about stalls bursting with produce, handmade earthenware, and sumptuous textiles. Enormous, steaming pots of rice smell of spices and herbs.

"Fresh figs from the southern orchards!" one cries. "Silk smooth as a lover's touch!" yells another.

Their stalls form a labyrinth of treasures, from pyramids of sun-ripened fruit to glittering jewelry that catches the light. Bolts of fabric shimmer alongside threads made from the finest fibers. I'd almost forgotten how many colors there are in the world after years in the muddy borderlands.

Even so, Caerwen's true nature lingers around the edges of the market, like the gray haze around a white cloud. As we pass darkened alleys, men rut against women with vacant eyes, and drunkards piss against the stone walls. Guards watch for pickpockets and beggars alike, to keep the "rats" away from the market.

From seemingly nowhere, my father's King's Guard materializes. They move with practiced efficiency, falling into formation around us without a word. Their presence parts the crowd like sharp shears through silk.

Of course my father already knows I'm in the city. He knows everything. So much has changed in my three-year absence and yet so much remains the same.

Their copper-plated armor glints in the sunlight, like the shells of iridescent beetles. I'd once asked my father why our family's color was copper. He'd stilled and said, "Because copper is the color of a fox. Thus, it is the color of the family that sits on the Fox Throne."

Of course, that wasn't good enough for me. "But why make your men wear copper-plated bronze, when everyone knows iron and steel are stronger?"

He'd narrowed his eyes and said, "Because a Fox Soldier does not *need* stronger armor. Their training is strength enough."

And that was that. The Fox King isn't the sort of father that suffers the ignorant questions of a child.

All around me, the market chaos fades as people notice the King's Guard and recognize me. Whispers ripple through the crowd.

"The heir," they murmur, their eyes wide. Some bow, while others shrink back, unsure what to do in the presence of the most notorious royal in the kingdom.

I keep my gaze forward, fighting the urge to deflate under their scrutiny. The weight of my return settles over me, as tangible as the humid air that clings to my skin. With each step toward the palace, I feel my borderland life slipping away.

When we arrive at the stables, I dismount with as much grace as I can muster. My thighs burn from days in the saddle and my rear feels bruised, but I won't grimace. I won't give any of my father's thugs the satisfaction of knowing my discomfort.

Grooms rush forward to take the reins of our horses in calloused hands. Chickens with rust-colored feathers scatter in panicked bursts, narrowly avoiding the path of hooves and mud-caked boots. The air is thick with the pungent mixture of horse sweat, fresh hay, and manure. It's a welcome mess compared to the blood-soaked tents of the borderlands.

I hear the heavy footsteps of someone walking toward me. My heart sinks as I straighten my posture to face my father, but it isn't who I expect. I do a double-take.

A tall, blond man around my age grins down at me. His copper-plated armor makes him look like some prince from the fairytale books I used to love as a child. A knight in shining armor in the midst of the grimy stable yard.

"Hunter?" I ask, the name catching in my throat. All

chaos seems to fade into the background for a moment. I'm suddenly acutely aware of how disgusting I am. My cloak, once a deep forest green, is splattered with days-worth of mud. The pungent mix of horse and sweat make me smell no better than the pigs in the sty just outside the stables.

Hunter surprises me by lifting me up into an enormous hug, spinning me quite literally off my feet.

"You're crushing me!" I laugh.

He sets me down, but keeps his hands on my waist. "Sienna. Sienna. Sienna." He won't stop grinning. It's a handsome grin, I'll give him that.

"I hardly recognized you," I lie. Gone is the gawky boy who used to hide away with me in the library. This man is two feet taller and at least twice as broad. His windswept hair glints like gold in the sunlight, but I'd recognize those warm, brown eyes anywhere.

"I have no idea what you're talking about!" he says, joking. His voice is deeper than I remember, more man than boy now.

My eyes drift down to the armor. The last time I saw him, he refused to join his father in the King's Guard, now he's dressed head to toe in copper.

I raise an eyebrow. "So ...?"

"It's different."

"That's an understatement." I bite my lip, not sure if too much time has passed for me to ask all the questions flooding my brain right now.

He grimaces. "You're wondering what the hell happened to me."

I nod. "You could say that."

Hunter shrugs, causing his armor to clang slightly.

"It's just," I start. "Your father ..."

"He won," he says, with only a touch of bitterness. "In the end, he always gets his way."

I really could have guessed as much, from the look of him, but it hurts to hear all the same.

"Fathers tend to have that effect on people," I say.

He nods.

I remember when we used to hide in the royal library to escape our fathers. Given that I'm the one who ran away, I have no right to feel a pang of nostalgia for our youth, but I do. We'd spend days hiding in the darkest aisles with only the glow of our own light to read by. I'd lose myself in the histories of Llwyn, reading about my ancestors who ruled with immense strength and power. Power that has since diluted in our bloodline, much to my father's disappointment.

Hunter always preferred stories with dashing knights saving lovely damsels, but he never thought he could be one. His father, Commander Malen, was one of my father's most trusted advisors. Still is, I assume. He was always the fastest, the strongest, the smartest man in any room.

He never let Hunter live it down that he, well, wasn't.

A blush creeps up Hunter's neck, staining his cheeks pink. "It's ... after you left, I ..." Hunter's voice falters, and for a moment, I see a flicker of the boy I knew—uncertain, abashed.

Suddenly, I'm confronted with all the damage I left behind. All the hurt I must've caused him is just below the shiny surface. The air feels thick, charged with unspoken accusations and apologies. We stand there, two strangers wearing the faces of old friends, not entirely sure how we ended up here.

"It's ok. I'm here now." I put my hand on his tall shoulder. "You can tell me all about it when the time is right."

His smile returns. I forgot how much I missed that good-natured grin. As different as Hunter may be from the boy I remember before I left, that, at least, is the same.

Hunter nods toward the palace door. "Are you ready?" he asks, his brows furrowed.

"Am I being summoned already?"

He gives me a knowing look.

Behind us, a horse whinnies and kicks a stall door. I flinch. The sound makes me think of the corpse wolves, of Nell's final shrieks echoing through the darkened woods, and of the horrible news I have to deliver to my father.

I sigh, resigned. "I'm glad he sent you to drag me to his chambers instead of one of his thugs."

Hunter's grin wavers slightly and I realize my mistake. When we were young, we used that term for the King's Guard, the knights appointed to protect the royal family and do my father's bidding. Only now he's one of them.

"Sorry," I say, flushing. "Old habit."

He lets me off the hook. "I get it. And ..." He stops me with a gentle hand on my arm. "I'm glad you're back. Truly."

I just nod because I'm not sure that *I* am.

We walk forward, memory guiding me down the familiar path. Hunter pivots toward the servants' halls, understanding that I don't want to be seen by the entire court yet. I'm sure the nobles would have fits if the heir traipsed through the great hall smelling of horse and looking like crumpled laundry.

I'm thankful for this small mercy. It gives me a few more minutes to gather courage to face them all, the people I ran out on three years ago without a word of explanation. I grimace, thinking of all their nosey questions and judgmental glances. But first, I must face my father, the Fox King.

Each step echoes like a countdown. My mind races, replaying a lifetime of lectures. I can almost see the familiar lines of disappointment etched into his face. My father spent my entire life complaining about me—wishing, out loud, that he'd had more than just one miserable child. That way, he could take away my birthright and give it to another, more responsible heir.

I remember standing before him countless times as a child, my chin high, tears threatening but never falling. I'd tell him I wish the same, because I don't want the throne. I never did.

After those fights, I'd always find Grandmother waiting for me, arms wide. I'd cry on her shoulder until the storm passed. She'd dry my eyes and give me that mischievous smile I loved so much.

"Come, Sienna," she'd say. "Let's have an adventure." And just like that, the world would right itself again.

We'd sneak through secret passages, our giggles muffled by cupped hands as we pilfered sweets from the kitchens. Under the cover of darkness, we'd dash across the moonlit grounds, our nightclothes billowing behind us like ghostly wings. Sometimes, in the dead of night, we'd slip into the throne room, its cavernous space feeling magical in the dim light.

Perched on the ancient throne, we'd dream up what sort of future we wished for Llwyn. One without war, she'd always say. And in the deepest, most secret part of my heart, I'd wish for a kingdom without my father. A world where the crown didn't loom over me like an executioner's axe. A future where I could just be Sienna. Not the heir, not the disappointment, just ... me.

In front of me, Hunter pokes his head through a hidden doorway designed to keep the servants out of sight.

"There's no one in the hall," he says, turning back to me. "Are you ready for this?"

I groan. "Never. But let's get it over with." I straighten, lifting my chin. I may not be the heir my father wanted, but I'm the only one he has. And this time, I'm not running away. Not while I still need answers about Grandmother.

Hunter steps out first, and I follow him into a corridor bathed in ethereal light. Tall, arched windows line one side, sunlight streaming through their leaded panes. The air here is different, still and heavy with the weight of history. It smells of aged wood, cool stone, and scented hair powders left in the wake of passing nobles.

Enormous family portraits hang in gilded frames along the opposite wall. They depict generations of great Fox rulers who've fought the Dead Queen for the past five centuries. They stare out from their canvas prisons with cold eyes. They're men and women with high collars and higher expectations. The famous auburn hair of our family blazes like dying embers in the slanting sunlight.

Predictably, my father's is the largest portrait of all. The most imposing. As in life.

Even here, captured in oils, his presence is suffocating.

I pause in front of a portrait of my mother, who died in childbirth. She looks down at us with an expression I can only describe as worried. The artist did nothing to hide the crease between her eyebrows or the slight downturn at the corner of her mouth. Her dark eyes are distant, as if she's thinking troubling thoughts.

"You look like her," Hunter says.

"Except for my auburn hair."

He nods.

As if on instinct, my eyes scan the hall for Grandmother's portrait, even though I know it isn't here anymore.

"That's because Áine isn't a royal," my father said when I pestered him about it. "She was little more than a commoner."

But I know that's not true. She had more power than Father likes to let on. Especially with the people who weren't nobles. After she died, everyone told me how sorry they were to lose her, from the bakers to the chambermaids. And they meant it. People loved her. The entire city was in mourning. All except for Father, who barely tolerated her.

My hand hovers over the silver moth blade hidden beneath my skirts.

Keep it safe.

I will. And, I'll find out what really happened to Grandmother.

Hunter steps up beside me and his natural calm eases my tension. He knows the roiling emotions in my heart. After all, it's how we met. Two motherless children, thrown together to comfort each other while the adults moved on. Grandmother took us under her wing, understanding full well that we needed each other as much as we needed her.

"Come," he says. "It's best not to keep the Fox King waiting."

Reluctantly, I tear my eyes away from my mother to face the guards stationed outside the king's grand doorway. I take a deep, steadying breath.

Without a word, the guards open the doors to let us in.

Inside the room, a fire roars in the enormous hearth, its flames crackling. The stone mantle is a masterpiece of craftsmanship. Foxes, our family's emblem, are carved into it with exquisite detail. In the firelight, they seem to come alive as they run, leap, and hunt across the stone.

My father stands in front of the fire.

For one long moment, we stare at each other. He looks just as unsettled by my changes after three years as I feel about his. His famous auburn hair has gone gray and his once-muscular frame has thinned. He seems diminished. Shadows emphasize new lines and hollows in his cheeks. They map his face like rivers on parchment.

Could the past three years have been as hard for him as they were for me? I doubt it.

One might think that after three years without a word to each other, a father and daughter would have a lot to say, but we don't. We just stare, the fire crackling behind us. The gulf between us was impassible even before I left. The years have done nothing to create a new bridge.

My father speaks first.

"Sienna," he says, the name echoing in the cavernous room, "it's been a long time."

It's not the opening I was expecting. I'm more used to tirades and bulldozing into long lists of disappointments, but I'm glad the tension is broken.

The large door opens behind us. Commander Malen walks in, the heels of his boots clicking on the stone floor. He hasn't aged a day since I last saw him. He's handsome, in a sharp, angled way. Stoic and cold. Nothing like his son.

My eyes drift to Hunter, where he waits silently by the door. Even from a distance, I can sense his unease in the presence of his father.

"My apologies, Your Highness," Commander Malen says. "I came as soon as I could."

Irritation rises in my chest. He's still the intruding overeager supplicant I remember him to be.

"I have urgent news," I say, unwilling to let Malen usurp this meeting.

My father looks puzzled. "Wasn't *I* the one who sent for *you*?"

"Yes, but you need to act quickly." My eyes dart to Commander Malen and I hesitate. I don't trust that man, never have. He stares at me with a pleasant expression on his face, letting me know he's comfortable in my father's presence in a way I've never been.

My father sighs as if I've disappointed him already. "Go on."

"We were attacked on the road. By corpse wolves." I watch his face closely for a reaction. He gives me none. "They've crossed into Llwyn territory."

The king's face remains impassive, but Malen's isn't. A small smile blooms at the corner of his insufferable mouth.

My heart sinks. "You knew ..." I start, but Father interrupts me.

"Of course, I knew." His voice is sharp. "Why do you think I had you sent back here?"

This hadn't crossed my mind. My father fetching me for protection? After three years of silence, it feels like a lie.

I bite my lip, chastened. A veil of mistrust settles over my heart. Just like old times.

Father walks toward me. Behind us, Hunter shifts. I'd nearly forgotten he was here.

"Your Highness," Hunter says. "Would you like me to leave?" Something in his voice sounds odd. Not afraid or mistrustful, but anxious?

Out of the corner of my eye, I see Commander Malen give his son a firm, subtle head shake.

I turn to look at Hunter. His face tells me all I need to know. He's never been good at keeping secrets from me, and right now his eyes are telling me there's more to my father's summons.

"No," my father says. "Stay. You should be here for this."

Alarm shoots up my spine.

"I don't ..." I begin to protest, but my father speaks over me.

"You're here to fulfill your duty to this kingdom, Daughter. Your duty as heir."

I watch the king closely, searching for hidden clues. "Duty" is a complicated word with him. Anything could be painted to be one's duty.

He reaches for a goblet and takes a long drink, eyeing me. Anticipating protest, no doubt.

I keep my voice calm. "And what, may I ask, is my *duty*?"

His eyes dart to Hunter's. My stomach drops with dread.

"Marriage."

I balk.

"Marriage?"

"Yes, that's what I said. Don't repeat me, Sienna." He takes another sip from the goblet in his hand.

Hunter flushes with embarrassment, his neck and cheeks turning a fiery red. Commander Malen looks smug.

No. He couldn't mean … "Hunter?" I ask, already knowing the answer.

"Everything has already been arranged, so do us all a favor and withhold your protests."

"But why?"

"There's no need to insult the man, Sienna. He's the best choice for this kingdom."

Behind him, Malen nods. That conniving, sneaky, overreaching … I refuse to be one of their pawns. Fury climbs up my spine, making the power in my sternum flare.

"He's from a rich family and the son of one of your favorite advisors, you mean."

"That's enough!" Father bangs the goblet onto the table. That's the angry face I know so well. His eyes narrow and his lips grow thin.

I glare at Hunter, who at least has the decency to look chagrined, like a child dressed up in play armor.

Father clears his throat. "I'd hoped that after your adventures, you'd be a little more accommodating. A little more respectful."

"Adventures?" My eyes widen with disbelief. "You call healing dying men at the border an *adventure*? Have you ever even been there? Have you even seen—"

He stomps back toward the roaring fire, waving a hand dismissively.

"It doesn't matter what you call your absence. The fact is, things have changed since you've been gone. Not the least of which is the stability of this kingdom." He lays a tightly clenched fist on the stone of the hearth. This is his tell. The thing he does when I know I've truly gotten under his skin: clenched fists.

He continues, "We need to give the people something to look forward to. We need to give them hope in the face of what's to come."

The corpse wolves, he means. Increasing war efforts against Annwyn.

"I am to be a martyr to the cause."

He laughs lowly, incredulous. "Call it whatever you want, dear daughter. As long as you don't put up a fuss." He takes another slow drink, then gives me a long look. "Your kingdom needs you."

"I—"

He looks back toward the fire. "I have very little patience with you, Sienna. Don't give me more of a headache today than I already have."

My mouth snaps shut. He's never had patience with me. Three years haven't changed that much.

Almost as an afterthought, he adds, "There will be an engagement celebration at the end of the week."

He knew the Dead Queen's unnatural army has been sneaking past our borders. And he wants to cover it up with parties and cakes.

I can't help myself. I scoff. He ignores me, preferring to stare into the flames. I look between him, Malen, and Hunter. I can't decide who I'm more upset with. Hunter's eyes plead with me to understand. To be accommodating.

To hell with being accommodating. I whirl around and march out of the room, slamming the door behind me.

Chapter 4

My old rooms are just as I left them three years ago. My fingers trail along the silk bedspread, cool and smooth to the touch. But the linens smell fresh, as if someone changed them in anticipation of my return.

When I open the carved wardrobe, its hinges creak. Inside, new gowns hang in orderly rows, a rainbow of rich fabrics and intricate embroidery. They're beautiful, yet impractical compared to the simple clothes I've grown accustomed to. Dresses this elaborate take weeks to sew.

Clearly, even the tailors knew I was coming home before I did.

I take my time washing and dressing into a court-appropriate gown. The skirts hang heavy, the fabric itchy and stiff against my skin. This is attire for a woman of leisure, not the working healer I've become. Nothing fits quite right, but it'll have to do. The sleeves are too tight around my shoulders and the bodice threatens to rip at its delicate seams if I bend too far. I've grown stronger from my years in the borderlands. Hard labor does that.

With a deep, steadying breath, I leave the sanctuary of my quarters.

Palace corridors stretch before me, a gauntlet of curious eyes and hushed whispers. Sunlight streams through the windows, casting long shadows across the polished stone floor. As I walk by stunned nobles, I nod politely, feigning nonchalance. From the corner of my eye, I see walking parties slow to a halt, their conversations dying mid-sentence.

The heir has returned.

My long copper skirts whisper against the stone floors as I pass, keeping my chin up and my eyes forward. I may as well let them all stare and get the shock over with. Soon, they'll hear of my engagement, then they'll have new gossip to entertain them.

I just want to go back to my old habit of hiding in the library while the nobles wonder what's wrong with me. The heir who detests her court.

I wish I could explain that I don't loathe them. It's everything else here. The parties, the gossip, the petty problems of the wealthy. The superficiality of it all. The allure of the castle intoxicates everyone. Everyone except me, the one person stationed to inherit it when the time comes.

When I reach the safety of the royal library, the tension melts from my shoulders like spring snow. I take a deep breath, drawing in the familiar scent of aged parchment and leather bindings.

Bookshelves line every wall. Their dark wood stretches toward cathedral ceilings so high they seem to touch the sky. Light glows from gilded sconces, creating a maze of shadows and illumination. The aisles of books extend so far they could be mistaken for a labyrinth.

The silence is welcome. Few nobles ever venture here, preferring the noise and glitter of social gatherings to the quiet of books.

I take my time reacquainting myself with the tall stacks, my fingers trailing along the book spines as I weave down the aisles. My footsteps echo softly against the marble floor.

In the distance, I hear the muffled rumble of wheels, likely a librarian pushing a cart. As the sound nears, an elderly man in brown robes turns down my aisle. I look up to greet him and he freezes mid step, nearly tumbling into his overflowing cart. His face pales as if he's seen a ghost.

"Sorry, to startle you," I say.

He closes his eyes and puts a hand to his chest. "No, Your Highness. It's just, for a moment, I thought you were your grandmother." A relieved smile brightens his face. "You look so much like Áine."

This small compliment takes me by surprise. In the court's hostility, I rarely expect to encounter kindness.

"Thank you," I whisper.

He nods. With quiet efficiency, he resumes his task, the soft creak of the cart's wheels fading as he disappears around a corner.

It seems I'm not the only one who still remembers my grandmother.

She used to tell me stories of the great deeds my ancestors did with our light and healing powers. My family inspired entire armies to fight against the northern Wolves, the Dead Queen's most gifted warriors. My great-great-grandfather lit the midnight sky to high noon for surprise attacks in our ancestral lands. Before I was born, my paternal grandfather famously survived the Kiss of Death from the Dead Queen herself—proof that light and life are stronger than darkness and death.

"Light power is inherently good," Grandmother always said. "You can never use it to harm." Unlike the corpse-makers in Annwyn, whose power is dark—raising the dead, manifesting shadows, and inflicting pain. This is why our kingdoms are forever at odds. Well, that and the fact that they keep moving into our ancestral lands. It's why my family has been fighting the Dead Queen for centuries.

Only now my father just sits in our gilded palace and plays war games with other people's lives. Like our citizens are nothing but living, breathing pawns in a morbid chess match. If you throw enough peasants at the corpse beasts along the northern border, you'll keep them too busy to attack the wealthy cities further south.

I'm no fool. I know my impending marriage is just another of my father's strategies. The real question is, to what end? How far is he willing to go to distract people from the threat lingering in the north? The same threat my grandfather fought, and his father before him. There's a long line of powerful, ferocious Fox Kings who've protected the Llwyn Kingdom from the Dead Queen and her corpse army.

This engagement shouldn't feel like a death sentence, but it does. I'm not ready for marriage. Especially not one that's foisted upon me.

Slow, steady footsteps echo along the library floor. I don't need to turn to know who it is.

"I thought I'd find you here," Hunter says.

I spin to face him. He's leaning against a bookshelf, rubbing his upper arm. It's an anxious habit he's had for years. He's changed out of his copper-plated armor and now looks more like himself, or at least like the Hunter I remember. His simple white tunic and brown breeches show the court's superficiality hasn't *completely* consumed him.

Then I look down at my gown with its cinched, silken skirts and realize I'm no better. Not that I have much choice over my clothes now that I'm back. Even less so as an heir about to be married.

"I'm sorry," he says, keeping his voice quiet so it doesn't

echo down the aisle. "I didn't mean for you to find out like this."

I close my eyes and hold in a breath. As much as I know this isn't his fault, it still hurts. I still feel trapped. Used.

"I know."

When I open my eyes again, he's giving me a familiar look. "Kind eyes" I used to call them.

"You look nice," he says. "Though I miss the smell of horse."

I snort. I can't help it. He knows me well.

He moves closer, closer than anyone else would dare, but this is Hunter, my dearest friend. And, if I'm going to be honest with myself, my old love. His closeness both comforts and tortures me at the same time.

I sigh. "Hunter, I ..." but I can't go down that road. It's a dangerous path. Instead, I look up into his brown eyes.

He waits, patient as always.

"How could you have let them blindside me like that?" I ask, all anger at him now depleted, like an empty waterskin. "Why didn't you tell me about the engagement the second I arrived?"

He reaches out to take my hand in his. I let him, my skin tingling at his touch. The familiarity feels both strange and thrilling after three years with no friends, no comfort, no touch. No one to confide in. At the borderlands, there was work to distract me from emotions. And more work. I learned to cut off any feelings of isolation or longing. I learned to not want companionship. Not to desire the warmth of someone else's skin on mine.

When you need to go without, it's best not to want. It's best not to need anything. Or anyone.

Hunter swallows hard, and his eyes drift down to our hands.

"I was just truly happy to see you, Sienna." He runs his

thumb over my knuckles lightly. "When you first saw me, your face lit up, like old times. I didn't want to ruin that. I hoped you'd remember what we had once. Before..." He shrugs. "I didn't want to be the one to disappoint you again."

And there it is. The "Before". I can see it now, the guilt that plays around the corners of his brown eyes. He betrayed me once. We have never been the same since.

I bite my lip. As much as I wish I'd had some warning, I can understand Hunter's reluctance to be the bearer of bad news.

He bends forward to catch my eyes.

"And, really, is this so bad?" His face is filled with timid hope.

My hand feels warm in his, and I can't decide if it's from our shared power or the heat that he used to ignite in me. Maybe some embers remain, buried deep beneath the scarred coals in my heart. The thought both thrills and terrifies me.

For a moment, I let myself wonder if my initial reaction to the engagement was just my usual rebellious response to my father. Maybe this could be something good. Maybe Hunter and I could rebuild what we once had, but stronger than before. The image of a shared future flashes through my mind —laughter, warmth, belonging.

But then reality hits me, cold and unforgiving. I remember why I came back here. This time, I'm going to find out what happened to Grandmother. Why she was in the borderlands. Why she never came back. I *won't* let my father keep his secrets. I can't allow Hunter or a royal wedding to distract me. There's no peace in domesticity for me, not when I still have so many unanswered questions.

Not when I suspect that Grandmother's death was no accident.

"I'm sorry, Hunter." I shake my head. "This isn't what I wanted. For either of us."

"What if it's what *I* want?" He asks softly. "What if this could be something truly great? You and me, like old times."

I can't do this. I can't marry someone of my father's choosing, no matter who the groom is. No matter that I feel the long-forgotten softening in my heart for a boy who understood me like no one else could.

I stiffen and take my hand away from his.

"Sienna, it's been three years. Haven't you punished me enough?" The pain in his voice takes me by surprise.

"Hunter, I didn't leave to punish you."

"Then why?" His voice has lost its earnestness now. He takes several steps back, bumping into the bookshelf. "Why did you abandon me here with *them*? Why else if not for what I did?"

My voice catches in my throat. He watches my face intently.

The truth is, as much as I loved Hunter—as much as I still love him—he broke my trust. He shattered my heart into a million pieces. I ran away because I had nothing left to lose.

He puts his hands on a high shelf and rests his forehead against the books, his eyes closed. He takes several slow breaths.

"I have hated myself every single day since you left." He stands up again to face me. "And I promise you, Sienna, that I will *never* betray you again." There's a fire in his eyes that I've never seen before.

He kneels down in front of me.

"No, Hunter ..." I try to pull him back up, but he takes my hands in his. I notice now that there are tears in his eyes.

Tears of guilt.

"Please forgive me, Sienna. We can move past this." He pauses. "It's been so long. We're both older, more mature. I know what matters now. Do you?"

Yes, I want to say. I do. But it's not him.

"It's us," he insists. "*We* matter, Sienna. You and me. We've always been what matters most. I forgot that once, but I vow to you, I will never forget that again."

I search his eyes, trying to find some way to convince him that his priorities may have changed, but mine haven't. I can't just ignore what happened to Grandmother. *That's* what's most important to me. And I can't hunt down her killer if I'm expected to be a docile bride.

Yet, I also know that father's decisions are final. I'll have to marry Hunter whether I want to or not. My life will be forfeited. I'll be sent to some remote fortress with my new husband, to live a domestic life away from the hustle of the Fox Court. Father will expect me to be an obedient wife and birth future Fox Heirs.

Goodbye, independence. Goodbye, freedom to search the kingdom for answers. Goodbye, Grandmother. For good this time.

But I won't go down without a fight.

I nod. It's as good an agreement as any to Hunter. He leaps up and spins me around again, like he did out in the stable yard. His good-nature is restored, like a tempest blown over.

I can't help but laugh at his renewed enthusiasm. That's the thing about Hunter. He's always been able to make me smile. And there are certainly worse qualities to have in a husband than that.

Chapter 5

"It's tradition," a seamstress says between a mouthful of pins when she sees my wide, horrified eyes staring through the gilded mirror.

I hate everything about this dress, from its enormous, cumbersome skirts to the fact that the royal tailors have clearly been working on it for weeks—long before I even knew I was engaged to be married. Most of all, I hate its color. A deep, seductive red.

"It's lucky," the seamstress says as she tugs the sleeve down my arm, smoothing out any wrinkles in the sheer fabric. "It means your marriage is blessed. That you will have many heirs."

"A litter of tiny red foxes," a pink-cheeked assistant giggles from behind us. She sifts through an ornate cabinet filled with buttons, clasps, and other fastenings. Mother-of-pearl, polished wood, and precious metals gleam from open drawers.

It takes great effort to keep from rolling my eyes. My own parents wore red from their engagement party through to the royal wedding, too. The color did nothing for their yield. All they got was me. One scrubby fox from hell.

Around us, bolts of fabric line the walls, arranged by color. Silks from distant lands shimmer like liquid jewels, while velvets in rich tones beg to be touched. Gossamer-thin chiffons and intricate laces are draped artfully over tables, to better display their patterns.

In one corner, a collection of dress forms stand at attention, each bearing a masterpiece. Half-finished gowns sparkle with partially sewn beadwork and glint with golden embroidery. They are undoubtedly beautiful. They just feel deeply wrong after what I've seen these past few years.

The seamstress waves for her assistant to hurry with the needle and thread. With only one day to spare before the engagement ball, we couldn't cut this last-minute fitting any shorter if we tried. She places a final pin in the hem of my sleeve.

"Ouch!" I flinch, pulling my arm away from her. A small drop of blood wells up at my wrist.

The seamstress looks horrified. She covers her mouth with her hands. "Your Highness, I am so sorry. Please forgive me!"

"It's fine." I wipe the spot away with my thumb. "It's nothing."

From the way the women's eyes dart toward each other, I know they don't believe it's nothing.

It's an omen, they're thinking.

Blood spilled before the wedding is bad luck. Like wearing the color red is supposed to be good luck. Never mind that I'd been performing amputations and healing gaping wounds for weeks before I even knew I was engaged. Superstitions are not logical in that way.

I hold out my arm for her to finish. She picks up silver shears with ornately carved handles to snip the ends of her thread. When she's done, she places it in a silk-lined box alongside golden thimbles inlaid with tiny precious gems and delicate crystal-tipped pins.

When the hem is secured, the women step back. They analyze every inch of me, from the high collar to the floor-length overskirt. I catch a glimpse in the gilded mirror. I look frightful, like a vengeful spirit here to curse the family. My grimace does nothing to dispel the illusion.

The seamstress must see my tension. She places a hand on my arm. "Your grandmother would be proud."

I know she means well, so I give her a smile. Still, deep down, I know she's wrong. My grandmother wouldn't be any happier with this arrangement than I am.

"Are we finished?" I ask, trying not to sound too eager. I have things to do today, on my last day of freedom.

The seamstress and her assistant help lift the gown up over my head as I wiggle out from underneath the tulle.

I make a quiet escape out the door while they fret over the proper way to remove the minuscule wrinkles I made in the fabric.

The palace is humming with preparations. Everyone seems to be infected with a sense of urgency. Everywhere I turn, there's a flurry of activity.

Decorators balance on tall ladders as they hang lush garlands. Along the grand staircase, more workers weave ribbons through the carved banisters. They create elaborate patterns that cascade down the steps like a frozen waterfall of royal copper and cream.

As I pass the kitchens, the air is heavy with the aroma of roasting meats and baking bread. Pots and pans clang like discordant bells, punctuated by the sharp commands of the head cook. A small army of kitchen boys toil over mountains of candelabras and ornate platters, their polishing cloths moving as quickly as a moth's wings.

Maids scurry up and down the halls, their arms full of fresh linens and downy pillows. They dart in and out of long-empty guest chambers, leaving behind the crisp scents of lavender and lemon. They dash past me, their faces flushed and eyes wide with a mixture of excitement and barely contained panic.

Clearly, I'm not the only one Father neglected to give an appropriate amount of notice for the engagement ball.

It's nearly noon, so I quicken my pace, knowing that father is about to break from his morning audience with his advisors. My heart races, partly from the brisk walk and partly from anticipation. I need to catch him in a good mood, before the stress of the day puts me at a disadvantage.

But when I arrive at the massive oak doors of the audience chamber, I'm left disappointed. The room is empty save for a few lingering nobles engaged in hushed conversations. They've already recessed for the afternoon.

A clerk emerges, his thin arms straining under the weight of papers and ink pots. His robes, once crisp, are now rumpled from hours of note-taking. He looks mildly alarmed when I approach, his eyes widening in recognition.

"I'm looking for my father."

He swallows hard, his large Adam's apple bobbing on his neck.

"The hounds," he says, his voice barely above a whisper. He nearly drops his papers in his haste to escape my presence.

Of course. I should have known. King Corsac cares more about his hounds than any natural person should. His obsession with those beasts borders on ridiculous, but right now, it's a blessing in disguise. At least I know where to find him.

I gather my skirts, the silk rustling as I bunch it in my hands, and break into a run. My soft leather shoes fall silent on the stone floors as I race for the nearest exit. Nobles gasp, startled, when I run past them, but I don't care.

I loathe the kennels. Calling my father's pets "hounds" is like calling the corpse wolves Pomeranians. The creatures are an unnatural species of fox, bred for centuries to be the most cunning, vicious versions of their kind.

The gate squeals like a dying animal as I open it to the underground staircase that leads to the kennels. This part of the castle used to be a prison before they built newer cells in the city. It's damp and dark down there, the air thick with the stench of decay and despair. Father prefers it this way. He says it makes the foxes more eager to please when he drags them out into the light for hunts.

Chitters and animal screams echo up the staircase long before I reach the corridor at the bottom. It's black as midnight down here, so I draw upon my light power. A small golden orb lights my path. Thick iron chains hang from the walls, rusty with age and what might be dried blood. I have to watch my step to keep my slippered feet dry from the puddles that pepper the ground,their surfaces slick with an oily film.

The smell of the kennel is overwhelming. Every breath makes me choke. Piss, feces, rotting meat—all mixed together in damp darkness. The stench seems to seep into my skin, and I know I'll be scrubbing for hours to rid myself of it.

My eyes glance warily through the iron bars of the cells on either side of the passageway. The foxhounds hiss and growl at me with hackles raised. They'd look like any normal fox if it weren't for the unmistakable feralness of them. Their dark orange fur is matted and covered in filth. Their copper, bloodshot eyes follow me with no fear in them at all. They stare me down as I pass.

Above the din, I hear my father's voice, a low, commanding rumble that sends shivers down my spine.

"Stay!" he commands. "Stay!"

Deep in the kennels, I see the glow of his light as it flickers against the crumbling stone walls.

I find him in an open chamber, a dead hare held out in one hand. Its glazed eyes stare accusingly at nothing. One of his foxhounds bares its teeth, revealing rows of needle-sharp fangs. The animal shrieks as it leaps into the air, a sound more befitting a demon than any earthly creature. The chain attached to the iron collar around its neck stretches taut, causing it to fall back to the ground with a meaty thud. Its long claws scratch at the stone ground as it rights itself again while keeping a wary eye on my father.

Father chuckles lowly, then throws the hare carcass toward the other end of the room. The foxhound stays low to the ground as it skitters toward the meal, moving with an unsettling, spider-like gait. I can see its ribs through its patchy, copper fur, and its skin is marked with scars and sores.

Father has always been fond of starving creatures into submission.

The king spots me and turns reluctantly from his plaything.

"Don't you have wedding preparations to entertain you?" His voice sounds irritated.

"I daresay the wedding planners have it under control."

He laughs humorlessly. "And here I always thought brides wanted to have some say in their flower arrangements and cakes and other such frivolities."

"If it's all so frivolous," I ask. "Why have an engagement ball at all?"

His eyes grow dark, unamused. "Don't start with me."

I resolve to change my attitude. I won't get the information I need by goading him.

Father picks up the bucket at his feet. It's overflowing with more limp hares. I follow him out of the room. He slams the iron door closed with a resounding clang that reverberates through my bones. The lock clicks into place as he turns a heavy key.

At the next door, he slides open a small hole. The metal scrapes against its frame with a screech that sets my teeth on edge. He stuffs a dead hare through the gap, its fur matted with congealed blood. On the other side of the door, nails scratch the stone ground as the foxhound grasps its meal. The frenzied sounds of tearing flesh and crunching bone fill the air, along with low, feral growls.

"I've been wanting to speak with you," I say, willing my voice to sound calm. Pleasant. Like my father prefers his women. It's difficult to keep a feminine, delicate air amid the oppressive stench and darkness, but I do my best.

"I gathered as much since you're standing here, watching me like a gaping piglet." He grabs another hare from the bucket.

My face flares and I bite my tongue so hard I taste blood. "Now that I've agreed to a hasty wedding for the sake of your subjects—"

"Which is your duty as heir," he interjects.

I grit my teeth. "Now that I'm doing my *duty*, I'd hoped we could discuss Grandmother."

He stills, hare carcass in hand. "What about her?"

My heart is beating rabbit-fast in my chest. "What happened to her."

He slams the pail down and whirls back around to glare at me. A dead hare trembles in his hand as he speaks. "I thought we'd finished discussing Áine when you left."

The hare's black, shining eyes stare at me from my father's fist. A smear of dark blood drips from its nose.

I stand my ground. "As I recall, it was never finished."

There's a long pause as my father studies me. "I didn't call you back here from the edge of the kingdom to have you disobey me again. Áine is not open for discussion."

"But I deserve to know—"

"You deserve nothing!" He yells, his voice echoing off the stone walls. Foxhounds scream and howl in response. The noise bounces off the inside of my skull, where a monstrous headache is brewing.

I realize I'm not breathing, so I force a steady breath, sucking in the putrid air.

"Your grandmother died in the borderlands," he says, his words tight and threatening as a bowstring. "If you *must* have someone to blame, blame the Dead Queen." He takes a few even steps toward me.

I hold my ground, refusing to move backward out of intimidation.

"But let me make one thing clear." His cool composure has returned. "We are *finished* chasing tails around the base of that tree. Do you understand me, Little Fox?"

Angry tears prick at my eyes, but I refuse to let them fall. Reluctantly, I nod.

"Good." He stuffs the hare between the bars of a nearby door. The animal inside lets out a yelp. We listen to it tear the carcass to shreds.

"If I hear that you've been asking around about your grandmother again, you will regret it." He puts a hand on my shoulder and squeezes, hard. It's a good thing that my engagement gown has sleeves. His grip will leave a mark.

He leans in toward my ear. The smell of his meaty lunch makes me turn my face away.

"Now, be a good heir. Smile at your party. Make your husband-to-be happy. And give the kingdom something to look forward to." He removes his hand and turns from me.

It takes everything I have not to scratch his face with my perfectly buffered nails. The darkness in his eyes tells me he won't budge. My hands clench at my sides as I turn from him, leaving without further argument. He'll never tell me what happened to Grandmother in the borderlands. I'll have to find my answers somewhere else.

I walk back up the damp stairwell and out into the

sunlight. The sudden brightness is almost painful after the gloom of the underground, and I squint against the glare.

When I'm far enough away from the kennels, I lean against the wall of an outbuilding. It's a potter's shed, by the look of it. A greenish film of grime covers the windows, but the wooden shelves are still visible within. They're filled with different sized pottery and sacks of soil.

The rough stone of the wall scrapes against my palms as I push against it, willing the rising fury to ease. There was a time when my father's cruelty made me crumble. When it made me sob into my grandmother's arms and complain about the injustice of having a king as a father. But now ... I get angry. Very angry.

All the awful memories from my youth pool back into the forefront of my mind, as vivid and terrifying as if no time had passed. The helplessness, the fear, the anger—they wash over me in waves, threatening to drag me under. I close my eyes and push the intruding thoughts aside, mustering my strength.

I should've known better than to come back here.

Beyond the potter's shed, nobles speckle the palace gardens. They're walking and gossiping without a care in the world, like they've never spent even a moment contemplating the war at the border. Or the villagers whom King Corsac sends there to die horrible deaths for our benefit.

There's a small group of women laughing, their voices light and carefree as they bend to sniff the late-autumn rose bushes. Their dresses are pastels in tones of lavender, pink, and blue. All except for one, a woman with silver-blond hair, who stands out in the traditional hues of the royal family—cream with copper accents.

I watch her from a distance, wondering how that woman has the gall to wear the royal colors without being related to the royal family. It's a fashion choice punishable by death.

She steps around the bushes and two things become immediately apparent.

First, I know her. She's Hunter's cousin, Elena. A once-shy girl a little older than I am.

And, second, she is pregnant. Very pregnant. A copper bow rests upon her distended stomach.

I'm not related to her, but I'd be willing to bet that I am related to the baby in her belly.

Chapter 6

Music and laughter leak from the great hall, traveling down the marble corridor to where I wait, dressed head to toe in a scarlet gown. The sound is ethereal, almost ghostly, as it echoes off the gray stone walls. Everyone is here for the biggest party in decades. It may be in my honor, but I feel very much like a lamb destined for slaughter.

One of my two guards taps his foot to the music. The soft clink of his armor keeps time with the distant melody. I wonder if he resents being stuck out here with me while everyone else is inside, partaking in the festivities. We're waiting for the music to change, the signal that it's time to prepare for my grand entrance. That it's time to "meet" my royal fiancé on the dance floor. Never mind that I've known Hunter since we were children. I suppose that's a luxury previous generations didn't have.

I try to plaster a smile to my face, but it's still difficult. I'm horribly distracted, as if I'm not really here. All I can think about is Grandmother and how she should be here for this day. How I'm still no closer to finding the answers I need.

Time is running out.

The music slows and the tempo shifts like the tide. The guards at my side straighten. It's time.

Reluctantly, I walk toward the closed doors that lead into the great hall. My heart flutters in my chest like a caged bird and the edges of my vision darken, threatening to pull me under. Wouldn't that be a surprise to the guests? An heir, lying unconscious on the ground in a pretty dress.

But when the music stops and the doors open, there's no time to daydream about an unconscious escape. The sudden silence is deafening, broken only by the collective intake of breath from the assembled crowd.

Hundreds of eyes watch me from behind black masks, a sea of faceless observers dressed as spider webs, peacocks, celestial beings, and even hens. This, too, is tradition. Everyone at the ball dressed as something else. All in midnight black, with masks to make the engaged couple stand out all the more.

Not that the simple color palate stopped the revelers from sparing any expense. Silks rustle, feathers tremble with each movement, and onyx jewels catch the light. Everything is dyed black, from the finest fabrics to the powdered hair arranged with sparkling pins.

Crystal chandeliers glow overhead, making all the jewels in the room sparkle. The effect is disorienting, like stepping into a dream world of black ice and starlight, until I see him. Hunter is standing at the opposite end of the hall. He's staring at me with a comfortable smile that seems to cut through the cloud of cold, calculating faces.

We are in this together, his expression says.

While some part of me is still angry, I find it impossible to blame him. None of this is his fault. As we stare at each other from across the ballroom, my irritation slips away like melting snow on a spring day. The only way through this storm is together.

The crowd parts as Hunter makes his way toward me. He

holds out his hand and I take it, grateful for a life raft in this sea of black-clad vipers. He leans in close, his warm brown eyes on mine.

"We can do this, Sienna." His voice is low and reassuring as he squeezes my hand. He steps through the crowd, leading me to the center of the dance floor with surprising grace.

Hunter places one hand on my waist, and it's a small relief to feel it trembling. I'm not the only one terrified under the gaze of a hundred eyes. He puts on a convincing performance, his back straight and his chin held high, but I can sense the nervous energy coursing through him.

The music starts up again, a haunting melody that seems to float through the air. Hunter leads me into the traditional marriage dance. My skirts swirl around us, a vibrant splash of scarlet against the night-black sea.

Our audience becomes a glittering blur as their masked faces meld into a dizzying kaleidoscope of black and silver. Eventually, the guests join in, their attention shifting away from us, like snowflakes blown away in a flurry—all except for one.

Hunter spins me again and my eyes land on a young man standing against a pillar, half in shadow. He's tall with dark hair. His black tunic has silver buttons running up to his high collar.

I don't recognize him as one of the other nobles around my age, which means he must be from outside the city of Caerwen. He watches me with undisguised curiosity. As our eyes meet, a shiver runs down my spine. He lifts his mask up to his face. It's a wolf with black fur, carved and adorned with tiny teardrop accents that glint in the light.

Hunter spins me again, the movement fluid and graceful. The room blurs once more, a whirl of midnight and candlelight. When I regain my bearings and look back to the pillar, the wolf is gone.

"You look unbelievably beautiful," Hunter whispers into my ear, breaking my distraction.

His warm breath on my neck makes me shiver. "You look nice, too."

He chuckles, moving me expertly through the dance. "Nice? That's all I get after hours of being poked and prodded by a half dozen tailors? These shoes alone have caused more pain than the training courtyard ever did."

I look down at his stiff red shoes. "Well, those are quite spectacular."

"Ah," he nods. "The shoes get higher praise than I do. I understand, they are remarkable ... or so the cobbler told me."

I smile, my anxiety easing away, like stepping into a warm bath.

A nearby couple bumps into us. They're dressed as a pair of black swans. They stumble, mumbling drunken apologies before they spin away.

"Sienna," Hunter says quietly, his voice barely audible above the swelling music. "I hope we can be friends again. More than friends. I want you to know that I plan to make you the happiest wife in the kingdom."

I laugh at the playfulness in his eyes. "That's a big promise for someone who has no idea what makes women happy."

He places one hand over his heart like my barb stuck true. "You misunderstand me, cruel one," he says, his voice low with a hint of desire. "Not women, plural. You. Specifically." He pulls me close, our bodies pressing together. The warmth of his chest seeps through the layers of crimson fabric between us. "I will make it my business to learn exactly what makes *you* happy, Sienna."

My heart flutters in my chest. I seem to have forgotten how to breathe. I laugh it off, taking a modest step back. "I look forward to watching you try."

He smiles wickedly. This is a different Hunter from the

one I remember. A brave Hunter, a confident Hunter. I'm not entirely sure what to expect from this new man in an old friend's body, but I'm excited to find out.

With a sudden movement, he grabs my waist, and we spin around the dance floor. My heavy skirts billow out around us, giving us extra momentum. The fabric catches the light, shimmering like liquid fire as we move. People around us chuckle at the youthful addition to the choreography.

Hunter nods at one man, who applauds in appreciation. My cheeks are flushed, and not just from the dancing. The air around us seems charged with electricity as Hunter returns us to the traditional steps. Our bodies move in perfect synchronization, as if we've been dancing together all our lives.

"In all seriousness," he says. "I think it would do us some good to give the people what they want."

"And what's that?" I raise an eyebrow.

"A gorgeously romantic royal love story."

I laugh so hard I snort. A nearby couple smirks at me.

Hunter leans toward them. "Isn't my betrothed charming?" He winks.

The man stutters as if he doesn't know how to respond to a royal couple. Hunter saves them by whisking me away to another part of the dance floor.

"Smooth," I say, somewhat breathless.

"So, what do you say?" he asks.

"To what?"

"To my romantic proposal."

"Your romantic proposal to be romantic?"

"Exactly."

My stomach is aflutter. Am I flirting with my longtime childhood friend-turned fiancé? I suppose I am. But ...

"If we're going to be friends again," I say. "If we're going to make an honest try for this ..." I'm not sure what to call it. Forced marriage? Friendship turned more than friendship?

Hunter nods. "This once in a lifetime love story that will make everyone jealous. Mhm, yes, please go on."

I roll my eyes and he pulls me a little closer.

"If we're going to put on a show of the greatest romance in a century, then I'm going to need one teeny-tiny favor." I hold my fingers up and make a pinching sign.

"Oh?" He spins me and the suddenness takes me by surprise. A genuine giggle escapes my throat.

Nearby couples give each other knowing glances as Hunter spins me back toward his chest.

I look deep into his eyes. "Then I'm going to need you to cover for me."

"Cover?" His eyebrows pull together in brief confusion. "As in, offer a distraction? What for, darling?"

"Subterfuge."

He dips me low, his mouth is a whisper away from my lips. "I'd love to."

He pulls me back up to my feet. "I think I'll need something from you, too. To make this convincing." He holds one of my hands as we glide forward in formation with the other dancers.

"And what's that?" I ask as we bring our bodies back together.

"A kiss."

I lift an eyebrow. "Are you bribing me for affection, Hunter? That doesn't seem like you."

"Not at all, darling." He does a silly spin himself. I cover a laugh with my hand like a polite court lady. He returns to grab my waist. "It's all a part of the illusion."

"Hmm ..." I try to smother my grin. "I suppose if it's for the cause."

"Oh, I assure you, it is." He nods earnestly. "But it will have to look convincing." He adds, as if an afterthought.

"I think I can handle that."

The song ends, its final notes lingering in the air. While everyone claps politely, I pull Hunter toward me, catching him off guard. The sudden movement causes a ripple of surprise through the nearby crowd. Dozens of black masks tilt in our direction.

I throw my arms around Hunter's neck, the fabric of his crimson tunic smooth under my fingers. Without hesitation, I press my lips to his with as much conviction as I can muster. His scent envelops me, a heady mix of fresh linen, citrus, and something uniquely Hunter. It takes a moment for him to register what's happening, his body tense with surprise. But then he softens, melting into the kiss. He wraps one arm around my waist, pulling me closer, while the other tangles in my long auburn hair. The sensation sends goosebumps prickling along my skin.

The surrounding crowd grows quiet, the sudden hush falling over the ballroom like a blanket of snow. The only sounds are the soft rustle of fabric and the distant tinkling of crystal as chandeliers sway above us. It feels as though time has stopped. Like even the room is holding its breath.

Kissing Hunter is nothing like the daydreams I had when we were growing up. His mouth is sweet, with a hint of champagne, likely sipped to bolster his courage before the ball. His lips are soft, kissing me with a tenderness that takes my breath away. And his body is warm against mine, solid and reassuring.

This is easy, easier than I ever imagined. What started as performance for our audience slips into something unexpectedly very real.

The kiss feels like the home I've always longed for—comfortable and safe.

When he slowly pulls away, I'm almost disappointed. He's looking at me, his face in mild shock. Then he puts a hand to my cheek and smiles. The expression transforms him, making him look younger, more like the boy I grew up with.

All around us, I start to notice the quiet whispers and nervous giggles. The sound ripples through the crowd like a gentle breeze. I break my gaze away from him and meet the hundreds of eyes watching us from behind black masks. The array is dizzying—glittering black rams with curled horns, peacocks with intricate feathered designs, delicate hares with long ears, serene doves, and sinuous serpents. The entire animal kingdom seems to be represented, all dyed with midnight.

But what strikes me most is their expressions. They smile kindly, in a way they've never smiled at me before. I'm so used to being the scorned one. The regretful, rebellious heir. The mistake. I've never experienced outward approval like this. Not since Grandmother.

Hunter was right. The world loves a love story.

I look back at Hunter and he winks. Then he faints flat out on the dance floor.

Chapter 7

There's a panicked rush to help my lovesick fiancé off the ground. I'm pushed out of the way, clearly not the court's favorite partner in this fairytale couple. It's like being battered by a tornado of black sequins and feathers.

"Someone get him some punch!"

"Fetch a healer!"

"Help me carry him!"

I allow myself to be pressed into the back of the crowd, unnoticed. Then, I slip behind a tapestry and out the nearest servant's exit. The thick fabric muffles the sounds of the ball as I pass through, like stepping from one world into another.

My steps echo down the narrow hall lit by dusty lanterns. When I look behind me, I notice my red skirts are trailing silver glitter, like stars escaped from a celestial ball. I give my dress a good shake, watching as the glitter falls to the floor, then I continue on. There's not much time before I'll be missed. This could be my only chance to find the answers I need.

I tiptoe past the kitchens with their fires blazing, the heat radiating through the walls. Through a half-open door, I see tables filled with cakes and pastries ready to be brought into the great hall. Cooks' assistants rush to and from the enormous wash basins, picking up discarded bowls and stirring spoons wherever they find them.

Feeling lighter than I have any right to in this heavy dress, I dash up flights of stairs. I gather my skirts to avoid tripping on the stone steps that have been worn smooth by centuries of use. My breath comes in quick gasps, the corset restricting my lungs as I climb higher and higher.

Finally, I reach the door near Father's chambers. I peek my head out into the corridor, my heart pounding. Two bored-looking guards stand at the opposite end of the hall from his grand doorway, making it impossible to sneak in without them seeing me. This dress isn't exactly discreet. I close the servants' door, the latch clicking softly.

Then, it hits me. If my father has kept a mistress secret long enough for her to be visibly with child, then there must be another way inside his rooms. I continue down the dim servants' hall. The further I walk, the fewer sconces line the walls until there are none at all. I summon my golden light from the depths of my core, holding it outstretched in my hand like an offering. It's no help. The hallway is a dead end.

Frustration builds up inside me. I pause to think. Why would a hallway lead nowhere?

It wouldn't.

I drag my fingertips along the seams of the stones running next to my father's quarters, searching for any irregularity, any hint of a hidden passage. The stone is cold beneath my fingertips as I feel the rough surface. A few feet back from the dead end, I feel a slight shift in airflow along a dingy tapestry. The tapestry looks like it's been in this dank corridor for decades, if not centuries. I hold my hands just above the surface of the fabric. It's moving gently in an invisible current.

It's a doorway.

I push the fabric aside. Beyond a hidden doorway, there's a short, dark stairwell that leads to the back side of another tapestry. Light glows around its outer edges. I scramble up the steps, lifting my skirts so I don't trip.

The only light in my father's room comes from several lanterns along the walls and a low fire in the hearth. Their glow is muted, casting long shadows that dance and flicker across the ornate furnishings. It's also chilly. The air carries a crisp edge that raises goosebumps along my skin. When I look around, I realize where the breeze is coming from. One of his windows is open, allowing the cool night air inside.

I run to his writing desk. It's enormous, with dozens of drawers filled with paper and notebooks scattered about. I don't know what I'm looking for. Anything to do with Grandmother's death. A letter, a journal, or a notice of some kind. As king, my father would need to keep everything, preferably in some semblance of order, which these clearly are not. It slows me down considerably.

I move to a nearby cabinet. More papers are strewn about in front of it. Royal decrees. Minutes from important meetings. Notes from his lovers, their perfume lingering on the delicate paper.

Nothing about Áine. This was my last place to find clues, but there's nothing here. The realization settles like a weight in my stomach. I'll never learn what happened to her. I'll never know why I lost the person I love most in this world.

I can't help myself; I kick the cabinet in frustration. Then I scrape my hands over the desk, scattering papers everywhere in my fury. The sharp edge of a document cuts into my palm, but I barely notice the sting. The papers float to the ground, pale ghosts caught in a breeze from the open window.

It takes me far, far too long to realize the papers I'm digging through chaotically are in no particular order for a reason. They're mixed and wrinkled. My father is meticulous in everything. He would never leave his papers in such disarray.

Another cold breeze blows past me. The hairs on the back of my neck stand up.

The window.

I whirl around, taking stock of my surroundings, but there's no one here. My eyes scan every dark corner. The room is quiet.

"I know you're here," I say.

Nothing.

Is it possible the other intruder already left? Could I be so lucky?

No, I could not.

A figure dressed in black steps out from behind a bookshelf near the fireplace, a lazy smile plastered across his handsome face. Even without the wolf mask, I know it's the man from the ballroom. The stranger.

"I'm impressed, Red," he says, his deep voice calmer than it has any right to be given the situation. "Shouldn't you be enjoying your party?"

I step toward him, my heart pounding so loudly I'm sure he must hear it. I hold up my fists like I know the first thing about brawling.

"What are you doing in my father's chambers?"

He chuckles lowly. "I could ask you the same thing."

I take a long moment to get a better look at this wolf in sheep's clothing. His black suit is cut trim, showing off his tall, muscled frame. This is a man who is used to fighting. I'd never be able to outrun him, especially in this infernal dress. His eyes are curiously pale. Gray, I think. They stand in sharp contrast to his dark, windswept hair.

My power is useless in self-defense. My family's abilities are inherently good—heal the sick, ease their pain, and light the world. It doesn't cause harm, not even against a threat. I've never been so vulnerable. The realization settles like a weight in my stomach.

He watches curiously as I fumble with my skirts. I keep one eye on him in case of an attack, my gaze darting between his face and his hands. With trembling fingers, I pull out Grandmother's knife from where I keep it strapped to my thigh. I immediately feel stronger, more confident with the silver handle in my fist. *This* I know how to use.

He smirks. "Well, that was ... unexpected."

"Who sent you?" I demand, holding the silver blade out. "Was it my father? Why are you following me?"

He raises a dark eyebrow. "I was here first. One might say *you* are the one following *me*."

"Who are you?" I demand.

He studies me. The slight smirk at the corner of his mouth is infuriating.

I scowl. "It seems only fair since you obviously know who I am."

"Everyone knows who you are, Red. That's hardly of consequence."

"Stop calling me 'Red.'"

He gives my gown a clear once over. "How about 'Little Fox'? That's what my people call you, you know. The heir that the Fox King wants to rid himself of." He runs a hand over the stone foxes on the fireplace mantel, calm and unbothered.

Anger flares up inside of me, hot and fierce. "You don't know anything about me."

He cocks his head, a predatory gleam in his pale eyes. "No?"

I am so, so tired of people assuming they know me. Assuming they know my wishes, my dreams, my desires. Assuming that a pretty marriage to a pretty boy will solve all of my petty problems. Assuming that I will grow up and forget the trauma of losing the person I loved most in this world.

No one knows me. Not really.

He takes a few slow steps toward me. "I know that you have secrets. That you're not pleased to be dancing with your charming groom-to-be."

"Lucky guess." My voice wavers, betraying my unease.

He smiles, welcoming the challenge. "I know that you'd rather read histories than fairy tales, even though your life looks like one."

My breath catches in my throat, but I say nothing. Did he watch me in the library? The thought sends a chill down my spine.

When he's only a few feet away from me, I shift, keeping my back to the hidden exit in case I need to run.

"I know that you had a very special bond with someone who was taken away too soon."

I just glare at him.

"I know that she's the one who gave you that pretty knife."

My limbs grow cold.

We stare at each other for a long moment, but he breaks first. His eyes flicker toward the window, assessing if he could make it there in time.

It's all the opening I need. I run toward the window and slam it closed, then hold up my knife again. "What do you know of my grandmother?"

His expression changes, softens slightly. "Nothing I can say."

I rush toward him, pointing my knife at his chest. He doesn't even flinch, like he's unafraid of a little girl with a little knife. What he doesn't know is that I have a lifetime's worth of anger inside of me. And that is far more dangerous than the blade.

"Tell me," I growl. It's a threat, and he knows it.

"Don't push me," he says quietly. "I don't want to use this."

I'm not sure what he means until I notice something. His hands. They're held up for what I thought was self-defense. I was wrong.

A dark mist swirls around his palms.

I take several hurried steps back, my eyes wide. I've never seen shadow power before, but there's no mistaking it. Where my power appears as a golden light, his is dark. Threatening.

"You want to kill me?" I ask.

"No."

"Hurt me?"

"I don't want to."

Fury ignites inside of me. This man is a Wolf, one of the Dead Queen's most powerful knights. The Wolves of Annwyn lead enemy fighters at the border. They're nobles who wield the most lethal shadow power. They kill for the thrill of it. My mind spins with memories of the mangled bodies brought back from the borderlands. The corpse wolves in the forest. The centuries-long war with no end in sight. My grandmother's death.

I *hate* this man.

I rush at him, my knife slashing at his pretty face. He narrowly avoids me, his eyes widening in momentary surprise. I lunge for him again, but this time, he's prepared. He grabs me from behind, wrenching the knife out of my hands.

"You're one of them," I hiss. "One of the Dead Queen's Wolves." The mask he wore at the ball lies on the floor near the window. How did I not suspect? Our enemy was hiding in plain sight.

"Yes."

"Your people killed my grandmother!" Hot tears of anger sting my eyes.

"Yes," he says again, less forcefully.

He releases me and I spin around. The Wolf stares at me with a curious expression on his face. It's almost like he's sorry. But his regret means nothing to me. We face each other at a standoff for several long moments. Me, in front of the window. Him, alight by the fire.

"Tell me," I plead. This stranger knows more about my grandmother's death than I do. I'm at his mercy. And it sickens me.

He swallows, hard. "I can't."

That's when father's doors spill open. A guard shoots a crossbow right into the gray-eyed man's chest. His blood splatters across my face. I stare wide-eyed as he falls to the ground.

Chapter 8

The foxhounds whimper at the scent of blood.

I follow my father's guards as they drag the Wolf down into the old dungeons, his feet scraping against the rough stone steps. An orb of light follows us, casting eerie shadows. The guards throw the Wolf to the ground in an empty cell and lock iron chains around his hands and feet for good measure. The foxes in the cells on either side yip and growl, sensing a meal.

A guard slams the door closed and locks it. The sound echoes off the damp stone walls of the dungeon.

"We can't send him to the jail in town. The other prisoners will talk," one guard says, his voice hushed and tense.

My father's low voice echoes behind us. "How fortunate that he decided to visit while everyone else was distracted."

The guards rush to attention. King Corsac steps toward the cell, but his eyes remain on me, cold and calculating. I can feel the weight of his gaze, heavy with suspicion.

"How fortunate, again, that the bride-to-be is the one who found him." He pauses, giving me a distrustful glare. "In my rooms, no less."

Father reaches into his pocket and hands me a kerchief. "Clean that blood off your face," he says, nodding toward a bucket of water in the corner.

Reluctantly, I take the kerchief from his hand and dip it in the pail. The water inside is cold, with bits of dirt floating on top. I scrub my face raw, hoping to get it all off. The kerchief is stained pink when I pull it away.

My father turns to one guard. "Tell me what happened."

Before the guard can answer, a foxhound leaps against its cell door, the metal bars rattling with the force of its impact. It barks and screams to be let out. To be given a taste of the blood it smells in the nearby cell.

The guard nods. "Your Highness, we heard a commotion in your rooms, so we entered and found the heir cornered. We shot the intruder."

"And how did not one, but two people enter my quarters without notice?"

The guard looks sideways at his partner. "We're not sure, Your Highness, but the window was unlocked and the curtains thrown open."

My father eyes my enormous gown and no doubt thinks the same thing I do. There's no way I could have climbed through the window in this dress.

"He needs to be healed." I nod toward the cell door. Through the bars, I can see the man still hasn't moved from the ground. Blood seeps around him, making a dark puddle on the dirt floor. "He could die from that wound."

My father studies me. "Then it would be one less traitor in the world."

My face flushes with anger. "That's not our way. The people of Llwyn heal. The Wolves are the ones who kill."

He turns his body to face me. "What is this man to you?"

I realize that they have no idea who he is. What he can do. I'm the only one that knows this man is a Wolf. That he can wield shadow power. If the stories are true, he could kill us all where we stand, too. I hesitate, the knowledge on the tip of my tongue. If he survives, he may very well be able to escape. If he does, my answers flee with him.

I decide not to tell them.

My father narrows his eyes.

"Nothing," I say. "He's no one."

"A *no one* who found a way into my rooms with my heir at his side?"

"No," I shake my head. "Not at his side. I followed him, like I said."

"She had a knife pointed at his throat when we entered the rooms, Your Highness," a guard says. I silently thank him, but I can tell my father still isn't convinced.

"Out." The king gestures toward the exit. "If he survives the night, we'll put him to questioning. He's no use to us as he is."

I stiffen. If the man dies, then I won't get the answers he clearly has. My eyes dart between the man lying prone on the ground and the king.

My father is testing me, I realize. A test of my loyalty. A test of my story. Proof that I truly don't know this man. That he means nothing to me ... except he does. I don't even know his name, but right now, that dying man means everything to me. I can't let him bleed out.

Father narrows his eyes again. "I said, 'out.'"

The finality in his tone leaves no room for argument. The lights in the sconces flicker out as we pass, plunging the kennels into darkness. Foxhounds wheeze and pull against their metal chains to reach the fading light. To reach us. The heavy kennel door slams shut, leaving the dying man in pitch darkness.

As we walk further away from the old dungeon kennels, the screams of the foxhounds fade into a haunting memory.

Our footsteps crunch over the stone walkway that leads back to the palace entrance. The air is cool, carrying the scent of autumn to our doorsteps—fallen leaves, damp earth, and the promise of colder days to come. Up above, the night is clear. Thousands of stars speckle the sky, as if nothing out of the ordinary has happened. As if my entire world wasn't just knocked entirely off kilter.

I went into the king's chambers expecting to find answers, and I found them. Or, rather, I found out *who* has them.

The Wolves. The Dead Kingdom. The one place I can't go.

"A deceitful bride and a fainting groom," my father says with a note of false wonder. "What an interesting evening."

I say nothing.

"I know a liar when I see one, Daughter. I will find out what that man is to you."

"I've never seen him before in my life." A truth. Hopefully, my father will see it for what it is.

He pauses, halting our small procession. When he looks at me, his eyes are dark. "You *do* understand that our family has protected this kingdom from Annwyn, from the Dead Queen, for centuries, don't you?"

I swallow hard and nod.

"Then you know what's at stake if we lose this war."

I nod a second time.

"Good." He turns and continues down the path.

The massive palace doors creak open when we approach and the guards step aside. A wave of noise washes over us as laughter and music spill out from the great hall. The party is still in full swing, oblivious to the dark undercurrents that threaten to pull us under.

My father holds out his arm to escort me back to the great hall. It's the last thing I want to do right now, but I lace my arm through his. Duty and secrets are what this little family is good at, after all. I can paint my face into a pleasant smile and be the heir he needs me to be. For now, anyway. Just until I find the answers I need.

Before we walk into the ballroom, Father gives me one long, assessing look. Slowly, deliberately, he licks his thumb. The action is so unexpected that I almost flinch when he raises his hand to my face. His thumb scrapes across my temple, the touch unsettling.

"Blood," he says, his tone maddeningly casual, as if he's commenting on a speck of dirt or a stray hair. He shows me his thumb. There's a smear of crimson there, stark against his skin.

Maybe, to my father, this small amount of blood seems inconsequential. But I'm starting to wonder if the old superstitions are true—whether blood spilled before the wedding day is an omen. A harbinger of strife, of unions doomed to fail, of kingdoms torn apart.

My impending marriage to Hunter may very well be cursed.

Chapter 9

For the rest of the evening, I can't escape my father's eyes.

After rejoining my fainting fiancé, I scan the crowd for an opportunity to slip away, but it never comes up. The King's Guards seem to have tripled since the party began, their copper-colored armor speckles the ballroom like cinnamon on black tea. Their eyes, like my father's, never leave me, tracking my every move.

Hunter squeezes my hand as we dance. I miss several steps in a row before a troubled look crosses his face. He leans in close, his warm breath against my ear. "I take it you did something naughty while I pretended to be indisposed." There's a hint of amusement in his tone, but I can hear the underlying concern.

I shake my head slightly. To my relief, Hunter doesn't press further, though I can see the questions forming behind his eyes. No doubt he'll corner me tomorrow, when we're away from prying eyes.

When dawn breaks, most of the guests have dispersed. Those who remain are barely standing, drunk on wine and palace gossip. I grit my teeth and curtsey to my father. He nods, granting me permission to escape.

Hunter takes my hand and presses a chaste kiss to my knuckles. Several nearby nobles cuddle closer to their partners, as if Hunter's affection toward me is contagious. I play the part of a lovesick lady and feign a pretty blush. They can't see the growing darkness in my heart.

When Hunter looks up at me with those dark brown eyes, I see exhaustion etched into his face. I'm sure he's as relieved the night is over as I am, though you'd never know it to look at him. His pleasant smile never cracks.

As I leave, several guards step forward to follow me. It's hardly a surprise; I expected as much. I won't be able to go anywhere without these copper-colored shadows until the wedding.

The revelers are still dancing, drunk and sloppy, as I weave through the ballroom. When I step into the quiet dawn, the clawing need to escape eases. Once we reach the gardens beyond the great hall, I can finally breathe again.

The world is pale with twinkling, golden sunlight. As I walk through the grass on my way toward my rooms, my dress leaves a trail of disturbed dewdrops, like a paintbrush across a portrait.

My copper tails follow at a respectful distance. When I reach the sanctuary of my room, I pause at the threshold, turning to face them. Without a word, I close the heavy doors, shutting them out. They'll remain out in the hall until I emerge again. Their armor clanks as they shift beyond the door, settling in for a long wait. They assume I'm off to bed, like everyone else.

My dress is heavy, and the hem soaked. It's a struggle to unlace and take it off alone, but I don't want to call for servants. Finally, the gown sinks to the ground at my feet and I take a deep breath. My ribs ache from the structured corset, and all I want to do is fall into the plush bed to sleep. But I can't rest now. The Wolf in the kennels could be dead already, taking the answers to my questions along with him.

From the bottom of my wardrobe, I pull out the simple stained gown I wore in the borderlands. I knew better than to trust it to the maids, who no doubt would've thrown it into the fire. I washed it myself in the bath, then hung it to dry in front of the fireplace, just like I had back at the encampment. It's wrinkled and stained, but all the better to blend in.

After changing, I clamber out the window and down the thick wisteria vines that climb up the stone face of the palace. The old habit feels good, like I'm just a silly girl again, playing at rebellion just to spite my father.

The hood of my brown cloak hangs low over my face as I cross the castle grounds for the third time in less than a day. Near the stables, I dodge hungry chickens pecking at the worms in the dew-soaked ground. I grab two filthy pails filled with water from the well. The stable hands seem slow and groggy after their night of toasting my impending marriage. One of them winces when a horse bangs his stall door with an impatient kick, eager for his breakfast.

My arms tremble as I approach the thick wooden door of the kennels, and not just from the weight of the pails. The guards barely notice me at all. To them, I'm just a lowly servant girl, sent to clean the kennels. They open the doors for me without question.

I hurry inside, afraid one of them might recognize me, but why would they? The heir they know has beautiful gowns and walks with the confidence only the highest nobles possess. My auburn hair is tucked under my cloak and I'm dressed like a woman to be ignored.

The guards close the doors behind me with a deafening clang. The first foxhound hisses in the darkness. I mentally reach for my power, where it rests in my core. The glow of my light helps ease the growing panic, but the stench chokes me when I take a deep, steadying breath.

I hurry down into the depths, water splashing from the pails as I go. Foxhounds leap at the doors of their prisons, chains rattling. Above the noise, I don't hear any sounds from the dying man. I might be too late.

An enormous ring of keys hangs on a nearby hook, so I pull it down. They rattle in my hands as I search for the correct number to unlock the Wolf's door. When I open it, my light illuminates the shadows within. The man hasn't moved from where the guards tossed him last night. Iron shackles bind his hands and ankles where he lies in a pool of filth. His face is as pale as death.

When I kneel on the ground next to him, my knees sink into the putrid, bloody mud. My hand reaches out to touch his pale face. He's breathing, but just barely.

He's also warm. Too warm. Fever has set in.

With a start, I realize the arrow is still lodged in his chest. Miraculously, it missed his lungs and heart, otherwise, he'd have been dead hours ago. I take a deep breath and think. My power is next to useless with the weapon still lodged in his chest.

This is just like the borderlands, I tell myself. Except there, when a patient died, it was tragic, but it wasn't personal. I have to keep this man alive.

Since the arrow entered through his back, I need to remove it through the exit wound in his chest. I rip open his soiled shirt, exposing pale skin mottled with bruises and caked with dried blood. The arrow tip isn't sticking out far enough for me to grasp.

"I'm so sorry," I whisper, my voice barely audible over the restless shifting of the foxhounds in nearby cells. I pull the Wolf onto his side and reach behind him, feeling for the wooden shaft. It juts out several inches where the guard broke it off last night, rough and splintered.

I can't push it through with just my hands; I need leverage. My eyes dart around the bare cell, finding nothing useful. In desperation, I remove my shoe, testing its firm sole. It's far from ideal, but it's all I have.

Thankfully, the Wolf is unconscious. I take another steadying breath and press the sole of my shoe into the arrow shaft. Slowly, agonizingly, the tip emerges from his chest.

The Wolf lets out a bone-chilling groan that echoes off the stone walls. I stumble backward. My heart leaps into my throat. His face twists in pain and sweat prickles his pale forehead, but he isn't conscious. Gritting my teeth, I press the shoe harder. The shaft slides through until I can't push any further. With effort, I roll him onto his back, the arrow's tip now protruding upward like a macabre flag.

The scent of fresh blood sends the foxhounds into a frenzy. Their chains rattle in the nearby cells as they scramble to get closer. I try to block out the mental image of them slathering and drooling in hopes of fresh meat.

My hands shake as I grab the shaft below the arrowhead and pull up. Blood squelches out of the wound and the Wolf groans again, but thankfully doesn't move. As I work, I can't help but wonder if this brush with death will give the Wolf a new perspective on the powers his kind wield so carelessly.

I toss the blood-slicked arrow aside. Stumbling to one of the grimy buckets, I rinse my hands with water that's tinged with rust. Then I pour some over his wound, washing away gore and grime to better assess the damage. What I see makes my stomach churn. The flesh around the hole is dark with poisoned blood. The Wolf is nearly dead.

With great effort, I roll him onto his side again. Placing one hand on each of his open wounds, I focus and reach for the power that's deep inside me. A faint, ethereal glow pools in my palms, casting a soft light that dances across the rough stone walls. I guide my gift toward the Wolf, feeling the familiar tug of energy as I heal him.

This isn't so different from healing an amputated limb or soothing a fever gone too far. I draw out the impurities, knit flesh back to flesh. He's lucky that no organs were pierced. Exhaustion makes the edges of my vision fuzzy. It's never good to heal without proper rest, but we don't have that kind of time.

Finally, his flesh is mended. I check both sides to be sure, pouring water over them to clean the Wolf's skin as much as I can. The black veins of blood poisoning have vanished. There isn't even a bruise.

Rolling him onto his back, I take stock of my situation. I'm alone in a cage with a Wolf. A Wolf who has every right to hate me when he wakes up. Judging by the shadow power he used in my father's rooms, he could be a *very* powerful Annwyn noble. If he can make shadows, he could kill with little more than a glance. Or, so the stories are told. I've never actually met anyone from Annwyn. Even so, a strange calm settles over me. I'm not afraid to die.

I pick up the remaining pail and splash the water over the Wolf's face.

He wakes with a groggy start, water droplets clinging to his dark eyelashes and full lips. His eyes drift as he takes in his surroundings—the iron shackles, the damp stone walls, the faint light filtering through the sconces in the hall, the barred cell door, and the discarded, bloodied arrow on the floor. Eventually, his eyes land on me. He doesn't look as afraid as he should when he props himself up on his elbows. I'm relieved to notice his arms are trembling. Hopefully, that means he's too weak to kill me on the spot.

"I just saved your life." I hope I sound braver than I feel.

As if an afterthought, he reaches up to his chest, his

shackles rattling with the movement. He feels the spot where the arrow once pierced. Now there's nothing but a starburst-shaped scar.

He raises an eyebrow. "So you did." His voice is hoarse.

I cross my arms, defiant as always.

He stares at me for a long moment. "Aren't you afraid of me? Knowing what I am?"

I scoff. "Killing me wouldn't help your position, seeing that you're locked up in a cell."

"I wouldn't kill you."

"Says the natural killer."

"You don't know me." He coughs, wincing.

"I know enough."

He doesn't respond, just lies back on the ground with a groan.

"What? Tired?"

He closes his eyes. "Turns out nearly dying is hard work."

"Try healing someone who's nearly dead."

He opens one gray eye to look at me. "*You* healed me?"

I put one hand on my hip. "Who else do you think pulled that arrow out of your chest?"

He looks around, feigning bewilderment. "Oh, I don't know. *Anyone* but the Fox King's daughter? Seems a bit beneath you."

I glower at him. "Well, maybe I stooped so low for a reason. And as payment—"

He turns his head to look at me squarely. "You charge for your services?" He scoffs. "So much for the holier-than-thou Llwyns who help others selflessly."

"Don't speak that way about my people." My voice is low, threatening. Not that I could do anything to this man if he tried to hurt me. "My fee is answering some questions."

He lets out a low, humorless laugh that I almost don't hear above the snarling of the foxhounds.

My heart thrums in my chest. "What happened to my grandmother?"

He closes his eyes and sighs, as if I'm too much. After a few moments, he sits up again and juts his chin toward the door. "What are those things?"

I pause, listening to the awful sound of the beasts growling low, scratching stone, and rattling chains against iron collars.

"Foxhounds." An anxious lump forms in my throat at the word. "They're my father's pets."

"They don't sound like normal pets." He eyes me, watching my face for signs of something, but I don't know what.

I will not be distracted. "You're surrounded," I say with feigned confidence. "And unless you'd like to become their next meal, I recommend you answer my questions."

"Listen." He gives me a pointed look. "I can't tell you what happened to Áine." He pauses, thinking. "But I know who can."

"Who?"

His pale eyes watch me closely. "The Queen. She was there when your grandmother died."

"You mean the Dead Queen."

"Some might call her that, yes."

"Why would the queen of Annwyn be at the border when my grandmother was killed?"

My heart races anew. Was it an invasion? No, Father would have used that information to his utmost advantage. He'd have sent criers to every village to tell them we were under attack. Then he'd spin it so the people knew that he would protect them. Even if that just meant sitting in his audience chamber, plotting, while he sent those very same people to the borderlands to die.

A scouting mission, then? Seems unlikely to be a queen's duty. Was Grandmother sent as an envoy for peace talks? I almost bark out a laugh at that thought. As if Father would ever trust her enough to speak for him.

For the first time, the Wolf in chains looks away. "It's complicated."

I narrow my eyes. "If you think you can trick me into setting you free, just so you can get out of answering my questions, you're sorely mistaken."

He holds a shackled hand up to his chest. "I would never. Despite what you may have been told, we Wolves live by a code of honor."

I scoff. "You call causing pain and murdering innocent people honorable? Or bringing corpses back to life to fight your battles for you?"

"There's honor in death, same as in life."

"Of course you'd say that."

There's a definite shift in the pitch of the foxhounds' cries. I stand up, on alert. I've been here too long. The real servants might arrive to feed the animals at any moment. My eyes dart to the Wolf. He studies me curiously.

"You're not supposed to be here, are you, Red?"

My lips pinch closed.

"You saved me when your father would rather I die a slow death."

I say nothing, but the panicked look in my eyes gives me away.

The Wolf sets his jaw. "You may be honorable, even if he isn't."

It's time to leave. I step out of the cell door and close it behind me with a bang. The Wolf watches me through the bars as I lock it.

"For saving my life, I would take you past the border," he says. "If you truly want an answer to your question, that's where you'll find it."

I glare at him, not sure how he suddenly has the upper

hand. In the cell behind me, a foxhound snarls and leaps toward his door, his chains rattle behind him.

The Wolf and I stare at each other through the cell door, assessing one another. Crossing the border into the Kingdom of Death is a fool's errand. It would only end in my own grisly demise.

And yet.

I believe he does know what happened to Grandmother. And that the answers do lie in the north. And he really would take me there, if I freed him. But if there's one thing I've learned from my years sewing people together again and bringing them back from the edge of death, it's this—Annwyn can't be trusted.

And if I dive that deep into my obsession for the truth, then I'm as good as dead.

Chapter 10

A KNOCK on my chamber door rouses me from sleep. When I open my eyes, the light has the honeyed hue of late afternoon. I'm surprised they let me sleep this long.

The knock sounds again. "Your Highness? There's a delivery for you."

I sit up with some effort, like I left my limbs behind in the realm of dreams. The silk sheets slip below my bare shoulders. I prefer to sleep naked rather than dressed in the frilly nightgowns the palace seamstress made for me.

"A delivery?" I call from the bed. "What kind?"

The maid giggles on the other side of the door. "It's a surprise, Your Highness. You'll like it."

Doubtful. I yawn. "Can you leave it outside the door for now? I'm not decent."

"I don't believe so, Your Highness. No."

I smother my groan into a fluffy pillow. "All right, give me a moment."

With great effort, I rise from the bed to throw on a dressing gown. If the maid saw I didn't wear the frilly sleeping gowns she ironed, she would be very disappointed.

But I can't sleep in that much luxury after everything I've been through on the border, everything I've seen. It haunts my dreams. The expensive bedding makes me feel guilty enough.

After checking in the mirror to make sure there's no drool on my face, I open the door.

The maid's eyes are bright, and I'm instantly suspicious. My eyes trail behind her to the parade of servants standing beneath enormous arrangements of red roses. My jaw drops. The sheer extravagance of the display is staggering, bordering on ridiculous.

The maid's face is flushed as she says, "They're from your groom, Your Highness! Isn't it romantic?" Her voice is high-pitched with excitement, as if she's living out some grand fairy tale, secondhand.

The most I can manage is a mumbled, "Mmhm."

The maid shoos me aside so the servants can take the entire greenhouse-worth of red flowers into my bedchamber. Bouquet after massive bouquet, my room fills until every surface is completely covered. The vanity, the writing desk, the window seats—they all disappear beneath a sea of scarlet petals. Even the floor is blanketed in vases overflowing with roses, forcing the servants to navigate between the arrangements.

The entire room has turned into a crimson garden. But this display doesn't make me think of romance and stolen kisses, it makes me think of thorns and open wounds. It makes me think of blood.

The thing is, I don't even like roses. And I'm pretty sure Hunter knows this. But this show isn't for me, not really.

"We'll give them a once in a lifetime love story," he'd said at the ball last night. It seems he wasn't kidding.

"They came with a note," the maid says breathlessly. She holds up a cream-colored envelope with my name scrawled on it in looping penmanship. The maid looks at it with hunger in her eyes. She clearly wants to know what it says.

"Go ahead," I say. "Read it to me."

Her eyes grow wide. "Oh, but I couldn't! It would be an intrusion!"

"It's all right, I'm ... too tired. To read." I flounder. "All that dancing."

The maid clutches her heart and gives me a pitying look, like I'm the most self-sacrificing heir that ever lived and she adores me for it.

"Yes, of course, Your Highness." She nods enthusiastically. "You must be exhausted. Please, sit. I will happily read the letter to you."

I shuffle to a gilded lounge chair. Its gold velvet upholstery blends into the sea of red roses. Settling into the cushions, I play the role of the beloved heir. My face arranges into what I hope is a convincing mask of romantic longing.

She breaks the wax seal with a flourish, her hands trembling as she unfolds the note. Then she clears her throat and reads:

To My Dearest Love,

These roses are but thorns compared to your beauty ...

I snort, the sound escaping before I can stop it. The maid's head snaps up, and she gives me an incredulous look.

Thinking quickly, I wave a hand in front of my face and add a slight cough. "My apologies," I say, with a note of polite embarrassment. "The pollen. I'll be fine."

Her face relaxes. She continues:

. . .

Waiting for our wedding day, when I can see your beauty bloom in our own shared chamber, feels like torture.

I roll my eyes and barely manage to stifle a groan.

The maid's face is pink, but I don't believe it's from embarrassment. She reads faster in her excitement, no doubt memorizing every word to repeat to her friends later. By nightfall, every servant in the palace will know of my lovesick groom. They'll be dreaming of our wedding night and the thousand roses he sent to remind me of all the beautiful things he'll do to my body.

I cringe at the thought. Thankfully, the maid is too engrossed in Hunter's saccharine words to notice me.

Your devoted groom,
Hunter

The maid is breathless, her eyes shining.

"Thank you," I say, dismissing her.

She turns to run out the door before remembering that she still has my note clutched close to her heart. Flustered, she returns in a flurry, hands it to me, then curtsies. As she finally exits, I hear the rustle of her skirts and the faint whisper of excited murmurs. No doubt servants are already spreading the tale of the romantic knight and his blushing bride-to-be.

Left alone, I sink deeper into the chair, the letter limp in my hand. If people didn't believe Hunter and I were some fairy-tale romance after last night's display, they will now. The thought should be comforting, our ruse works perfectly. Instead, I feel a weight settling in my chest, thick as the scent of a thousand roses.

By the time I'm dressed and ready to leave my chambers, it's almost evening. My stomach grumbles, but my hunger is laced with a pang of guilt. I have the luxury of accessing the kitchens whenever I please. The Wolf in the dungeon kennel isn't so lucky.

When I enter the kitchen, the clang of metal pans and the rhythmic chopping of vegetables greet me. Steam rises from enormous pots, carrying the rich aroma of simmering broths and stews. I narrowly avoid colliding with a cook's helper hoisting a giant pot of broth, its contents sloshing dangerously close to the rim. He grumbles at me before recognition dawns on his face.

"My apologies." I swipe a still-hot roll from a cooling griddle.

He attempts to bow with his enormous, boiling pot in hand.

"No, please," I say. "There's no need."

As the smell of roasting vegetables and sizzling meat wafts toward me, my thoughts return to the kennels. My stomach sours at the memory of the stinking foxhounds and the decades of excrement and gore that coat the floors. Even if I healed the Wolf this morning, no man could survive long down there in that filth. Especially not if my father sends his questioners in to torture him.

Will my father even think to feed the Wolf in the kennels? Not likely. With renewed purpose, I grab several more rolls, their crusts crackling as I stuff them into my skirt pockets.

A kitchen maid notices me and raises an eyebrow.

"A picnic." I turn to leave.

Her face transforms, skepticism giving way to excitement. "Wait, Your Highness!"

I pause in the doorway.

The maid grabs a basket and scurries around the kitchen, ducking under pans held high and weaving around cooks with bowls filled with chopped vegetables. She returns with a basket overflowing with hard cheeses in waxy rinds, savory preserved meats, and colorful ripe fruits. Nestled among the food are two delicate porcelain plates, crystal glasses, and a bottle of wine from the royal cellars.

"For the prince-to-be," she says with a curtsey. "And you, of course, Your Highness."

I may still be an afterthought, but the gesture is so kind I'm at a loss for words. I glance around the kitchen and notice several eyes watching me in anticipation. "T-thank you."

Hunter's charms seem to have power over everyone in this palace. As his bride, it appears I get to feel the afterglow. I'm no longer the irritant underfoot. With Hunter, I'm invited, welcomed, even celebrated.

For a second, I daydream about marrying Hunter. It could be a good life, being adored by my people, with a loving man at my side. But then I remember that the food is a deceit. It's not for my betrothed or a secret, romantic picnic. It's for the Wolf among sheep. The enemy in the dungeons.

After I leave, I deposit the basket of food in my chambers, hiding it behind a large rose bouquet. It will have to stay here until I can figure out how to get it to the Wolf. But just as I leave the room, closing the door behind me, I hear the clang of armor approaching down the corridor.

My hand freezes on the ornate door handle. I step aside to allow them to pass, but they don't. The footsteps halt abruptly. Four King's Guards stand before me, their polished armor gleaming. My heart sinks.

"Your Highness, we need you to come with us." The knight's voice is gruff, leaving no room for argument.

I can feel the blood drain from my face. Does my father know I healed the Wolf? Did someone recognize me in the kennels this morning?

At the back of the group, a familiar tall, blond figure catches my eye.

Hunter stares meaningfully, as if he expects me to protest. He shakes his head so slightly I wonder if I imagined it. His eyes are wide, meaningful.

Swallowing hard, I curtsey to the knight that spoke to me. "Of course."

To my surprise, they don't lead me to the king's chambers. Instead, we head outside. The warm afternoon sun feels at odds with the chill of dread running through me. It takes several moments for me to realize where we're headed.

The kennels.

My heart drops. As we near the entrance, a figure emerges from behind an ancient oak tree, its gnarled branches casting dappled shadows across the ground.

"Daughter." The king does not look happy to see me. But, then again, does he ever?

"Father."

We stand off for a moment, both refusing to reveal our thoughts. The sounds of the castle—distant laughter, the clang of practice swords, the rustle of leaves in the breeze—seem muffled, as if the world is holding its breath. I search his face for any sign of what he knows, but he is stoic as ever.

"I thought we could revisit our conversation from last night." Father says, gesturing for the guards to open the kennel doors. "Pay our friend a visit."

The moment the heavy doors creak open, the foxhounds sense my father and begin howling. Their voices echo up the stone staircase like a haunting song.

I keep my chin high. "As you wish." My voice is steady despite the fear gnawing at my insides.

We descend into the damp darkness, led by orbs of light cast by father's noble guards. The scent of mold and decay intensifies, mingling with the metallic tang of old blood. Our footsteps echo off the stone walls as Father leads us. He pauses outside the Wolf's door.

"Shall we see if our friend survived?" he asks, a taunting note in his voice.

I shrug, like I couldn't care less. "He is no friend of mine."

The iron keys clang together as he opens the lock and I flinch when the door's rusty hinges screech open. We all lean in, peering through the cell's gloomy darkness. Father ignites a ball of light, momentarily blinding us before he sends it into the cell. It pauses in the middle of the room, just above the drying puddle of blood.

I watch with secret pleasure when Father's eyes widen, a flicker of surprise breaking through his usual stony mask. He scans the cell.

The Wolf sits propped up in the corner, grinning like a mischievous boy caught stealing an extra slice of cake. Despite the filth and grime covering him, there's a defiant spark in his gray eyes.

"Interesting," Father says, his voice deceptively calm. "And here I was sure you wouldn't last the night."

The Wolf shrugs, as if we're not discussing his brush with death.

My father pauses long enough, a few of the guards shift uneasily. I search for Hunter in the back of the group, but he watches my father, his face unreadable.

The king lifts a hand lazily. "Hold him."

Two of the copper-armored guards step forward. They grab his arms, wrenching him off the ground. To the Wolf's credit, he doesn't look afraid.

To my left, I feel the cool approach of armor as a knight moves closer. I glance up to find Hunter, a worried look on his face.

"Who sent you?" my father asks.

The Wolf just stares him straight in the eyes.

My father looks unperturbed. "Are you an assassin?"

Still, the Wolf says nothing.

My father sighs. "Fine, have it your way." He curls his finger toward the guards still standing next to me. One man starts forward.

"Wait." Father holds up a hand. The knight halts mid-step. Father looks at me as he says, "Hunter."

The man steps back, but Hunter hesitates.

The king raises an eyebrow. "Is something the matter?"

"No, Your Majesty," Hunter says. His eyes dart toward mine before he steps forward.

My father gestures with his chin. "Hit him."

Hunter holds up his fist, but hesitates again.

My father's voice is deceptively upbeat. "I have to say, Hunter. I'm not enjoying this game we're playing where I have to ask you to do everything twice."

This is another one of my father's notorious, sadistic tests. He wants to see how far Hunter's loyalty will go. How far he can push him into obedience. My father watches me for a reaction.

Hunter punches the Wolf in the stomach. The Wolf doubles over as much as he can with both of his arms restrained.

"Let's try this again," Father says. "Who sent you?"

The Wolf coughs, but doesn't speak.

Father gestures for Hunter to hit him again. "Are you an assassin?"

Still, nothing. Father nods for Hunter to continue. The next punch lands on the Wolf's jaw. The clank of Hunter's metal gauntlets makes me wince.

"Did you plant something in my rooms?" Father asks.

The Wolf spits a wad of blood toward my father's expensive shoes.

"Hm." Father looks to Hunter.

Hunter punches him on the chin again, this time breaking the skin along his jawline.

"Again," Father says.

A third punch makes the Wolf yelp in pain.

"Again."

Punch.

"Again."

This one lands on the Wolf's stomach with a dull thud. He groans, but doesn't say a word.

My stomach churns, bile rising in my throat. I'm afraid I'll vomit right here on the damp stone floor. The guilt is overwhelming. This is *my* fault. I'm the reason he was discovered in Father's rooms. I'm the reason he's healed, fueling Father's fury. I'm the one Father truly wants to break with this display of cruelty.

"We can do this all night, if we have to," Father says. The light above him casts deep shadows across his face. "I will stop at nothing to ensure the safety of my kingdom."

Another punch. Then another. I involuntarily whimper when I hear a sickening crunch as Hunter breaks the Wolf's nose. Fresh blood spatters onto the floor.

Father steps right up into the Wolf's face, so close their noses almost touch. "Why was my daughter there with you?"

Blood drains from my face. The room seems to spin, and I might pass out.

Hunter looks toward me, his brown eyes wide, pleading, but I'm not sure for what. Mercy? Understanding? Forgiveness?

I don't know the Wolf. But I *do* know what he is. The question burns in my mind: Why won't he use his power to defend himself? Is it to keep his identity a secret? He could kill us all with nothing more than his bare hands. He could call upon his own shadow power and inflict pain on everyone in this room. But he doesn't.

Another thing I can't seem to work out is why he trusts me, the Fox King's daughter, to keep that secret for him. I'm supposed to be his mortal enemy. Why does he assume I won't tell?

Then it hits me. The Wolf knows I won't tell his secret because he has one about me as well. He knows I didn't just follow an intruder into my father's ro'oms. He knows I was looking for answers. That I want them so badly, I broke into my father's chamber through a hidden entrance, during the middle of my engagement party. I have secrets too. And the Wolf knows it.

For now, both are safe. So long as neither of us breaks. But that's the thing about secrets, somebody always slips, eventually.

The Wolf looks toward me, grimacing through blood-smeared teeth. Those pale, full moon eyes full of pain ... and determination. He will not talk. Not even if it means his life is forfeited.

Father rushes forward, grabbing him by the neck. They stare into each other's eyes, each daring the other to act first. My father releases him and stomps past me, out of the cell.

The knights shift, uneasy. My father never gives up so easily. We listen to his footsteps as they walk down the hallway. Moments later, he returns with a blade in hand.

"Strip his shirt."

Hunter reaches forward, ripping the stained, thin shirt. In a moment of shock, I realize it's still the one from his wolf costume. The black silk hangs in tatters, and its crusted with mud and dried blood.

My father takes a step back when he sees the Wolf's chest. The starburst scar from his arrow wound is on full display. Father's eyes narrow, then dart toward me with suspicion. I feign surprise as best I can.

"Who else was in here?" Father yells.

The guards' faces pale. "No one, Your Highness!" Of course, they would never suspect a scullery maid to be a 'someone.'

"Well, he didn't heal himself, did he?"

Father lurches toward me, his face purple with fury. "What did you do?" he growls.

The foxhounds yip around us, attuned to his moods.

I shake my head. "N—nothing!"

"Do you take me for a fool?" he asks lowly, almost a whisper in my ear.

"I don't—"

"That man was at death's door only hours ago." He points toward the Wolf. "And now he's completely healed." Father brings his head closer to my ear. "You and I both know, not just *anyone* could have brought a dying man back from the dead."

I keep my face neutral, but my growing fury shows up in other ways. Sweat prickles at my temple and my hands tremble.

Suddenly, I'm a child again, standing in front of Father's fox hearth as the flickering flames cast sinister shadows on the walls. He's just told me that Grandmother is dead, torn apart by a pack of corpse wolves at the border. I'm shaking and I've wet my skirts. He calls her death "unfortunate" and chalks it up to a "tragedy." Yet another death to blame on the Dead Queen of Annwyn.

Someone less familiar with him might believe his act of grief, but I notice how the corners of his mouth turn upward slightly. He's delighted though he tries to hide it. My terror transforms into something more powerful. Rage overtakes me for the first time. I want to kill him. I want to claw his eyes from their sockets, take the nearest sharp object and thrust it through his grinning mouth.

"Of course, a big man like you would torture a frightened girl."

My eyes snap open at the Wolf's voice, dragging me back to reality.

Father turns slowly, his eyes burning with cold fury. "What did you say to me?"

The Wolf raises his head, squinting through swollen eyes that gleam with defiance. He spits a glob of blood onto the filthy stone floor. "I said, pick on someone your own size."

My father smiles. It turns my insides into ice.

Father takes a few steps forward, rolling up his expensive silk sleeves. He pauses in front of the Wolf. "All right." He punches the Wolf in the nose.

A sickening crunch makes me flinch. I can't take it anymore. I leap toward my father, grabbing his arm with a feral growl.

"Enough!" I scream. "Llwyn is supposed to be better than this! We're healers, not torturers!" In mere seconds, a knight grabs me by the waist, pulling me back. My limbs flail, punching, kicking, scratching at copper armor—to no effect.

The king rights himself and leans forward, inches from my face. "Llwyn only survives because *I* do whatever it takes to protect it." Then he turns and attacks the Wolf, like a man possessed. He grunts with each blow, landing punch after punch into the Wolf's face until it's bruised and bloodied, like a slab of meat.

My body flinches with each hit. Bile rises in the back of my throat and I'm not sure I'll keep the tears of fury at bay much longer.

"Release him," my father orders, finally. The Wolf drops to the ground like a limp sack of grain. My father continues to kick his motionless body where it lies curled up on the cold, filthy ground.

"Stop!" My voice shakes. "What good does it do to beat an unconscious man?" I grit my teeth in rage.

There are smears of blood on Father's hands and chin. "It does me a great deal of good, Daughter. He will continue to feel my wrath for days." He shrugs. "Weeks, perhaps." His eyes grow dark. "Unless someone disobeys my orders again and heals him." His voice sounds like a threat. Or maybe it's another one of his tests. Either way, I can't stand to watch him beat this man anymore, enemy or not. I can't stand to bear witness to my father's cruelty again and again.

I was safer on the borderlands, among the war-wounded and the corpse wolves.

"Let's go," Father says. He nods and the guards release me. My arms ache from the ghosts of their fingers on my skin.

Most of his guards follow him out the door, but Hunter hesitates, watching me as I kneel on the filthy ground. I make sure the Wolf is still breathing. He is, but it's labored and shallow. In less than a day, he's on death's door again. And that's my fault.

"I said, go." My father's voice is low.

There's nothing I can do for the Wolf now. I can't heal him with my father standing nearby. He'll kill him if I intervene. I remember the bread roll from the kitchens in my pocket. My voluminous skirts block it from sight as I tuck it close to the Wolf's chest. I doubt he'll be able to eat when he regains consciousness—if he regains it at all—but this is the best I can do.

"My patience is growing thin," Father warns.

Hunter steps forward and holds out a hand to help me up from the ground. I'm glad to see it's shaking, though his face is brave. I take it. He gives my hand a gentle squeeze before releasing me. He positions himself between me and the king as we walk toward the exit of the kennels. The Wolf's door slams closed behind us.

My limbs feel heavy when we reach the fresh air outside. It's all I can do to stay standing on trembling knees.

Father leads us into the nearby gardens. Nobles avoid our eyes as we pass, and I know why. We bear the unmistakable marks of people involved in intrigue. My skirts are filthy from the kennel floors and my father's knuckles are bloody, his sleeves still rolled up to his elbows. Father doesn't seem worried about the gossipmongers. No one would dare question a bloodied king.

Father halts near the fading hydrangea bushes. He gives Hunter a pointed look. "Leave us."

Hunter hesitates, then nods. He watches me warily as he retreats toward the stables. The three other knights follow, their shadows stretching long in the fading light.

Father turns to me, haloed in the setting sun. "I do not trust that man in the cell. And it's not because we found him sneaking around my rooms like a thief." He squints at me, his eyes dark and calculating. "Do you know why I don't trust him, dear daughter?"

I permit one sharp shake of my head.

"I do not trust him, because I do not trust *you*."

"I swear, I don't know him." My voice is quiet, lost behind the choking rage.

"Let us both hope that's true," he says. "Now run along, Little Fox. I believe your beloved is waiting for you."

I turn to retreat, relief spreading through me like ice through my veins.

"Actually, one more thing," he calls me back.

I pause mid-step, my hands clenching into fists at my sides.

My father clucks like a mother hen. "A deceitful heir should be careful, lest she lose her throne." He turns from me, then pauses. Almost thoughtfully, he adds, "Or even her life. One cannot be too careful with these dangerous games. Best to wed and live a happy, domestic life. Wouldn't you agree?" He raises an eyebrow at me.

I grit my teeth and nod.

"Good girl," he says, like he speaks to his foxhounds when they cower at his approach. "An obedient daughter is a rewarded daughter. Remember that next time you try to deceive me." He leaves me among the dying autumn flowers.

When he is out of sight, my knees crumble and I fall to the ground. I do my best to stifle the gut-wrenching scream into my filthy gowns. Angry tears blur the world around me. Not even the brilliant orange sunset along the horizon can distract me from the darkness growing in my heart.

Part Two

The Knight

CHAPTER 11

THE TWILIGHT around me is eerily quiet. Twisted branches and overgrown hedges cast dark shadows on the ground. I'm crumpled in the dirt, focusing on steady breaths, when someone wraps their arms around my shoulders. The metallic scent of copper mixes with the aroma of night-blooming flowers. It smells like a nosebleed in a garden.

Hunter's armor digs into my arms uncomfortably, but I don't push him away even though we're in full view of anyone passing through the grounds.

"Sienna, I'm so sorry." His voice hitches.

I shut my eyes, trying to banish the memory of Hunter hitting the Wolf again and again. Of the sickening thuds echoing off the stone walls of the decrepit cell.

"I didn't want to do it," he says. "Please believe me."

I do. But that doesn't stop the memory from playing in my mind like a bad dream on repeat. I rub my hands over my face and take a deep breath, trying to get ahold of myself. I've spent my entire life inventing new ways to outwit my father. I can beat him at his own, vicious game. I just have to figure out how.

But this felt different from his usual cruelty. This felt like a test especially for me and Hunter. A test of our loyalty at another man's expense. A man who refused to fight back.

That's not how the stories go.

In the lore about Annwyn, the Dead Queen rules with an insatiable blood lust. Her people kill for sport, using shadow power in creative ways to induce torture and pain. Llwyn nannies tell stories of horrible creatures brought back from the dead and sent to naughty children who refuse to behave. As far as I've been told, the Annwyn people are monsters.

But today, *we* were.

Everything I thought I knew is wrong and I feel like I can't breathe. My thoughts are racing so fast I can hardly make sense of them. I'm the only one who knows the man in the kennels is a Wolf. He could have killed us all, or at the very least, revealed my secret. But he didn't. My father nearly killed him, but he protected me. Why?

The twilight deepens as the last rays of the sun cast an eerie glow. Fireflies flicker among the stalks of dead flowers. An icy breeze causes the dried topiary to shiver in a death rattle. Somewhere in the distance, the unmistakable giggle of a lovers' tryst reminds me we aren't alone.

I pull away from Hunter. His face is worried, his eyes wide. The cracks in his knuckles are still stained with blood. I shake them off and stand, brushing the dirt from my red dress.

Hunter scrambles up after me. "Sienna, we need to talk." He tries to catch my eyes. "Somewhere away from here. Where no one will listen."

The last thing I want to do right now is talk to Hunter, but I know this wasn't his fault. He is as much a prisoner of the Fox King as I am. We can't just sit here in the dirt, falling to pieces. That's what my father wants. That's how he wins.

I straighten and nod. "Meet me in the cemetery."

"The ... cemetery." He nods. "Yes, that would work. No one there to listen."

"Look for my signal." I turn toward the palace with its glowing windows and harden my heart. "It's time to get dressed for supper. We're expected." Then I head back to my rooms to burn this dress that's tainted with the smell of the kennels and the memory of a tortured Wolf.

I sit through an entire supper next to Father, wearing a new red dress and a placid smile like nothing happened. I can't stomach a single bite. Everything reminds me of the Wolf, from the roasted pig with its splitting flesh to the ripe, red fruit with oozing juices. The dark wine looks so much like the Wolf's spilled blood that, for a moment, I can't help but wonder if this is another one of my father's sick tests.

My mind keeps returning to the man in the kennels. Guilt gnaws at my insides like maggots feasting on dead flesh. The Wolf is likely dying because of me. Again.

When it feels like I've been present for an appropriate amount of time—like a pretty display pony all dressed in red—I excuse myself from the table. The chair scrapes against the floor as I stand, drawing unwanted attention. I force myself not to flinch, my smile still plastered in place. From across the room, I give Hunter a look that I hope anyone witnessing would assume was an invitation for a secret lover's rendezvous.

Back in my rooms, I change out of the voluminous red skirts and back into my stained woolen dress from the borderlands. It's still damp from my most recent bathtub washing, but it will have to do. This time, when I climb down the wisteria outside my bedroom window, I have the enormous picnic basket over my shoulder. The night air is cool with a breeze that makes me shiver. A few apples fall to the ground below when I lose my footing. The soft thuds echo in the stillness.

I don't light my path as I cross the palace grounds toward

the outskirts where the royal cemetery lies. The moon peers out from behind thick clouds, and it's enough light to see by. I don't want to draw attention to myself. If anyone notices me in the dark, I'll just look like a silly palace maid off to a secret picnic with a forbidden lover.

Gravel crunches underfoot as I enter through the large, black gates surrounded by ancient, moss-covered walls. This is where most of my ancestors are buried. The air is thick with the smell of autumn decay and damp stone. Enormous gravestones pepper the ground. They're etched with images of knights doing daring deeds and ladies wearing elaborate gowns, all last-ditch attempts to frame the dead in veils of glory. In truth, most of them spent their lives in gossipy parlor rooms or in wine-fueled gambling dens.

I never come here. I'm not proud of the family I hail from. The one person I'd love to visit isn't buried here. She isn't buried at all. The story claims there wasn't enough of her left to inter, not after the corpse wolves finished with her.

Determination fuels my steps. We should have had more time together. I should have been there when she died. But I wasn't. No one was. Carved stone and grand mausoleums don't tell you what sort of person a deceased ancestor was, the legacy they left behind does. And for my grandmother, *I* am that legacy. I continue down the cemetery path as my resolve solidifies into something hard and black as obsidian.

I have to reach the Wolf. I have to know what happened to her.

I move quickly, the oppressive darkness pressing in on all sides, my footsteps muffled by the soft, damp ground. As I weave through the maze of gravestones, twisted trees, and mausoleums, their shadows stretch like they're reaching out to ensnare me. I feel the weight of the past bearing down on me, the whispers of long-dead ancestors rustling through the leaves. Their judging eyes seem to follow me, their disapproval palpable even in death.

There's a pond in the center of the graveyard that seems like the most obvious place to meet Hunter. As I grow closer, I hear the telltale songs of bullfrogs singing to the night, followed by the splash-plop as they jump into the water.

A single, white marble mausoleum stands at one end of the pond, overlooking the reeds that serve as home to waterfowl. It's decorated with delicate-looking moths carved into the stone by expert hands.

It belongs to my mother.

I've never felt drawn to this ornate house of the dead before. I never knew my mother, the queen, but I respect her as the daughter of the greatest women I've ever known. For just a moment, I feel a pang of sadness and loss pierce my heart. How different would my life be now if she had lived? If I hadn't been born, she would still be alive, possibly bearing heirs that Father wanted.

Through the windows of the mausoleum, the outline of a statue waits inside. I squint, trying to make out the graceful features of a woman I'm said to resemble. But I see no familiarity in the smooth, white skin and empty eyes. She is nothing but someone else's memory etched into stone.

A faint mist rises from the pond, swirling around the base of the mausoleum. The silence is oppressive, broken only by the occasional splash of a frog or the distant call of a night bird. Until footsteps sound in the distance.

I step away from the mausoleum as my eyes strain in the darkness.

"Sienna?" Hunter whispers.

In the moonlight, he looks more like my old friend again. The stress on his face melts when he spots me. He walks faster to meet me at the edge of the pond.

"I was afraid I'd never find you out here," he says. He's

changed out of his copper and bronze armor and into a warm tunic to protect from the autumn chill, back into the casual wardrobe of a common man. The way I prefer him.

His eyes pass over my wardrobe change. A shiver runs down my spine, and I pull my cloak tighter around my body.

"Most people would hardly recognize you," he says.

"But not you."

"No, I could never forget your face." He reaches out to caress my cheek with the tips of his fingers. He treats me like I'm a piece of art, fragile and precious.

For just a moment, I forget everything and everyone else. We are just two souls, learning to love each other all over again. What I wouldn't give to go back in time, to start anew with him before the world destroyed me. Before Grandmother was murdered. Before he was trained to be my father's copper-clad pet. Before I fled to the borderlands. Before he betrayed me and broke my heart.

But we can't go back. Living in a fantasy won't fix anything.

I clear my throat and turn to face the pond. Hunter drops his hand, a small sigh of disappointment escaping his lips. A muskrat stands in the shallows, watching us.

"I have to ask." I study his face. "Did you know about Elena?"

His face stills, then falls. "Yes." He sighs. "Everyone knows. But no one is foolish enough to say anything."

I nod. "My father has many spies."

"More like nobles hungry for his approval."

"How long has she been his mistress?"

Hunter shrugs. "It's difficult to say. My father is very discreet about organizing their ... meetings." He frowns. "She's been wearing copper for several months now."

"I expect I'll have a little brother or sister soon."

He doesn't say anything.

I look at him from the corner of my eye. "She just seems like an odd choice. She was always so quiet when we were children. So reserved."

"I doubt she had much say in the matter." Hunter's voice has an edge to it. He's never liked his father's many ploys to gain the king's approval. This is just one of many. Like our impending marriage. Commander Malen will stop at nothing to ensure his place in my father's inner circle.

We spend a long time staring out at the still pond. The quiet cemetery offers a welcomed peace. I wish I could stay here and never leave. My eyes drift to my mother's mausoleum with the beautiful moth carvings along the doorway and I remember that, someday, I never will.

Hunter breaks the silence. "Are you still hungry?" he asks, with a note of confusion. He looks pointedly at the picnic basket.

"Oh, this." I shake my head and hold it up. "I have a favor to ask you."

"Another one?"

I scan his face to gauge his reaction, but there's no malice or judgment there. Just curiosity.

"Hunter, please, you have to go back there. You have to help him."

As a noble, Hunter has *some* healing powers, though they're nothing like mine. Still, he can heal minor scrapes and bruises. He did it for me all the time when we were children. It's better than nothing, and it might just be enough to save the Wolf from death.

Hunter winces. "I can't do that, Sienna. Your father will notice."

"But he's going to die down there if we don't do something."

"Yes, because your father nearly *killed* him." His mouth is stern. "All because someone healed him. What do you think your father will do to him this time, if someone fixes him again?" He releases a groan of frustration and runs his hands through his blond hair. "Besides, you know I can't heal that level of injury."

I shake my head, refusing to think of the gruesome possibilities. "It just has to be enough to keep him from dying. It wouldn't be enough for my father to notice. Just don't let him die."

"Why not?" Hunter asks, an edge of irritation in his voice. "Why do you care so much about a man you claim you've never met before?"

I close my eyes, willing my guilt to ease. "Because this is all my fault."

He's silent for a moment. The sounds of the night fill the void—a breeze blows through the reeds, frogs jump into the pond, an owl hoots in the distance.

"What do you mean?" he asks.

"I healed him the first time." It comes out as a whisper.

Hunter doesn't look surprised.

"I just ..." I stammer. "I couldn't watch him die. Not after all the soldiers in the borderlands. Not when I knew I could save him."

Hunter's concern melts away, leaving worried eyes in its wake. I know I'm playing to his sympathies, but I don't care. There's too much at stake to worry about morals now.

He nods. "I'll try to heal him, for you. But you have to tell me one thing, Sienna." He moves to catch my eyes. "Why were you in your father's rooms that night? Why did you ask me to cover for you?"

I start to give him the same fake explanation I told father, that I'd spotted the suspicious intruder and followed him.

"No." He shakes his head. "The truth."

My jaw snaps shut. As much as I want to trust Hunter, we have a complicated history when it comes to trust. And something in my gut tells me not to share this secret with anyone. Not yet, anyway.

After a few long moments, he sighs. "Fine." His shoulders droop with disappointment. "But whatever you're up to, please be careful. Your father is dangerous."

"I know," I whisper, looking at the ground.

Hunter watches me for a long moment. He reaches toward my face and lifts my chin so I meet his eyes. "Someday, I hope you'll be able to trust me again. Until then, I'll do whatever I can to prove that I'm on your side."

Warmth pools low in my belly at the touch of his fingers on my skin. "Thank you."

His eyes are etched with concern. It makes him look like a man twice his age. I hate that I'm the reason those lines are there.

"I hope you know what you're doing," he says. "Because I will follow you straight into the fire if I have to."

He holds my gaze for a long, long time. There's something between us that I can't pretend away. It's the spark of an ember that I thought we'd extinguished a long time ago. When he looks at me like this, my heart thumps wildly in my chest. I start to forget myself.

"Sienna," he says, taking a hesitant step closer to me. His voice is breathy and low. He shifts his hand on my chin, moving it back to cradle my jaw. His fingers tangle in my loose hair. "You know how I feel about you, right? How I've *always* felt about you? It hasn't changed."

A shiver runs through me, and I'm not sure it's from the cold.

The cemetery glows with moonlight and the insects sing a song of love for summer's end. The early autumn breeze moves my hair across my face and Hunter brushes it away like a caress. He leans forward, placing his forehead against mine. Then he closes his eyes and takes a shaky breath.

"I love you, Sienna."

For a moment, I let myself be swayed by this unfamiliar feeling of adoration. I want to fall into this, into him. I want to be in love and blind to all consequences.

But I'm not that person anymore. And I'm not willing to sacrifice the woman I've become to live in a fantasy. I don't trust my father's intentions for arranging this marriage, and I can't allow myself to get distracted. I need to uncover the Fox King's secrets. If I don't, no one else will.

Hunter opens his deep brown eyes and stares into mine. He pulls me closer, so close I can feel his heart beating next to mine. My body is aware of every inch of his skin beneath his clothes, from the firm muscles pressed against my softer flesh, to the ragged breath that causes his chest to rise and fall.

He leans his face down toward mine. "Sienna." His voice is deep with longing.

Despite everything, I give in to the wave of desire that surges inside of me.

Hunter kisses me deeply, and the world falls away. I melt into him instinctively, my arms winding around his neck as if I've done this a thousand times before. His lips are soft and warm, and the way they move against mine makes my heart ache with a bittersweet, homesick kind of longing. Something deep inside me stirs, hungry and impatient.

I'm no stranger to intimacy. I've been taking herbs to prevent pregnancy since I was old enough to learn what they are. I've had my fun in the hay bales with clumsy boys who didn't know where to put their hands. I've let battle-shocked soldiers in the borderlands fumble against me in the dark, desperate to feel alive. They never really saw me, and I never let them. It was touch for the sake of touching, shallow and fleeting in the shadows. It was a way to forget the horrors of war.

But this ... this is altogether different.

My fingers grasp the front of Hunter's shirt, clutching him closer, as if his body is the only thing keeping me from coming undone. Our kisses grow more desperate, the air between us charged. This is scandalous and, if truth be told, a long time coming—and there's no one here to see us. Warmth grows inside me, pooling in a low, delicious ache. I want this. I want *him*.

He leans down to kiss along the curve of my neck, and I shiver. I grab his hair in my fist, urging him to kiss harder. Something in me longs to feel the bite of teeth on my skin, the sting of need. I tilt my chin up to expose the length of my neck. He brushes his lips along my racing pulse, and I moan.

My breath comes out in ragged bursts as I shift my hips against his, feeling a delicious thrill at his hard length. He moans against my lips, and the power I have over him makes my entire body flush hotter.

Hunter guides me several steps backward until my spine presses against the stone mausoleum wall. I gasp at the shock of cold, but it only makes the fire inside of me burn hotter. There's a delicious, aching need that's tightening inside me. I wrap one leg around Hunter's waist, my skirts falling to expose my skin to the cool air. He grips my thigh and digs his fingers into my flesh. The pain makes my lust ignite, growing into an uncontrollable blaze inside of me. I tighten my fist in his golden hair, desperate for more pressure. More heat and friction.

Every thought disappears, and I am left breathless. I am lost in this flurry of passion that feels too strong for me to stop ... until I open my eyes. Through the mausoleum window, my mother's marble statue stares down at us, haloed in moonlight.

What am I doing? I'm forgetting who I am, what I stand for. And what must be done.

I release him and turn my head away from his desperate

kisses. His eyes are unfocused, his lips swollen, his cheeks flushed. But Hunter is every bit the gallant knight—he doesn't press me, doesn't try to reason or coax. He leans one hand on the wall behind my head and for a few moments we both pant, collecting ourselves. We listen to the night around us as we wait for our beating hearts to settle.

"Too fast," he says, misinterpreting my reluctance to continue.

"Yes," I whisper.

He leans his forehead against mine again. "I'll wait for you. As long as it takes."

And what if it takes forever? I think, but don't say.

When I look into his chestnut eyes, there's a sincerity there that's startling. He deserves a nice girl. One who will be content being his wife and having his babies, not one who sneaks into dungeons and brings the wrath of the king wherever she goes. This man will follow me to the edge of the world before he would find another, better girl to love. But I can't let that happen. I can't drag him down with me.

Someday, I will have to hurt Hunter. Badly.

I just hope I'm strong enough to do it.

Chapter 12

There was a time when the fae lived among mortals. They feasted together, worked alongside each other, and, in rare cases, wed one another. The great human kings and queens of old took fae husbands and brides, wooed by their enchanting powers and captivating beauty. From their unions, the seeds of shadow and light power sprouted.

Sunlight bleeds through the library window, creeping across the page of my open book as I read. I've spent the better part of the afternoon delving into the origin story of corpse wolves. I'm trying to discover how they came into existence, how long they survive in their state of constant decay, how many there are ...

How to kill them. Again.

As centuries passed, men grew more bloodthirsty. They stole, they lied, and they fought. They started wars and killed each other over greed and power. Eventually, the fae grew tired of their human neighbors and fled north, where humans were few and far between. But the power that they left behind in the hearts of human kings remained, giving more fuel for fire between them.

As the power of light became the dominant strain in the blood of men, shadow power became something to be feared. So, the light wielders saw the opportunity to push the dark ones north, to follow the fae who fled centuries before. The power of light grew strong in the southern lands, while the north grew ever darker in its wake.

At the front of the library, the large oak doors open with a clang. I bristle as footsteps echo on the marble floors, interrupting my concentration. I try to block them out as I read.

No good southerner knows for certain when the Dead Queen was reborn, or how her shadow powers morphed into reanimating the dead. However, one thing is forever true: To travel north into the Kingdom of the Dead is certain—eternal—death.

The footsteps grow closer and I try to will them away, but it's no use. I'm tempted to hide in the shadows, but my scarlet gown is hardly discreet. A palace messenger in copper and cream livery rounds the corner. He spots me sitting on the window bench and heads in my direction, a look of relief crossing his face.

"Your Highness," he says when he stops in front of me. "Your presence is requested in the gardens."

I raise an eyebrow. "Since when does my father request an audience in public?"

He shakes his head. "No, your majesty, it's your betrothed."

It's out of character for Hunter to send someone to fetch me instead of coming to the library himself. Suspicion grows in my stomach, but I'm desperate to know if Hunter snuck into the kennels last night. If the Wolf survived.

I close the cover of the book in my lap and set it on the window seat for later. "Do you know what this is about?"

"No, Your Highness." The small smile at the corner of his mouth suggests otherwise.

I stand with a sigh. "Take me to him then."

It's not a far walk to the royal gardens. The gravel paths are full of courtly ladies and men promenading in fine silks and velvet. Everyone here is out to see and be seen by the biggest gossips of the court. As a general rule, I avoid the gardens. They remind me of a web with fat, glittering spiders searching for their next juicy meal.

Hunter waits at the center of the garden, near the bubbling fountain depicting a dancing maiden with foxes nipping at her heels. He isn't in his shining copper armor. Instead, he's dressed in a red tunic with black trousers, as dapper as any royal fiancé should be. When he sees us approaching, he smiles and holds out his hands.

"My beloved, what a pleasure to see you this morning." He nods to the messenger, dismissing him.

I raise an eyebrow. "Hunter, what's—"

He grabs my hand and kisses my knuckles lightly. Some distance behind him, a woman in fluffy pink taffeta sighs. I see what this is. We're putting on a show for the court.

"Is this really necessary?" I ask.

He presents his arm and I hold the crook of his elbow as he leads me in a casual stroll around the fountain. His only response is a wicked grin.

"Were you able to meet with our dear friend last night?" I ask, hoping Hunter will understand. I lift one eyebrow, urging him to take the hint.

"Yes. Yes, I did." His voice is upbeat, as if we're discussing a beloved aunt.

Nobles mill about, watching us from the corners of their eyes.

"And … how was he?" I keep my voice calm, casual. There's nothing in my tone that shows the fear buried in my heart.

"He lives."

I breathe a sigh of relief. "What did he say?"

"He said, 'Thank you.'" He pauses to think. "That's about it."

That can't be all. "Did he *do* anything?"

"He drank that expensive bottle of wine rather quickly." Hunter inclines his head toward a man who tips his hat in our direction. "Not that I could blame him."

"Did you, you know?" I move my hands around in front of us, like a healer who has no idea what she's doing.

Hunter smirks. "Dance with him? No, darling. There wasn't time for that."

I give him an impatient glare then lean toward his ear, like I'm whispering a lover's secret. "He isn't going to die, is he?"

Hunter shakes his head. "No, my love. Not today." He straightens. "I have a gift for you." His voice is louder than necessary, for the benefit of the people walking by. It's no accident that everyone in the garden seems to be meandering closer to the fountain, like none are immune to the gravitational pull of royal gossip.

From the ledge of the fountain, Hunter grabs a small, flat rectangle wrapped in fabric. He hands it to me and I take it gingerly, like it's dangerous. He nods for me to open it. All around us, nobles crane their necks to see.

Wrapped inside the cloth is a small, green book.

I can't help but laugh. "You requested I leave the library so you could present me with a book?"

His smile doesn't waver, but he lowers his voice to a whisper. "Well, no one would see your gift in the library."

My fingers glide over the gilded title embossed on the soft cover, "Love Poems for the Ages." I raise an eyebrow at him. "I never knew you liked poetry, Hunter."

"There are many things you don't know about me. I am a man of mystery." He kneels in front of me and a gaggle of ladies near the willow tree put their hands over their hearts and swoon.

"Hunter," I say between gritted teeth hidden behind a forced smile. "What are you doing?"

"I'm reciting love poetry to you. It's every courtly woman's dream." He pauses. "Or so the kitchen maid told me when I asked her for tips about wooing."

I want to laugh. Or scream. I'm not sure which, but the humor in his eyes softens me. "Let's get on with it then."

"Fear not, good lady. 'Tis a short one."

I narrow my eyes at him, sensing a joke. "How short?"

He fishes several leaves of parchment from his belt pocket and unfolds them with a snap. "A mere fifty verses."

I groan as my smile falters. "Make it quick. For the love of …"

Hunter clears his throat, then projects. "The great poet, Archibald, once said that true love comes but once in a generation." Hunter pauses as nobles gather nearer to listen. "We must be those lucky few, my sweet, for our love is one for the ages."

The growing audience claps politely.

I attempt to flee, but Hunter reaches for my hand and holds me in place. I lean down to hiss into his ear. "I won't let you forget this little stunt, if it's the last thing I do."

He turns his head to whisper back, his nose nudging my ear like a caress. "I'm looking forward to it." His eyes shine with laughter.

I sigh, hoping the courtly ladies think it's from adoration rather than frustration.

Hunter continues, "So here I kneel, ready to pour my heart out to you in verse. I wrote it this morning as I gazed into the depths of your eyes over our breakfast porridge."

I close my eyes, thinking murderous thoughts. My fingers grip the edges of the green poetry book. I briefly consider smacking Hunter with it.

He clears his throat.

What beauty is a flower when compared to your sweet complexion?

What softness is velvet when set next to your soft skin?

What sweetness does a berry compare to your lips?

I raise an eyebrow, and he gives me a slight shrug. He tosses one hand up toward the sky theatrically.

None! I say.

For thou art more beautiful, more soft, and sweeter than anything yet known.

I am but a humble man, who knows not many things.

I try to hide my scoff behind the book. He continues on, reciting something about birds and rainbows—or maybe it's honeybees and dewdrops?—I'm far too embarrassed to pay attention.

Finally, the torture ends to scattered applause. The ladies in the garden have flushed cheeks and stars in their eyes. Hunter stands, wiping the dirt from his knees, and bows to the audience. When they've turned their heads to giggle and whisper together in small groups, Hunter leads me down a path of impeccably trimmed boxwood shrubs.

"I'm reluctant to praise you for this little stunt," I say. "But if the point of this exercise was to endear us to the people, I think you might be something of a genius."

He laughs. "All I heard you say was that I am a genius."

I groan.

He bumps his shoulder into mine. "It's easy to give the people what they want."

"Speak for yourself," I grumble. "Public humiliation doesn't come naturally to me."

"It's less about humiliation and more about humility."

I give him a skeptical look. "Nothing about that poem screamed 'humble.'"

He snickers. "No, I guess you're right. What I meant was, it's less about *you* than it is about *them*. People want to believe in love and hope. Is it really so bad to give them that?"

I purse my lips, but say nothing. Hunter has always been a bigger person than I am. Less selfish or single-minded.

"Anyway," he says, nudging a stick out of our path with the toe of his shoe. "That book wasn't the real gift. It was just the public one."

I tilt my head to look up at him. "Oh? And what is this 'real' gift?"

He fishes another small box from his pocket and hands it to me.

"You know, you don't need to give me presents."

"I promise you'll like this one."

The box is white with a thick, red ribbon tied around the middle. I remove the lid and my breath catches when I see what's inside: a silver moth on a thin chain.

"Hunter ..." I'm at a loss for words. The necklace looks so familiar, but it takes a moment to sink in.

"It was your grandmother's."

My eyes shoot up to his. "How did you get this?"

The boyish humor is gone from his eyes, replaced by genuine sincerity. "While you were gone, I found it and kept it close. It was ... how I stayed near to you, even though you were so far away." He rubs the back of his neck and a very real blush colors his cheeks. "I know that may sound silly."

I shake my head. "That's not silly at all." With one finger, I trace the delicate silver curves of a wing. It's the same moth that's carved into the stone around my mother's mausoleum. The same one that decorates Grandmother's knife.

He nods. "I recognized the moth the second I found it."

"But where?"

His eyes dart around to see who's listening. A smile brightens his face as if we're not discussing the belongings of a dead woman. I look up and spot two of my father's guards nearby.

"I'll bring you there," he says.

"When?"

He takes the necklace gently into his hands, then waits. I lift my hair off my shoulders and turn away from him. When he reaches to clasp the necklace around my throat, I close my eyes. The metal is cool against my skin and Hunter's scent is all around me, fresh and bright like a citrus grove after a rainfall. His fingers linger on the skin at the nape of my neck.

"Tonight," he whispers, his warm breath on my ear.

He steps away and holds out his arm for me to take. I do and we continue walking down the garden path.

We sneak away from the palace after supper, our red court clothes left behind. I pull the hood of my brown cloak up to hide my auburn hair, lest anyone recognize me. An autumn breeze blows, making me shiver. Soon, this cloak won't be warm enough for the impending winter.

Hunter leads me down the darkened city streets. Dim lamplight reaches through shuttered windows and onto the cobblestones below our feet. Most shops are closed now, except for the odd tavern and house of ill-repute. The myriad of smells from market day are long gone, replaced by cool stone and garbage left out to rot.

"Where are we?" I ask. I've never been to this part of the city before. It's a long way from the main roads that lead straight to the palace.

"White's End," he says. "It's ..." he pauses, thinking. "One of the less desirable neighborhoods in the city." A rat squeaks by, getting underfoot.

"What were you doing here?"

Hunter pulls me closer, lowering his voice as we walk. "The King's Guard often has ... special assignments. Out of uniform." He pauses as a drunken man stumbles by, swearing loudly about being booted from his favorite drinking hole.

"Such as?"

"I can't say, Sienna. I'm sorry." His mouth is a grim line, ever the loyal knight.

"I understand." But I don't. Why would Commander Malen send his men into the city in disguise? They're sworn to protect the king, not masquerade with the city's unsavory nightlife.

"So, you were on a different mission when you found my grandmother's necklace?"

"More or less." He nods noncommittally. "Here." He points toward a shop with filthy windows half covered in old, molding newspaper. Lamplight still glows from the interior.

"Why would that shop be open at this time of night?" I ask, suspicious.

"Exactly my question when I went inside last year."

Hunter puts his hand on the oxidized doorhandle and pushes it open.

Inside, the shop is a mess of overflowing shelves with dusty odds and ends, everything from books and children's toys to rusty tools and antiques. Along one wall runs a scratched, glass cabinet displaying some of the shop's more precious items. Old coins, knives with dulled edges, and broaches shine under the dull lamplight.

"What do you want?" a gruff man's voice calls from behind a black curtain covering a doorway in the back of the shop.

Hunter clears his throat. "Hello, sir. We're here to inquire about a necklace."

"Unless you're here to buy one, I don't want anything to do with yous," the voice says. "I'm done giving out charity for other people's trash."

Hunter and I share a look.

"I think you misunderstand—" Hunter begins.

The curtain behind the counter is thrown aside as a small, old man with a ruddy face appears. "I don't misunderstand nothin'. Now go!" When he sees us, he pauses, considering. "You lot don't have the look of White's Enders."

"No," Hunter says. "We're not."

The old man eyes us with suspicion from underneath bushy gray eyebrows. "What is it you said you want?"

"Information," Hunter says.

I step forward. "What do you know of this?" I take the silver moth out from beneath the neckline of my dress.

The man freezes, holding his breath.

"You know it?" I ask.

His eyes remain on the moth for longer than necessary. Then he makes a decision. He grabs a filthy rag from behind the counter and begins dusting the shelves. He kicks up a veritable cloud in his wake.

"No." He spits on the ground. "Can't say that I know it."

Hunter leans forward across the counter. "I purchased this necklace from your shop last year."

The shop keeper shrugs, avoiding our eyes as he wipes around a ceramic dog figurine with a chipped nose. "I get a lot of baubles in here. I can't be expected to remember every single one of 'em."

"Do you remember the woman who might have given it to you?" I ask. "Her name was Áine."

He shakes his head, but the tension in his neck muscles gives him away. He's nervous, but trying not to show it. "I don't know nothing about no one. Now, best be on your way."

Hunter puts a hand on my arm and turns me back toward the exit. "Come on. He isn't going to tell us anything."

But I'm not ready to give in so quickly. It's been years since I had any leads about Grandmother and I'm not about to walk away. Suddenly, something catches my eye near the door. A few inches above the scratched floor, there's a small carving in the dingy baseboard.

A moth.

We've been asking all the wrong questions, I realize. I turn back to the old shopkeeper, who cringes.

Hunter pauses in the doorway. "Sienna, what are you—"

I stomp back up to the counter and look the wrinkly old man straight in the eye. "Then what about moths?"

The silence that follows tells me one important piece of information: the shopkeeper is afraid.

Eventually, he swallows. "Are you implying somethin'?"

I hold his gaze. "Only if moths mean something to you."

He sucks his teeth, then leans forward over the counter toward me. He smells of tobacco and old paper. "I think you'd best leave my shop before I call the king's men for shoplifting."

"We didn't steal anything," Hunter says, indignant.

The shopkeeper points his chin toward the silver moth around my neck. "Says who?"

I glower at him. "Fine." I turn to leave. *For now.*

After we leave the filthy shop, I pause to peer through the newspaper-cluttered windows just in time to see the old man dart toward the door and lock it behind us.

Chapter 13

When Hunter finds me the next day, I'm in the library again. This time I'm sitting on the floor of the nature section, books about insects scattered around me. There's something more to the moth around my neck than meets the eye. I know this now. My new problem is, I don't know how to learn what that "something more" is.

Footsteps echo across the marble floor before Hunter peers down the aisle, spotting me. He's in his King's Guard armor. The copper gleams in the sunlight cascading through the windows at the far end of the aisle. He looks every bit the dashing hero, ignited by unnatural powers and noble purpose.

He smiles at me where I sit on the ground. "I thought I'd find you here."

I gesture to the towers of books around me. "I am nothing if not predictable."

He chuckles, reaching out a hand to help me to my feet. "I don't think anyone would call you 'predictable'." He looks down at the open book in my hands. Its pages are covered in sketches of moths, facts about their lifecycles, and mating habits—but nothing about their mysterious purpose carved into the paint of an old pawn shop.

I rub my tired eyes with my free hand. "I suspect I'm in the wrong section entirely, but I have no idea where else to look."

He chews on the inside of his cheek, thinking. "I'm not sure either. And by how the shopkeeper reacted, I don't think it would be wise to tell anyone we're looking."

I rub a hand over the back of my neck where it aches from hours spent bent over tomes, flipping through page after page of moths. "That man can't be the only one who knows."

He nods, thinking.

"Hunter," I ask. "Have you seen the moth symbol anywhere else during your assignments throughout the city?"

He shakes his head. "I'd tell you if I had."

"Would you?" My voice sounds harsher than I intend it to. "Even if it's related to whatever your father is up to?"

He gives me a long look. "Sienna, I ..." He sighs. "I want to tell you everything. I truly do. But I'm a knight. My honor is all I have. You can't expect me to—"

I shake my head. "No, I know. I'm sorry." I'm being unfair. I know this. And yet I can't help but long for the days when Hunter and I shared everything. There were no secrets between us before I left for the borderlands.

"It's just ..." I sigh and close the book, tucking it under one arm. "Sometimes I don't know how to handle the fact that you're one of them now."

He reaches out to grab my free hand. "Sienna, I swear to you. I can be loyal to more than one person."

"Can you?" The words slip out with a bite I wasn't expecting. I thought I'd forgiven him for his betrayal, but maybe I'm still holding onto some small slice of resentment. Some ember of heartache that's hiding in the shadows, deep inside of me. Forgotten, but not entirely gone.

His face softens. "I can be a knight *and* your husband."

"And my friend?" The implication is there. The fact that most husbands and wives have very different power dynamics than ours. Friendship isn't usually part of the equation in arranged marriages. The woman is expected to obey the man in all things, but I won't. He knows that. That's never been me. And it's never been us.

And I'm terrified marriage will ruin that.

He draws his lips into a thin line, then takes a step closer to me. "Sienna, do you think it's wise to dig further?"

A small fire of irritation rises in me. "Are you willing to give up already?"

He shakes his head. "No, that's not what I mean. It's just ..." His eyes scan the gaps between the bookshelves on either side of us, to make sure we're alone. He lowers his voice. "Your grandmother died under very odd circumstances. Yet her necklace shows up in a strange shop in the middle of White's End." He gives me a knowing look. "A shop that turns out to have a carving of that very same moth, despite the shopkeeper insisting he knows nothing about it."

The implication hangs in the air between us, unspoken. We could be the next to die if we keep this up.

I try to relax my shoulders, to put on an air of someone who isn't worried. "I've spent my entire life trying to find out what happened to her. I can't stop now." I give him a long look. "You, of all people, should know this."

He nods, sighing. "I do."

Guilt pools in my chest. I've sacrificed the last twelve years of my life, devoted to this cause. Every time I think I'm getting closer to finding the answers I need, I encounter more curiosities. More questions without answers. It's infuriating and all-consuming. This doesn't have to be Hunter's life, too.

My mind flickers back to the Wolf in the cell. More and

more, it seems, he is the only one who can help me. As much as I hate it. As much as I loathe the idea of trusting one of the Dead Queen's Wolves. They're the same people who've been killing mine for centuries—but I'm running out of options.

"Hunter, you don't have to help me." I swallow. "You've been a true friend. I appreciate everything you've done for me." My hand reaches for the moth resting against my chest. "You've given me the breakthrough I've needed. I could never thank you enough."

Hunter reaches forward and takes the book of moths from me. He studies an open page for a long time before closing the cover and setting it on a shelf. His eyes meet mine.

"I will help you. To the very end. Until we find out what happened to your grandmother and fix what's broken between us." Hunter reaches over to a shelf and plucks another book from it. Its cover is rusty brown and engraved with faded black lettering that's too damaged to read. He opens it to the first page. "I suppose we both have a lot of reading ahead of us then." He smiles at me and I smile back.

He turns another brittle, dried page in the book, then abruptly drops it. "Damn." He opens his palm to reveal a paper cut, already beading with blood.

I grab his hand, then reach for the power sleeping inside me. It flows easily. I've always been comfortable around Hunter. Until recently, anyway.

Power spreads from my core like liquid sunshine, up through my chest. It travels through the veins in my arms until it pools in my open palm. I touch my fingertips gently to Hunter's bleeding cut. We both watch as his skin knits together, becoming so smooth it's as if there was never an injury to begin with.

How I wish heartaches could heal as easily.

I wipe the blood from his palm with my thumb. When my eyes travel up to his face, Hunter is studying me with a familiar look. It's adoration mixed with a dash of wonder, as if I'm some miraculous, precious thing. A secret that he's privileged to know.

Heat, very different from my dissipating power, flushes my cheeks. I hold his gaze. It feels like a dare. Something forbidden, yet tempting.

"I have to know," he says, swallowing hard. "Is this all part of the act?"

I blink, trying to process his question. "There's no one here to see ..." My voice comes out as a whisper.

He lifts his healed hand slowly, as if he's afraid I'll run away if he moves too fast. "Has it *ever* been an act?"

I hesitate, wiling myself to say, *Yes. I've been playing along this whole time*. But there's a lump in my throat that won't let me lie.

"Has it been for you?" I ask.

His face grows fierce with longing. His eyebrows knit together and his lips part in a way that I find utterly intoxicating. "Never." He brushes his thumb along my jawline. "Nothing about this has ever been a lie."

When he kisses me, my knees grow weak. I forget to resist, forget everything except for him. Hunter. The only man who has ever loved me. The only person who will follow me through all of my harebrained schemes and adopt my dream as his own. I know this is wrong. It's cruel to hold him like this when I don't want 'forever' with him. Even if I wish I did.

He wraps his other hand in my loose hair and I grow lightheaded with lust. He presses his body into mine, pinning me against the bookshelf. I want to rip the copper-plated armor from his chest. To feel the warmth radiating from his skin. My mouth aches to drink him in, to taste every inch of him. I want to trail the tip of my tongue over his broad chest, down the muscles of his stomach, to the low line of his breeches.

Instinctively, my fingers search for a gap in his armor,

along his waistline. There has to be a buckle or maybe some laces to release. My fingertips brush the skin of his hip, beneath the edge of his armor. Hunter moans, his mouth pressed to mine. Heat coils tight between my thighs, hot and insistent. I want to reach down into his breeches and grasp his—

Hunter's lips break from mine as he takes a step back.

The change is so sudden, I'm left feeling dizzy. I have to brace myself against the shelf. I give him a baffled look, but his focus isn't on me anymore. Instead, he's staring down the library aisle. Someone clears their throat and I understand.

The elderly librarian stands there, a sheepish grin on his face. "Many pardons, Your Highness." He nods to Hunter. "Sir Hunter, the Commander sent word that you're to meet him in the training yard. Immediately."

Hunter stifles an infuriated sigh before nodding at the librarian. "I understand. Thank you for delivering the message."

The librarian bows to me before turning back down the aisle. He pauses at the end, then looks back over his shoulder at us. "Perhaps, next time, I will say I've not seen you." He gives me a kind look. "Either of you."

Hunter clears his throat. "I would appreciate that."

When the librarian is out of sight, Hunter turns back to me. He has the smirk of a mischievous boy who's been caught doing something naughty, but who intends to do it all again.

We both burst into mortified laughter. I try to stifle mine in the crook of his neck as he pulls me back toward him, tenderly this time. He places a kiss at my temple, pausing to breathe in the scent of my hair.

"I'm sorry, but I have to go."

I nod. "I know."

He meets my eyes. "We'll continue this conversation later."

I raise an eyebrow. "Was this a 'conversation'?"

We both grin.

He kisses the tip of my nose. "Perhaps we'll continue *all of it* later."

"Perhaps."

He squeezes my hand as he turns to leave. Only when he's gone do I realize my hand is still smeared with his blood.

Chapter 14

This time, when I sneak into the pre-dawn kennels, I have a burning mission inside of me. I'll get the Wolf to tell me about my grandmother.

Now.

I can't help him escape. If he wants to live, he needs to play by *my* rules. I have the upper hand here. Answer my questions, or die in the kennels.

The guard outside the kennel is too sleepy to ask many questions of the girl with a hood pulled low over her face. I lug a pail of well-water through the door, careful not to spill it on the stairs as I descend.

The kennels are eerily silent while the foxhounds sleep. My light casts shadows through the bars and into their cells as I walk down the aisle. Mixed into the filthy, scattered hay on the stone ground are gnawed bones and carcasses. Rabbits, mostly. Flies buzz around them, taking the opportunity to feast on the dead flesh.

In the furthest corners of their cells, the foxhounds sleep. They're curled up in tight balls of matted copper fur. To the unwise, they might look like nothing more than household pets. But when one of them lifts its white-tipped tail to peer at me from the shadows, the illusion is broken. His copper-colored eyes shine with hunger. A low, rumbling growl follows me as I hurry past.

The Wolf isn't asleep in the back of his cell. He watches me through swollen black eyes as I set down the pail of water and walk up to the barred door. I won't risk opening his cage. These bars are my best bargaining chip.

"You haven't died yet," I say, by way of greeting.

He laughs humorlessly. "No. Not yet." He squints at my orb of light, trying to adjust from the pitch darkness he's been sitting in.

I reach into the bag that I strapped underneath my cloak. I pull out the bread I stole from the kitchens late last night. "Hungry?" I ask.

He doesn't move.

I wait.

"I expect there's a price." He watches me through the curtain of dark hair covering his face. There's a long, grisly cut along his cheekbone that's sealed together with dried blood, and the skin around his eyes is mottled with purple bruises. Probably from the broken nose, though it looks like he straightened the cartilage back into place.

I shrug. "Isn't that true with everything?"

His face doesn't betray his thoughts. He merely waits.

I hadn't intended to show my hand just yet, but I suppose the sooner the better so I can retreat before I'm discovered.

"I need information."

His iron chains rattle as he slowly stands, never showing the pain he must be in. Hunter doesn't have strong healing power. He couldn't have done much more than keep the Wolf from dying.

"As I said before, you can get it." He holds my eyes in his cool, gray gaze for a long moment. "For a price."

"Escape."

He nods. "Escape."

"I can't offer you that."

He lifts an eyebrow. "Can't? Or won't?"

"Both." My voice is calm. Matter of fact. "But I can offer you some life-sustaining bread."

He tsks, shaking his head slowly, but his eyes drift to the food in my hand. There's hunger in his eyes that he can't hide.

"Do you expect me to beg, Red? To crawl on hands and knees and offer you my entire kingdom for a slice of bread?" His words are bitter, mocking.

"No. I expect answers."

He turns his back to me, staring into the dark corner of his cell. "As I said before, the only answer you seek lies with the queen in Annwyn."

"You don't know the question yet."

He turns to watch me, wordless. He's right to suspect a trick. I am a Fox, after all.

I reach back into my bag to retrieve a book of moths. Something tells me not to show him Grandmother's necklace where it hides beneath my clothes. I fumble with the book, opening it up to a page with a sketch that resembles the silver moth. The same one I found scratched into the shop's paint.

"What do you know of moths?" I ask.

There's a slight change in his face that I'm sure is unintentional. Lines deepen around his mouth and his gray eyes darken.

"That they are beautiful but elusive creatures susceptible to a whack with a swatter. What of them?"

His indifference can't fool me. I sense a new layer of tension in the air between us. He knows something.

"Try again." My voice is full of unearned confidence.

He watches me for a time, assessing. A Wolf calculating the success of a potential target. "Maybe you could be more specific?" His eyes drift to the food in my hand and I know I've got him.

"More *specifically* ..." I lean toward him. "Why have I seen these moths in secret places all around Caerwen?"

I haven't, of course. But I'm willing to bet they exist. If there truly is something more to these moths, there's no way they exist only on my grandmother's necklace and the dirty wall of an old pawn shop.

The corner of his mouth twitches. "You expect a Wolf to know the secrets of a Fox's den?"

I lower my chin, staring harder into his eyes. "Yes."

The Wolf walks back toward me with a slight limp, sizing me up like a predator. His chains rattle as they drag along the ground. He grabs the bars on his cell door and leans forward. I resist the urge to back up, standing my ground.

"Do you even know what you're asking, Little Fox?"

I don't blink, don't swallow, don't breathe. Nothing to give away my position. "That's inconsequential. I want to know what *you* know."

He holds his hand out for the bread. I rip off one small square from the loaf and place it in his hand. He chuckles as he stuffs it into his mouth, wincing slightly as he chews. After he swallows, he pushes himself off the bars and takes a few steps back toward the shadows of his cell. For a moment, I think he won't tell me anything, but then he speaks, his back still facing me.

"Moths are curious creatures, aren't they?"

I say nothing.

"They emerge gloriously from the husk of their former selves. Reborn from little more than worms." He looks over his shoulder at me. "You, Red, are no worm. And thus, no moth."

"What is that supposed to mean?"

He laughs in that infuriating way of his, low and taunting. "It means you could never be one of them."

"Them?" I cross my arms. "So, the moth represents a group of people?"

He turns to face me again, his eyes dark. "Yes."

"People who some might consider worms." It's not a question. That explains why we found the carving in the filthy shop in White's End. "Commoners."

He waggles his head noncommittally. "Yes ... and no."

"You're not really holding up your end of the bargain," I warn, irritation flaring.

"Aren't I?"

I dig through my bag and take out a hunk of preserved meat. The Wolf stills. I can practically see his mouth watering.

"If you want this food, then you'd better talk."

"What happened to the helpful little fox who saved my life?"

"She's grown tired of your evasive answers," I snarl.

The Wolf paces in his cell, thinking. He turns to look at me. "Do you trust me, Red?"

"No," I spit out so quickly it has to be the truth.

"Then why would you come to me, your mortal enemy, for answers about a pretty little bug?"

"Truth for truth?"

He nods.

"Because I have no one else to ask."

"Hm," he says. "Like your questions about Áine." He returns to the bars, staring into my eyes with a ferocity that's both terrifying and somehow thrilling.

My heart jumps in my chest. I'm not afraid of this man, the shiver running through my veins is something else entirely.

His words hiss like a snake. "The moth is the symbol of the underground. The Llwyn that hides in the shadows."

I shake my head, confused. "Why must they hide?"

He tuts, mockingly. "Why, from you, Little Fox. And your great Fox King."

My head is whirling. Why would the people of Llwyn need to hide from the monarchy? My father hardly pays attention to the actions of everyday people. To say he cares what a shopkeeper in White's End thinks is to compare him to a great bear who interests himself in the affairs of an ant.

I glower at the Wolf. "I don't believe you."

He shrugs. "Suit yourself. But we traded a truth for a truth." He holds out his hand, expectantly.

For a moment, I consider not giving him the food. But in the end, my guilty conscience wins. I toss the bread and meat through the bars, past his outstretched hand.

"What good are veiled answers from a Wolf in a cage?" I ask.

He stares at me through the bars.

I step closer, our faces only inches apart. He could bite me now, if he tried. "I'd be careful of trying to outwit a fox," I warn. "The fox always wins, eventually."

He grins. "Unless she's devoured by a wolf first."

The Wolf's proximity sends a reckless thrill through me, unfamiliar and exhilarating. It's power, I realize with a shudder. Maybe I'm more like my father than I care to admit.

I smile at him as I turn to walk back out of the kennels, taking my light with me. The first foxhounds stir from sleep around me. Their snarls echo up the stairs as I walk, thinking of moths and foxes.

And hungry Wolves that look at me like they want to taste my flesh.

Chapter 15

I'M SITTING at a long table covered in sweets: powder pink treats; pies piled with mountains of fluffy, white meringue; and crystal cups filled with silky, blue and yellow mousse. Near my elbow, there's a bowl of candies decorated to look like foxes. Their little beady eyes stare at me blankly.

I vaguely wonder if I've stepped into a confectioner's dream.

"Everything must be perfection at the royal wedding," a tiny man in a chef's uniform says. "We cannot be lackadaisical about cakes."

Next to me, Hunter whispers. "No, certainly not that."

I elbow him for what feels like the fifth time in as many minutes. He laughs, his eyes light and playful in a way I haven't seen in a long time. He's wearing a traditional red shirt of the royally betrothed. My scarlet dress pinches my ribs. It's not exactly the most comfortable choice for an afternoon sampling wedding cakes.

"First up," the chef says. "Is the cake that I call the Heavenly Highness." He gives a grand, full-body gesture toward a servant, who quickly brings two dessert plates from the back of the room. The plates display perfect slices of white cake topped with pink frosting and a tiny candy-spun strawberry.

I raise an eyebrow as Hunter immediately pops his sugar strawberry into his mouth.

"Mmm," he nods. "Heaven, indeed." He picks up his fork eagerly.

The chef beams. "I will leave you both to discuss." He steps backwards about a half-dozen feet to give us "privacy". Why anyone needs privacy to eat a cake is beyond me. It's not like we're ingesting political secrets. Though, maybe ...

I keep my face controlled as I place a napkin over my lap like a proper lady. "Have you read anything interesting lately?" I ask with one eyebrow raised. I play with the silver moth around my neck pointedly.

Hunter looks up at me, his cheeks full of white cake. "I haven't had time," he says after he swallows. He scoops another huge fork full.

While Hunter's been busy with King's Guard duties, I've hardly slept. I spent the past day and night reading everything I could find about moths. There are plenty of ancient field sketches and biological notes from insect enthusiasts ... but nothing about their symbology or potential relevance to a woman I believe to have been murdered.

My disappointment must show on my face.

"Your Highness?" the chef asks. "Is it not to your liking?"

I blink up at him.

"The cake." He gestures toward my plate.

"Oh!" I pick up my fork. "My apologies, I was lost in ... my ... my betrothed's eyes. That's all." I shove a forkful into my mouth. My groan is genuine. My eyes roll as I taste strawberries and cream in baked form. I swallow. "Light as air."

The chef beams.

Next to me, Hunter scrapes the remains of pink frosting with his fork. "Amazing."

"We'll have that one at the wedding," I say decisively. "It's perfect."

The chef shakes his head and tuts. "No, no, no. There are a dozen more to try before you decide."

"A dozen?" I ask, not sure if he's joking.

"A dozen." The chef nods. He gestures to the servants to clear the plates and bring out the next round. They buzz about like late-summer bees in black and white uniforms. Silver platters clink and fabric swishes softly as they move with practiced efficiency.

This cake is as dark as the forest at night with a glistening chocolate glaze on top that's smooth as a mirror and reflects the warm sunlight. The rich aroma of cocoa and toasted nuts wafts through the air, making my mouth water.

"Toasted almond and chocolate," the chef says, beaming with pride. "I call it The Lover's Tryst."

"I love getting married," Hunter says, taking a bite. "And you, of course," he adds as an afterthought, his words slightly muffled by the cake.

I can't help but smile.

The chef steps away again to give us some space. The heels of his shoes click against the polished floor as he leaves.

All around us, the servants bring even more confectionary treats to the table. Jellied white rabbits, their sugar-coated bodies glistening in the light. Cookies shaped like delicate snowflakes, so intricate it seems a shame to eat them. Pale blue mini-cakes sprinkled with powdered sugar like snow, their cool hue a stark contrast to the warm golds and reds of the room. Perfect for a winter wedding.

My eyes dart toward the window. Autumn has arrived in full, finally. The sky is gray and heavy with the promise of rain, and the wind rustles the changing leaves in the trees. They dance in a mosaic of green, russet, gold, and crimson.

I clear my throat and pick up my fork. "And have you

checked on our friend?" I ask Hunter, trying to keep my voice steady. When he stares at me blankly, I add, "Our new puppy."

His eyebrows draw together with confusion.

I lean closer to his ear and whisper. "In the kennels."

His eyes widen with understanding. "Oh. No." He rubs the back of his neck. "Sorry. I haven't had the opportunity."

A servant steps forward to bring a copper-colored sun tart to the display on the table. Its flaky crust glistens with a sugar glaze, and the scent of cinnamon and nutmeg adds to the already heady mix of aromas in the room. I barely take a bite of cake before a server whisks away the chocolate almond slice and replaces it with another that's yellow with fluffy, pale frosting.

"Lemon," the chef says, his round cheeks pink with excitement. My father might be right about one thing: people love a royal wedding to fuss over.

The chef watches, waiting as we both take our first bites. The tart sweetness instantly transports me to the golden sunrays of summer. I close my eyes to savor it.

"Thoughts?" the chef asks.

"Gorgeous, delicious ..." I say, at a loss for words.

He smiles encouragingly, waiting for more.

My brain scrambles to think of a better response. "... But maybe not right for a winter wedding?"

He nods his approval. "Very wise, Your Highness. A perfect cake in all respects, but one. It is out of season." He chuckles, then whispers. "But still worth the taste, no?"

Hunter hums, his mouth full of cake. "Definitely."

The chef claps his hands together. "I will let you two get acquainted with Madame Sunshine while I fetch more champagne!" He disappears into the kitchen.

"I like him," Hunter says with a grin.

Seconds later, the chef returns carrying two twinkling champagne flutes. "For the lovebirds."

We thank him and clink our glasses together gently. They chime in the way only the finest crystal does. I take a sip. It's like crisp fireworks in my mouth.

"Beautiful," Hunter says. "Many thanks."

I take another sip, trying to ease my anxiety. Then another.

"Ah, ah, ah!" the chef says. "Not too fast. You have ten more champagne bottles to sample as well."

I swallow, my eyes wide.

The chef leans in conspiratorially. "One can not serve the first champagne one tries."

"No, definitely not." Hunter drains his glass and sets it down on the fine white tablecloth. "This is the best day ever."

After at least six more cakes, a messenger dressed in familiar copper livery enters the room. The lighthearted atmosphere dissolves instantly.

The messenger approaches me and bows, but I already know what's coming.

"Your Highness, your father awaits you in his audience chamber."

I sigh and stand. "Thank you," I tell the messenger. Then I turn to the chef, who's wringing his hands anxiously. "My apologies, sir, but I must attend to King Corsac." I gesture toward Hunter. "I leave you in excellent hands. My beloved will choose the cake. He knows my tastes well."

Hunter stands abruptly. "I'll accompany you." His good-natured smile is gone now, replaced by a stern line of worry. I hate that I've ruined this experience for him.

"I'll be fine," I tell him. "Stay. Pick out a good one."

Hunter looks torn between duty and the new cake a server just brought to the table: white with purple frosting and blue berries. "I'll do my best."

The large doors of the audience chamber echo when they close behind me. My father stands at the head of a long, polished table, a glass of dark, amber liquid in his hand. Next to him, Commander Malen looks up, peeved at the interruption. He holds a stack of papers in his arms.

The only other people present are the guards at the door.

"Daughter," Father says, his voice smooth as silk but with an underlying edge. "My apologies for interrupting your wedding planning. I hope you and Hunter are enjoying yourselves."

I grit my teeth.

He chuckles lightly, then finishes what's in his glass. "The joys of youth. Young love and all that." He shares a lewd grin with Malen, eyebrows raised as if he knows anything about love. He's much too selfish to have ever truly loved anyone, even my mother.

Father sets his glass on the table with a soft clink, then gestures for me to sit next to him. My limbs are stiff as I walk forward. I sit in a chair of my own choosing, several feet away. He notes my small disobedience, his eyes narrowing almost imperceptibly, but says nothing. He sits down himself. For a long moment, we just stare at each other.

Finally, he speaks. "Do you have anything to say to me?"

Panic rises in my sternum. Does he know I asked Hunter to heal and feed the Wolf? I do my best to appear calm.

"You should have tried the cake."

Father lets out a bark of a laugh, but there's no genuine joy in it. "Such a comedienne, Little Fox. You've always been amusing."

"But?"

He watches me, then shrugs. "I suppose there's no point in drawing this out any longer." He gestures toward Commander Malen, who bangs his fist against a nearby bookshelf. It opens with a groan to reveal a hidden door. Two copper-clad guards enter, dragging the Wolf between them.

I stand so quickly my chair falls out behind me. Father watches me with interest, one eyebrow raised. After my momentary panic, I control my face to be neutral, my hands clenched at my sides to stop them from shaking.

The guards toss the shackled Wolf onto the ground. He lands with a dull thud, a small groan escaping his lips. He's still visibly weak, but his coloring is much improved. His skin is no longer bone white and his eyes have lost the glassy sheen of the starved. The swelling around his nose has subsided and his bruises have faded to green.

"Ah." The king claps his hands together. "Our honored guest has arrived." My father uprights my chair and presses on my shoulder, forcing me down into it. He gestures for the Wolf to take a seat next to me.

The Wolf watches him, his pale eyes like a storm cloud, veiled and haunting. He gets up from the floor on shaky limbs and takes a seat next to me, his chains rattling with each movement. There's a tension in his body, like a coiled spring ready to release.

"Wine." Father commands.

Two servants appear from behind a tapestry. One carries a decanter and crystal goblets, the dark red liquid sloshing gently as he moves. The other balances several plates of grapes, breads, and cheeses. They serve us with practiced efficiency and back away, their soft footsteps fading as they disappear behind the tapestry once more.

My father watches the Wolf, predicting his next move like this is a game of chess.

The Wolf doesn't eat.

"Come now," my father says, like he's speaking with an incorrigible child. "You must be famished after all of your ... adventures."

The Wolf stares at him coolly.

I can feel the fury radiating off the Wolf beside me, like heat from a raging fire. His hands curl into tight fists, the cracks in his knuckles caked with dirt and dried blood. Killing hands. I know, deep in my gut, that he could unleash his shadow power and slaughter us where we stand. And yet, he hasn't.

Why?

Briefly, I think I must have a death-wish, keeping a man like this alive. But I've long known that I don't fear death. There's little left in this world that I care for. It was all taken from me, replaced with parties and an eager groom whom I didn't choose. There's a tiny voice inside of me that thinks I would like the Wolf to kill us all. I've dreamed of Commander Malen's death a thousand times for the cruelties he inflicted upon Hunter when we were children. And I'd truly relish the sight of my father dripping in his own blood, even if it was the last thing I ever saw.

"Suit yourself," Father says as he grabs a handful of purple grapes.

I hope he chokes on them, but he doesn't.

Father shakes his head like he's forgotten something. "What are we, beasts?" He snaps at a nearby guard. "Remove his irons. This man is our honored guest today."

The man takes out a key and the iron shackles clatter to the ground. The Wolf barely reacts.

Father leans forward, his elbows on the table. "Who are you?"

"Tristan."

I startle, realizing I've never asked his name. I'd grown used to thinking of him only as "the Wolf".

"Who sent you?"

The Wolf—Tristan—narrows his eyes. He leans forward on the table, mirroring Father's posture. "A ghost."

Father rolls his eyes. "And what does this 'ghost' require of me that he sent you to invade my personal chambers?"

"An end to the invasion of Annwyn." He says it so calmly that, for a moment, I think I misheard him.

My spine tingles. *Us* invading *them*? I've been to the borderlands. I've seen the carnage. If anything, it's the Llwyn people who are in peril. For generations, Annwyn has creeped into our territory, our land. At least, that's what I've always been told.

I spare a glance for Malen, who glowers at the Wolf from the shadows. I know that look. It's one I've seen a thousand times whenever Hunter did something that he disapproved of. That look is a promise to make him pay for the misstep when no one is watching.

Father gives Tristan a pitying look. "A sympathizer then."

This makes no sense. I turn to the Wolf and ask, "Sympathizer for wha—"

Father snaps. "Be quiet or I'll have your tongue ripped from your face!"

My jaw clamps shut. My face heats to what must be a fiery flush. I can feel the Wolf's eyes on me.

Father picks up a small knife from the cheeseboard. He twirls it in his hands for a moment, then asks. "Is this one a sympathizer, too?" He points the knife's tip in my direction.

The Wolf stays silent.

Father's eyes narrow, and he stands abruptly from his chair. "I grow tired of your games, Tristan. I only like mine." He speaks as he walks briskly toward us. I think he's heading to Tristan, but he pivots at the last second. He wraps one arm around the back of my chair, pinning me to it, while his knife meets my throat.

"Let's see how little you truly know or care about my heir." He presses the knife closer to the delicate skin of my neck. The cool metal nips at my throat like a lover's kiss.

The Wolf stares at the king with cool indifference.

"What?" Father asks. "Do you think I'm bluffing?" He laughs. "My daughter and I have no great fondness for each other. Isn't that right, dear daughter?" He tilts his head to look at my face, but I close my eyes against the tears that threaten there. I have no doubt that he would kill me. It would solve one of his many problems. He could just blame it on the Wolf.

But if there's one truth universally known, it's this: A king without an heir can't keep his throne for long. A usurper would seize the opportunity sooner or later. And that, I know in my soul, is the single thing that has kept me alive all these years.

"What a small man you are."

My eyes pop open to see Tristan studying us.

Father just laughs. "You've known no suffering until you've had a disobedient child." He presses the knife closer. "Now tell me. Who do you work for and how is my deceitful heir involved?"

"She isn't." Tristan says simply, with a shrug. "I'd never seen her before that night."

"Then what was she doing in my rooms with you?"

A warm bead of blood trickles down my neck. Tristan watches it fall. The drop catches on the delicate silver chain that hides Grandmother's necklace beneath my dress. His face grows dark, the only emotion he's shown throughout this entire test.

"She followed me."

The Wolf stands up from his chair and my father pulls me closer into the back of mine, threatening. Guards make a move to grab Tristan, but father shakes his head. The Wolf leans one hip against the table and finally reaches for a grape. He pops it into his mouth, as if this were a mere chat instead of an inquisition laced with murder.

I've never noticed how tall the Wolf was before. Maybe

because I've mostly seen him sprawled out on the ground, too weak to stand. The night I encountered him, we were both in elaborate costumes, but now we're just two people facing a monster, unadorned. He's weak, but under his worn clothes, his muscles are tense, ready to pounce. His dark hair is messy, like that of a man who's just been properly tumbled. But most noticeable are his eyes. They're pale gray and cold like the moon.

Tristan smiles. "I, however, was in your room to find information."

"And did you?" my father asks, his voice low.

Tristan pauses, thoughtfully. "I don't know. Possibly. It's still difficult to tell."

"Stop playing games," Father hisses, his patience waning. "Tell me plainly. What were you looking for?"

Tristan squares off to face us, a slight smile at the corner of his mouth. "I was looking for the Heir to the North."

Father actually laughs. He looks to Malen for backup.

"Very amusing, Your Highness," Malen says, ever the good little bootlicker.

Father turns his attention back to Tristan. "Fables and baby stories? In my chambers? You'd have better luck in that infernal library this one hides in." Father puts his face close to my ear. I can feel his hot breath on my cheek. It smells of spirits and old cheese.

The Wolf considers this, tilting his head. "Perhaps."

"The truth." Father presses the knife further into my neck and I feel the flesh splitting. Slick, hot blood trickles over my collarbone. Ludicrously, I think how fortunate it is that it won't stain my dress too badly, since I'm already wearing red.

The Wolf stiffens.

I can feel my father's grin next to my face, like the creep of a spider. A chill runs down my spine. "Ah, there's more to this than you've said." Father tuts. "And here I thought we were developing a bit of honesty between us."

The Wolf's pale moon eyes give nothing away, but he clenches his jaw in barely restrained anger. "For generations, your family has stolen land, food, resources. All to fill your own palace coffers."

"Typical sympathizer nonsense." The king laughs it off, like it's nothing but a rumor in the wind.

The Wolf's fists clench at his sides. "You've killed men, women, and children—even your own people who you call 'sympathizers'—just to feed your greed." His eyes dart to mine and I know what he's secretly telling me.

Grandmother.

The Wolf is saying Grandmother was murdered for being an Annwyn sympathizer. How could that be? I'm heir to the throne. She wouldn't have undermined me like that. Father, yes. But not me.

The Wolf continues. "Families in Annwyn died—continue to die—of starvation, disease, and the blades of your soldiers."

My stomach tightens. No. That can't be true. I've healed thousands of soldiers who were attacked by Annwyn warriors and their undead monsters. It was self-defense, not aggression. But then I wonder, why did the camps always move north, into newly reclaimed territories? I've never seen a map with border lines on it. I never knew for absolute certainty who's land we were on. My breath catches in my chest as doubt creeps through me like a shadow.

Is it possible the corpse wolves aren't on our land at all? That we are on theirs?

Father scoffs. "The queen's Wolves can just bring the peasants back to life, if they so please." Like it's nothing to kill a child. And, to him, maybe it isn't.

Tristan's voice lowers to a growl. "We do not reanimate people."

At the word "we" father's arms stiffen against me. The Wolf has finally played the card I knew he'd been hiding—the confession that he isn't dealing with a sympathizer, but an actual Wolf.

Across the room, Commander Malen stills, his hand reaching for the silver and copper sword that's ever at his side.

Even with the blood soaking into the neckline of my dress, I feel a small thrill of glee. If my father's terror is the last thing I see on this earth, then it will be a good death.

Father's voice shakes. "Guards! Guards!"

They're slow to respond, not fully comprehending what my father and I both know: Tristan isn't an ordinary man. He is a Wolf among Foxes.

"You want to know why I was really in your chambers that night?" Tristan says, taking a step toward us. "I was looking for a way to end you."

The knife slices into my throat as Father leaps away from Tristan. Blood spills over my chest in a hot gush, and I fall to my knees. At the sight of the blood, I try not to let panic take over. I can't heal myself, and I don't know what to do.

The guards have reached Tristan now, their bronze swords pulled from their sheathes. But they don't do any good, because in an instant, we are all cloaked in a veil of darkness. The guards shout and I hear scuffling. Someone cries out in agonizing pain and I flinch. The blood loss makes me lightheaded.

Someone pulls me up from the ground and drags me toward a wall, away from the chaos. For a moment, I'm afraid it's my father, back to finish the job while cloaked in shadow. But even though I can't see him in the darkness, his hands are too careful with me, too gentle to be my father or even a guard. They have to belong to the Wolf.

"Red," Tristan says. "Red, are you okay?"

With all the blood loss, I can't tell if I'm losing my grip on reality or if he's actually concerned about my wellbeing.

"I don't know," I whisper back, honestly. At least I can still speak. That has to be a good sign. But when I look down, I'm not so sure I should celebrate yet. My dress front is wet with blood, my hands sticky and trembling.

The guards yell for reinforcements as they bump into furniture, blind in the darkness.

"I can't heal you," Tristan says. "What should I do? Where should I take you?"

"Go." I try to push him away. "You won't get anywhere with me."

"I can't leave you here to die with these monsters."

A laugh bubbles out of me at the absurdity of that. Us, the Llwyns, being called monsters by a Wolf?

"They'll heal me as soon as you're gone." I shake my head. "But you won't get far without help." I slump into him, the blood loss truly weakening me now.

"Red!" His whisper is panicked now. How kind it would be to die next to someone who actually seems to care, even if we're as good as strangers.

Swords clang in the darkness and a heavy piece of furniture crashes to the ground.

"There's a cemetery," I say. "Near the northeast side of the grounds. Find the mausoleum at the pond. I'll meet you there. I'll help you reach the borderlands."

"No. I can carry you. Tell me where to take you—"

"Go!" My voice is raw and the strain makes me cough. The pain in my neck is staggering, and my vision is beginning to blur at the edges. I'm struggling to keep my panic at bay.

Tristan hesitates, but eventually lays me on the ground. "I'll wait for you." And then his hands leave me. Moments later, a slight breeze breaks through the chaos from a window that someone threw open. I relax in relief, knowing Tristan got away.

From where I'm lying slumped on the ground, I watch the darkness in the room slowly dissipate. The Wolf is truly gone. Everything sounds fuzzy in my ears, like an echo of real life. I'm vaguely aware of the reinforcements arriving as they burst through the chamber doors, swords drawn. Then Hunter sprints toward me, his face fearful as he draws upon his own healing power to staunch the blood flowing onto the palace floors.

Just before I black out, it strikes me that my father and Commander Malen are nowhere to be seen. Across the room, an innocent-looking tapestry lies on the ground, exposing one of my father's many secret passageways.

Chapter 16

I DREAM OF MOTHS.

Or maybe it's less of a dream than a deathbed memory.

Once, my grandmother woke me in the middle of the night, a finger pressed to her lips to keep me quiet. Without hesitation, I followed her through the empty corridors, our bare feet making no sound on the cold stone. She led me out of the palace, across the gardens, and out into the forest beyond, all the while saying nothing. She didn't need to. I would have followed her to the edge of the earth with nothing more than a wink.

The hem of my nightgown grew heavy with dew as we walked, and twigs scratched at my bare feet along the forest floor. Eventually, she paused. Dappled moonlight illuminated the forest floor where night flowers bloomed and moss sparkled with dew.

"Go," she whispered. "There's a clearing ahead."

I stepped forward, determined to show her I wasn't afraid. There, in the middle of the forest, was a small clearing speckled with wildflowers. But that wasn't what made my breath catch in my chest.

It was the moths.

Thousands of them.

They covered every stone, flower, branch, and leaf. Every variety of moth that nature could imagine from garden-variety cabbage whites to elusive, pale green lunas. Their wings fluttered and waved, as silent as the moonlight, as if it was a gathering of graceful, midnight dancers.

"What is this?" I asked as I spun slowly in place, unable to take my eyes away from them. The spots on their wings blinked with each flutter, like the eyes of fae.

"Moths are solitary creatures," Grandmother said, her voice full of reverence. "But when I was a child, I stumbled upon this gathering. As far as I know, it only happens once per year, on the first full moon of midsummer."

"But why?" I asked.

Grandmother just shrugged. "Who can say? The moths don't tell me their secrets. Many don't even have mouths."

I turned to her, my eyes wide. She laughed.

"It's true. They survive off the food they ate as caterpillars. They don't live long as majestic, winged creatures." She tilted her head up toward the stars and closed her eyes. "But while they live, they are a wonder."

We laid there on the wet grass, showered with moonlight and speckled with moths until the sun rose. As the birds sang their morning songs, the moths silently floated away in the wind, taking their many secrets with them.

I awake in my silk-covered bed, moonlight streaming through my window. My hand clutches Grandmother's moth necklace so tightly, the silver bites into the flesh of my palm.

Slowly, as if through a fog, the Wolf's escape returns to my mind. I bolt upright, gasping. My hands grasp at my neck, remembering the wound there, feeling the thin scar that's replaced it. A palace healer must have attended to me.

"Shh!" a voice whispers. I turn to see Hunter scrambling up from a nearby chair, next to a small lantern lit low. He's wearing a rumpled white shirt and brown trousers. It's the sort of thing he'd wear to the training yard. A glint of metal behind him draws my eye. Copper-plated bronze. He'd tucked his King's Guard armor behind an arrangement of red roses on the floor.

He kneels next to the bed and places a hand on my cheek. "Everything's alright now, Sienna. You're safe."

"Have they captured him?" I ask, panic rising in me again. It makes me woozy and I fall back into the downy pillows.

He doesn't respond.

The room still smells ludicrously of a thousand roses. The romantic gesture feels like a distant memory now. Yet here we are, surrounded by a veritable garden as proof that it did, in fact, happen.

When the nausea passes, I look sideways at Hunter. His face twists with concern, his lips pursed like he's holding something back.

"Well?" I ask, impatient after my brush with death. "Did they?"

"Do you wish they had?" His face is unreadable in the low light. "Or are you asking because you hope he got away?"

I make an impatient sound that causes my neck to burn, like there's still a tear beneath the surface. The noble-born healers did their best for me, I'm sure. The external wound healed, but there's still significant damage under the skin. Only time will heal me completely. Well, that or my father. We share the same inherited power, after all. But considering he's the one who sliced me, I doubt he's eager to fix his own handiwork.

Discomfort must show on my face. Hunter grabs a small

tin of salve from the nearby table and hands it to me. I take it without comment and smear some of the honey-smelling ointment onto my neck. The skin is tender, and the medicine does nothing for the burn.

"I told you before," I say when I've finished. "I don't want him to die because of me."

"Did you know he was a Wolf?" Hunter asks, an accusation laces through his words like thorns through one of the bouquet of roses.

I nod.

"And you would still help him? After he nearly killed you?" Hunter says, incredulous.

"What?" I hold up my hands as if I could stop that thought. "No. He didn't try to kill me. Father did."

"That's not what the other King's Guards are saying."

"And whose employ are they under?" I ask, challenging him to believe the lies over me. "If anything, he saved me."

"Why would he do that?" Hunter shakes his head, still not willing to believe a Wolf on the loose would have spared the heir to the Fox Throne. And, honestly, I don't blame him. It hardly makes sense to me and I was there.

"I don't know." And I don't.

Tristan could have killed Father and been gone in an instant if it hadn't been for me. If he hadn't stopped to care for me, then he'd have fulfilled his mission and been well on his way to the northern border by now. But he didn't.

"*I'll wait for you*," he'd said. Why?

I rub a hand over the scar on my neck. "I'm not sure I understand any of it. The Wolf said some ... confusing things."

Hunter's face twists in wariness. "What kinds of things?"

The low light casts shadows across the ridiculous floral arrangements throughout the room. I'm tucked into this soft, warm bed, healed and lovingly cared for ... but I still don't feel safe. I never do in the palace.

I throw the blankets off of me. "I don't know, but I'm going to find out." I move to get out of bed, but Hunter places his hands on my shoulders.

"Whoa, whoa. Hold on, Sienna. You nearly died!"

"Which is why I need some answers."

"Can't they wait until morning?"

"No." I fight away a wave of lightheadedness. "They can't."

I step off the bed, grateful that someone put me in one of those god-awful frilly nightdresses or else I'd be standing in front of Hunter in the nude. He blushes anyway. I grab a dressing gown from the closet, throwing it over my sleep clothes to make me appear more presentable. It's not at all to my taste, too many bows and pastels for my liking, but I don't have time to change into something less ridiculous. I tuck Grandmother's necklace under the fabric.

"Can we at least talk for a minute?" Hunter asks, looking alarmed by my sudden resolve.

I reach for the door handle, then pause. "You can come with me. You need to hear this, too."

I throw open my chamber door and two guards stand at attention. Hunter scrambles after me, looking like he hasn't slept in a decade.

"Take me to him," I say to the guards.

"He's in hiding," one says. "From the Wolf."

I lower my eyes. "I am the heir to the Fox Throne. And I said, 'take me to him.'"

They do.

We take the hidden passageways, guided by our own light. The luminescent orb bobs ahead of us, showing the way through the narrow stone corridors. After several turns and downward spiraling staircases, we're deep in the palace's underbelly.

The guards lead us to a thick wooden door that opens on

squeaky hinges. We pass through and emerge into a mildew-smelling chamber with at least a dozen more guards standing at the ready. There are no windows, no other doors. My father is truly in hiding, afraid of the Big Bad Wolf. His fear makes me brave.

Even though it's the middle of the night, Father isn't sleeping, either. He's sitting at a desk, writing furiously. When he hears the door open, he stands abruptly.

"Who let you in here?! I said no visitors until the Wolf is found!" He sounds unhinged in a way I've never heard before. It's both alarming and deeply satisfying to witness.

"I forced them to bring me." I say, standing tall. I'm not afraid of the Wolf, after all. "I see you're relieved to discover that I survived my injuries."

He doesn't even have the decency to look flustered. "My congratulations."

This room feels like a prison. Maybe it is. No one would ever find a person locked away down here. The walls glisten with dripping condensation and there's a collection of emerald green moss and fungi growing in the corner. The air down here is thick with the smell of earth, as if fresh air never reaches these depths.

I take several leisurely steps toward Father's desk. "Rumor has it, the Wolf sliced my throat and spilled royal blood—nearly killing your heir." I stare at him, allowing my eyes to do the rest of the talking.

We both know the truth.

Father doesn't react. "He's a menace and a villain."

"Hm." I purse my lips. I'll keep his secret for now. Not that anyone would believe the truth from me, except for maybe Hunter. Behind me, he shifts, unsure what to do. I gesture toward him. "I brought my betrothed."

"I can see that." Father's eyes narrow on the guards who

brought us. They'll be punished, but I can't worry about that now.

"I have questions for you."

"As always." His voice is unamused.

I step toward him. "Is it true that we're the aggressors in this never-ending war, not Annwyn?"

Father rolls his eyes. "You've always been a petulant child."

"I'm not a child anymore. And I won't follow you blindly."

"Since when do you follow me at all?" Father's scowl deepens. "Your entire life, you've been angry and needlessly rebellious. You make life harder than it needs to be, then blame others for your misfortunes."

"Like Grandmother's murder?" It's a challenge, and the look on his face tells me he knows it. He doesn't respond.

It feels slightly absurd to stand in this moldering dungeon arguing about murder and deceit while wearing my frilly nightgown and velvety-pink robe. I should be clad in armor if I'm the only person brave enough to defy this beast.

"It's time you stop living in the past and start facing your responsibilities." He clenches his fist on the desk. "This kingdom does not protect itself. It needs a strong ruler to save it from the Dead Queen. And here you are, sneaking around with her spies."

"That's not what happened."

He pinches the bridge of his nose, like he has a headache. "Do you know what the corpse queen wants? She intends to overthrow the Fox Throne. To bring horror and chaos to Llwyn. Doesn't that matter to you at all?"

I set my jaw, refusing to take the bait.

He looks at the guards near the door. "Get out."

I feel the steadying presence of Hunter behind me, unmoving. It's a brave thing to stay behind in the face of an angry king. An immense wave of gratitude washes over me.

The guards leave and close the heavy door behind them. They look like copper insects skittering away from a hungry lizard.

Father breaks the following silence. "Let me ask you a question." He tinkers with the inkwell on his desk, thoughtfully. "What use would healing powers be if there were no fools on the verge of death? If there were no wounded soldiers on battlefields?"

The questions are rhetorical. He lowers his eyes at me. "This war is how we keep our family on the throne."

"You mean, this is how *you* stay on the throne?"

"For. My. Heir." He glares at me. "Or, it would have been, if you hadn't been such an infuriating, embarrassing failure."

There is an implied threat in his words. For the first time, I wonder if maybe he'd intended for me to die yesterday. If he wanted to bait the Wolf and make a scene, to kill me and blame it on the prisoner. My hand instinctively reaches up to my throat to feel the tender scar there.

"You think I only exist to gratify you," I say, incredulous. "To make you look good. To keep *your* seat on the throne."

Father shrugs. "It's all a matter of your point of view."

"Murdering people and stealing land for personal gain isn't what a *good ruler* does."

"Good?" He raises an eyebrow. "Define 'good'. Our people are fed. They have homes and clothes on their backs."

"All won through theft and lies."

Hunter reaches forward to put a hand on my elbow. "Sienna, maybe—"

Father steps closer to me. "Do you honestly think the comfortable housewife cares where her food comes from, as long as her brats are fed? Do you think the silversmith cares what his weapons are used for, as long as the work keeps coming?"

I stare at him in horror.

Father leans in close to me. "No, they don't." He scowls. "A good ruler takes care of his own people. That's what I do. I will damn Annwyn if it means Llwyn thrives. A good father does what he must to protect his family."

The word "family" rings in my ears. It is hollow and meaningless coming from his lips. How has he protected me? I'm his only true family and I've never felt safe a day in my life. Especially not from him.

All this time, *we* were the monsters—The Fox Throne and Llwyn.

We were the ones stealing land, killing families, causing pain and misery. All to keep my monstrous family in a golden palace.

And I helped him.

In my determination to run away, become a better person than my father, to help my people, heal them, save them ... I was helping *him*.

"I can't do this." The whisper comes out of me before I've had a chance to really think it through.

In my peripheral, I see Hunter look at me in alarm.

"Can't do what?" he asks. But I think he already knows.

My father lowers his eyes at me and the shadows of this dark room dance around the creases in his face.

"Any of it." I shake my head and turn to Hunter. "I am so sorry, Hunter. But I can't marry you."

Hunter's face pales. He stands frozen, like he's trying to register my words, but he doesn't understand them.

Maybe in another life, this could work. If my father wasn't trying to force me to marry him, if I wasn't stuck with this royal burden, if Grandmother hadn't been killed ... If. If. If. A marriage won't work under that kind of pressure. As much as I wish it weren't so, I need to end this. For both of us.

I reach out to put a hand on his arm. "I am so, so sorry."

Little by little, his face melts into a pool of sorrow. His brown eyes glisten. "Please, we can talk about this. Don't let that Wolf ruin everything we have."

I shake my head. "This isn't about the Wolf." I turn to look at Father and force myself to stand taller. "It's about *him*."

Father smiles patronizingly. "And what will you *do* with the rest of your life, if you refuse to be an obedient wife and heir?"

"I'll return to the borderlands." Even though I say it out loud, I know it isn't true. I'd rather become a hermit in the forest than help Father unwittingly again.

Father's laugh is hollow. "And you believe I'd permit a rebellious heir to just waltz about the kingdom, living life as she pleases?" his voice grows low, threatening. "That is *not* how kingdoms work."

I glare at him, trying to untangle the veiled threats in his words.

"An unruly heir is a danger to us all," he says. "An heir must obey the king, or else she serves no purpose. Or else she threatens the security of an entire nation."

"I don't want the throne." I lift my chin. "Find a new heir. I've heard whispers that you already have."

Both Father and Hunter stiffen. Did he really think he was hiding his pregnant mistress from anyone? A pretty, young, unmarried woman walking around the palace with a distended belly, all decorated in the royal colors? So much for a master strategist.

"Your mere existence is a threat!" Spittle flies from Father's mouth as he speaks. Silence echoes in the tiny, secret room. After a moment, he holds up his arms to gesture to the dripping stones around us. "Take a look around, Little Fox. This could be your future instead of a soft marriage bed."

My blood goes cold. "You would lock me in a forgotten dungeon for disobeying you?"

His smile is malicious. "I've done worse to protect this kingdom."

Grandmother.

My fists clench the silk of my nightdress to keep from grabbing the silver moth hidden beneath it. Suddenly, I understand something I should have a long time ago. The enemy isn't Annwyn. It isn't even Llwyn. It's my father. And something deep inside of me tells me he's the one to blame for Grandmother's death. I just need to find out how. And why.

"Leave me," Father's whisper is as loud as a shout. "And pray that you come to your senses."

Hunter and I walk out of the damp chamber, slamming the door behind us. We follow the guards back down the narrow corridors, stepping over crumbled wall stones and puddles. Our footsteps echo ominously through the dark.

Finally, when we've climbed back up the spiral stairs and the passageways look familiar again, I speak.

"I'm sorry," I whisper to Hunter. "I wish I knew a better way."

Hunter just nods, refusing to look at me.

"It's just ..." My voice shakes with emotion. "I can't be bound to that monster for my entire life. If I marry you, I will be."

After a long pause, he says, "You're wrong."

I stop walking and turn to him. The guards halt a few paces away when they notice we're not following.

"Please," I beg. "Tell me how I'm wrong about this. If I marry you, I'm just another one of his puppets. He gets to tidy me away, like a forgotten wedding present. Out of sight. Beholden to another man. Another man, who is equally beholden to *him*."

Hunter swallows, looking away. "I never wanted to become one of his puppets, you know."

I shift to meet his eyes. "I know that, Hunter. We were going to make our own paths. Our own lives away from this awful place." I sniff. "I don't understand what changed."

Hunter scoffs. "What changed is you left, Sienna."

He could have slapped me and it would've hurt less. I try to stop the tears of shame from spilling over my eyelids.

"What changed is I was alone. With them! What else was I supposed to do? Be the rebellious son forever?" He scoffs, shaking his head. "I don't have the protections you do as heir. I don't have the privilege to run away and survive on my title or my naturally born talents." He looks me straight in the eyes with a seriousness I've never seen in him before. "You and I are not the same. We are not on equal footing. We played and pretended when we were young, but it was all a lie. A fantasy, Sienna."

It hurts, but it's true.

His voice is raw with emotion. "And you have the audacity to blame me for it."

"No, I don't blame you, it's just—"

"No," he closes his eyes. "You do. All my life, I've tried to make you proud. Except for that one stupid mistake that made you run away. I've told you that I will spend forever trying to make it up to you. But still, I am not enough."

I'm ashamed because he's right. I do blame him. And I know how awful that makes me sound. How unforgiving and intolerant. Like my father.

"I chose the pink one, by the way," Hunter says.

I shake my head, confused. "What?"

"The cake." He clears his throat. "It's the one that made you smile the most. So ..." his voice trails off.

A sob threatens to cut off my voice. "What a waste of a good cake."

He nods. "What a waste of a good life."

My vision blurs from the tears. "I'm truly, truly sorry."

He nods. Then turns and leaves. The guards shift, allowing him to pass without comment. I listen as his footsteps echo, growing fainter, until a door slams behind him.

I am alone. Again.

And it is all my fault.

Chapter 17

In late morning, when even the laziest courtier has emerged from their beds, I dress in my red skirts and take a leisurely stroll in the palace gardens. I carry a woven willow basket in one hand and delicate floral shears in the other, the very picture of domesticated grace. My red hood is pulled back, allowing the weak sunlight to warm my face and ensuring everyone can see me admiring the last of the autumn blooms.

And, as always, my copper-armored tails follow at a short distance. Four. How can I lose four of father's copper guards at once? I watch them out of the corner of my eye, the gravel path crunching beneath my feet as I wander between boxwood hedges.

There are other nobles here, as I had expected. They're all vipers dressed in rich velvets and fur-lined cloaks. Jewels glint at their throats and wrists, catching what little light filters through the overcast sky. One might think they're out to get the last of the fresh air before the world grows cold, but I know better. They're out to be seen, just like I am. And to hear the most recent gossip, whispered through lips painted in shades of pink and red.

They try not to gape at the angry, red scar across my throat. I wonder what the palace story is, how they will explain away my injury. If the nobles knew about the escaped Wolf, they wouldn't be out here prancing around the garden. For one brief moment, I allow myself to imagine what these people would do if a corpse wolf appeared on the lawn. Gnashing teeth, blood-soaked silks, screams, tears. Would they finally abandon their petty intrigues then?

"Your Highness," a young woman curtsies as I snip a wilting rose and drop it into my basket. When I look up, I realize it's Elena. Her pregnant belly stretches the taut copper fabric of her dress. Her silver-blond hair is intricately braided and pinned, glinting in the weak sunlight.

Eyes follow us, soaking in the gossip to spread around court later. The king's pregnant mistress, talking to his heir in the garden. How insolent.

Elena doesn't appear to notice that she's overstepping. Or doesn't care.

"You're taking advantage of the last of the year's flowers, I see." She bends slightly forward to smell a bloom still attached to the vine. "With all the roses in your personal chambers, I'm surprised to see you in the gardens. We all heard about the gorgeous display my cousin sent you."

Nearby, her ladies giggle prettily, the sound like delicate bells. I can practically see their ears straining to hear my response.

So, no mention of the broken engagement. Father must not have told anyone. News like that would've spread faster than the pox. Perhaps he's planning to force me into this marriage. It won't work.

I hold up my basket of autumn roses. "For my late mother," I say, with just a hint of sadness.

Elena's perfect composure slips, but just for an instant. "Oh, I'm so sorry. I didn't realize ..."

"That I was making the last bouquet of the season for my mother's grave?" I give her a pitying smile. "No, you couldn't have known." I watch her reaction as I add, "She died in childbirth, you know. Doing her duty to give the king an heir." I snip the head of another rose, then straighten to look Elena in the eyes. "Me."

Her face pales slightly. "I hear she was an exceptional woman. As was your grandmother." She rubs her hand over her distended belly. "You remind me of her, actually."

Her kindness takes me by surprise, especially after my cruelty. My hand slips, pricking my finger on a thorn. A drop of blood blooms bright on my skin. I wipe it away with my thumb.

"I'm nothing like my grandmother." I snip more blooms. "Everyone adored her."

"Do you know why?"

When I look at Elena, there's an openness to her face that I didn't expect. I fear a trap. After all, I'm so used to them here in my father's court. I'm primed for trickery.

"She was kind," I say. Simple, yet truthful.

Elena smiles faintly, then takes a step closer to me. Her whisper flutters against my ear. "She wasn't kind, Sienna. She was *strong*. She was strong for our people. Your people." She takes a step back, her placid smile hiding whatever intention she had in telling me this.

"You might be more like her than you know." Elena curtsies, her silver-blond hair glinting in the sunlight. "I will leave you to your mourning, Your Highness. We keep the late queen and her mother in our thoughts."

All I can do is nod as I watch her glide away to her crowd of fluttering maidens. They send curious glances over their shoulders as they head toward the topiary garden. A giant green hare and fox watch over them as they pass.

There must be some reason the king's mistress broke decorum to speak to me about my grandmother, but I can't discern what. Is she trying to unnerve me? Psychological torture isn't above my father's purview. Could it be her specialty as well? Maybe the sweet, smiling mistress is not what she initially seems.

At least I accomplished one mission this morning. If anyone sees me visit the cemetery later, no one will question it. That is, if I can ever lose these infernal copper tails.

A guard eyes me from behind the trickling fountain several yards away.

I spend an hour walking the perimeter of the gardens, trying to come up with a plan. All around me, twisted stems reach up from the ground, their tips dead-headed by gardeners unwilling to permit the decaying flowers to sit proudly upon a throne. It's a silly way to feel about flowers, but I pity them. Peonies, roses, chrysanthemums, and dahlias—all with lives cut short because they don't meet the expectations of perfectionists and masochists.

At the edge of the royal gardens, the labyrinth's shaded entrance catches my eye. In an instant, a plan forms. It's so foolhardy, it just might work. I discreetly scan my tails. The closest one is still several yards away. I maneuver through the garden to put as many obstacles as possible between us. He doesn't appear to notice.

This may be my only shot. I make a sudden turn for the labyrinth. Before they even notice, I'm inside, the yellowing hedges tall enough to hide me. The second I round the first corner, I run. It only takes a moment for the guards to realize where I've gone, but the twists and turns of the labyrinth conceal me. The guards' armor clanks wildly behind me.

I skid to a halt in front of the labyrinth's many exits and make a quick decision. If I leave now, I'll never get far enough to escape to the cemetery unseen. Instead, I grab a handful of flowers from my basket and toss them out the exit, then run deeper into the labyrinth. At my first opportunity, I tuck myself behind the first statue I see, a mournful maiden draped in stone silks. My heart pounds in my chest so fiercely I might pass out. I focus on quiet, slow breaths as their steps grow closer.

Suddenly, a guard yells. "This way! The southern exit!"

I listen as their armor clanks further and further into the distance. The labyrinth grows quiet. Not only have I lost the tails, but they're heading in the opposite direction from the cemetery. It'll take them hours to catch up with me. By then, I'll have rendezvoused with the Wolf. With any luck, I'll be even closer to finding out the truth.

As I move to leave, a figure darts past the stone maiden's sanctuary, heading deeper into the labyrinth. I peer out into the passage beyond, just in time to get a better glimpse. It's a woman wearing a voluminous cloak, her hood pulled low over her face. Just as she rounds a corner, a gust of wind blows her cloak open, exposing a flash of copper fabric stretched taut over a swollen belly. My breath catches.

It's Elena.

Her presence in the gardens isn't what's odd. It's her solitude. No woman carrying the king's child should wander the grounds alone. And I highly doubt she outran her tails the way I just did.

Curiosity takes over. I abandon my plan and plunge deeper into the labyrinth. Its walls seem to close in around me. Elena has vanished. I hold my breath to listen. To my right, there's a whisper of gravel and hurried footsteps. I turn to follow her, keeping my steps as light as I can, pausing to listen at each crossroad. Just when I think I've lost her, I hear a breathless whisper.

"Now is not the time to second-guess anything. We're too far along to turn back now."

It's a man. A shiver of horror runs down my spine. I know that voice. It's Commander Malen.

Then, Elena. "But what if he doesn't look like him?"

"Do you think the king will care what his son looks like, as long as he has a new heir?"

My eyes widen in shock. I strain to look past the thick hedge walls, but I can't see them through the leaves.

"If he suspects the baby isn't his, I'll be killed." Elena's voice is edged with fear.

"And if he doesn't," Malen says, "we'll have the wealth of an entire kingdom at our disposal."

"How easy for you to say, when it isn't your neck on the line."

"Enough!"

I press my ear into the prickling hedge, straining to hear every word.

Elena's voice is barely audible. "I'm afraid."

A pang of sympathy stabs my chest. Some small part of me knows I should hate this woman. But I don't. Maybe it's because I don't want the throne to begin with. Maybe it's because I know what it's like to belong to a man like my father. She's trapped in a poisonous snare that she'll never be able to escape now. Not unless death claims her first. Like my mother ... like my grandmother.

All the women in the king's circle die. All except me. So far, at least. And right now, I'm not sure how long that will last.

Malen's voice is sharp and cruel on the other side of the hedge. "What do you possibly have to be afraid of?"

"It's coming. The baby."

"That's what babies do."

"What if I die in childbirth, like the queen?"

My heart sinks. That is my mother's legacy, a fearful story that expectant mothers worry over. A monster under the marriage bed. A ghost who haunts every birthing room. It's tragic.

I wonder if my comment in the garden has something to do with the anxiety in Elena's voice. Guilt slides through my chest, thick and black as tar.

"Then you die a hero," Malen says, impatient. "A lowly woman who gave the king a new heir. A chance to put our family on the throne for generations to come."

"This was a terrible mistake."

"Too late for that."

My foot slips on the gravel, and I freeze, cringing at my carelessness. The maze grows silent.

"Who's there?" Malen calls out.

I turn and run, twisting down identical pathways until I burst from the labyrinth. Too late, I realize my basket has spilled. Dark red roses litter the path behind me.

Chapter 18

By the time I reach the cemetery, I'm out of breath and my side aches. I lean against a crooked tree, hoping no one saw me.

Worry clouds my mind. Not for myself or the fate of the Fox Throne, but for Elena. If Malen put her up to this, it's her neck in the noose, not his. She's the one parading a bastard as the king's child. It will end badly for her. It always does. She's yet another woman trapped in the Fox King's sticky web, and I can't help but pity her.

I curse and throw my basket of flowers into the pond. Geese scatter away from the assault.

"I was afraid you'd died."

I whirl around to see Tristan a mere three feet behind me. It strikes me that I've never seen him in broad daylight before. Our previous interactions had always been in damp dungeons and dim chambers. He's younger than I originally thought. Possibly mid-twenties, though the bruising and swelling around his face makes it difficult to tell for sure. His eyes though, look ancient.

"You waited." My words come out on a breath.

Now that I'm alone with the Wolf, free of shackles, I know I should be afraid ... but all I feel is relief. I'd expected him to make a break for it, to vanish. That would've been the smart thing for him to do. Hiding on palace grounds seems highly illogical. Especially if he's waiting for a stubborn heir who may turn around and betray him.

He steps closer. "I said I'd wait for you. Wolves always keep their word."

"Yes, the code of honor. You mentioned that."

He nods.

"Why?"

He tilts his head to the side, very much like the animal he's so often referred to. "Why live honorably?"

I shake my head. "Why wait? Why risk your life for a woman you don't know. Who's the daughter of your sworn enemy?"

His jaw clenches, but he doesn't turn his pale eyes from mine. "Because I need your help."

I cross my arms and frown. "You travelled all the way to Caerwen alone. What makes you think you need my help going back?"

"Because this time, I have the Fox King on my trail." His tone is even, honest. "And you know the way to the borderlands better than most in Llwyn."

I narrow my eyes, studying him. If he's lying, he's good at it. I don't see any telltale signs of deceit. No wavering eye contact or fidgeting. Still, I don't believe him. He's a Wolf, he would be fine without me. There's more at play here.

The question is, can a Fox outwit a Wolf to get what she wants?

"I'll consider it," I say. "But I need *some* answers first." I glare at him. "The truth! No more lies and deceit. I've had enough of those to last me a lifetime."

In the pond, a frog jumps into the water, creating ripples that spread slowly, but unstoppably across the entire surface.

"Alright," he says, finally.

I square off. "Who is the Heir to the North?"

He sighs. "I'm not sure."

"You crossed Llwyn and risked your life in a king's palace, all for something you're not sure about?"

"It's complicated."

"How?"

"Given the centuries-long war, the last of the royal bloodline disappeared some time ago. But rumors reached us in Annwyn. They say the heir still lives. Only ..."

"Only?"

Tristan sighs. "Only it's difficult to confirm without proof."

I jut out my chin, defiant. "Then how do you know the rumors are true?"

He gives me a sideways smirk. "Suffice it to say, they come from a credible source."

I nod, sensing he's telling the truth. "Who are the sympathizers my father mentioned?"

"Southerners who think your family should be ousted." His eyes grow dark. "That your father's cruelties against Annwyn are grounds to usurp him."

"How many are there? Who are they?"

He just shakes his head, either because he doesn't know, or he isn't willing to tell me. How can there be an entire group of people who hate my family, yet I never knew about them? It's not a secret that I'm no fan of the king's. Wouldn't someone have told me?

Even as the thought crosses my mind, I know the answer. No. No they would not. Because being royal is the loneliest position in the world. Everyone wants to be seen with you, but no one trusts you.

If I can't trust anyone in my own homeland, I may as well try trusting someone from Annwyn. I'm out of options.

"Fine." I nod. "I'll take you to the border." I expect to feel regret the instant it's out of my mouth, but I don't. Instead, I'm filled with an odd sense of calm, like I'm finally choosing the right path. "I'll help you escape, in return for one thing."

His eyes are hard, but he waits for me to continue.

"The truth. You must tell me everything you know about my grandmother and the sympathizers." I swallow.

"Not until I reach Annwyn."

"I understand that."

His nostrils flare as he mulls it over. Then he nods.

I take a deep breath, inhaling the chill of autumn. I likely just signed my own death warrant, helping a criminal escape. Worse, I'm helping the king's would-be assassin go back to Annwyn.

"Tonight," I say. "I'll gather supplies and meet you back here at midnight."

———

I'm in my rooms, stuffing a sack with basic necessities for the journey, when I hear a knock on my chamber door. I still, my soiled borderland dress in hand. Perhaps, if I pretend I'm not here, they'll leave.

The knock sounds again. I stuff the dress into the sack, then toss the whole thing under the bed before turning toward the door.

"You may enter."

I expect to see one of my father's many messengers, or possibly even Hunter, but I'm completely wrong. When a small, old man in brown robes steps inside, I have to do a double take. It's the librarian.

He gives me a bashful smile. "Many apologies for interrupting you, Your Highness. I hope I'm not too much of an inconvenience."

"N-no. Not at all. Sir ... um."

He smiles, good-naturedly. "No 'sir', my lady. Just Merle. I am but a humble servant to the muse of books." His quiet, casual nature puts me somewhat at ease.

"I'm glad to finally learn your name."

He nods his appreciation. "I won't take much of your time. I heard a rumor that you were looking for something."

He takes a small, worn book out from inside his voluminous sleeve. He holds it out to me.

I take it in my hands and stare at the cover. There are no words on the leather, just the thin, silver outline of a moth. The same moth that now rests against my breast bone, beneath my dress.

I look up at him, wide-eyed. "How did you ..."

"The books, ma'am.," he says matter-of-factly. "The ones you left behind in the library when Sir Hunter was called away."

A blush spreads across my face. For a moment, I genuinely thought he'd heard about my interest from the shopkeeper in White's End, as ludicrous as that would be. A royal librarian would never mix with the likes of a pawnshop owner.

He waves away my embarrassment, likely chalking it up to modesty. He did walk in on Hunter and me in the library, doing quite a bit more than reading. "Fear not, your secrets are safe with me."

For a moment I wonder whether he means my compromising situation with Hunter, or my interest in moths.

Merle bows, slightly. "I'll take my leave." He turns and opens the door.

I hold up a hand. "Wait, please."

He hesitates, his hand still on the doorknob. "Yes?"

"This book," I hold it up. "The moth ..." I shake my head,

trying to find words that make sense. "You once told me I look like my grandmother."

A nostalgic smile spreads across his face. "I did. She was a great lady. One of the best."

My heart twists in my chest. "Yes. She was." I run my fingers over the book cover. The fabric is as soft as a moth's wings. I make a reckless decision and pull the necklace out from beneath the neckline of my gown.

Merle doesn't react, just watches me with curiosity.

"Do you recognize this necklace?" I ask. "It was hers."

He nods, just once.

"Do you know anything about it?"

Merle watches me for a long moment, weighing what must be a million answers before he speaks. "I know that it was very precious to her. And that she would be proud to see it around your neck." For the briefest moment, his eyes linger on the scar at my throat before he bows slightly and closes the door behind him.

In the silence of the room, all I hear is the blood roaring in my ears. I sit on the edge of the overstuffed bed and open the book's cover.

The Silver Moth Society

A treatise on the demands of the Llwyn people in favor of the permanent destruction of the Fox King and all future despotic rulers.

On the inside cover, someone penned a list of names. The first one sends a bolt of lightning into my chest: *Áine.*

My hands shake so violently, I drop the book to the floor. In a blind panic, I scramble beneath the bed and claw up the loose floorboard where I used to hide treats as a child. I toss the little book inside as if it were a hot ember, then scramble backward until my spine is pressed against the wall. My breath comes in ragged gasps as I try to make sense of this.

I am the heir to the Fox Throne. And yet ...

My grandmother was an Annwyn sympathizer.

Chapter 19

The feast hall is nearly empty at supper aside from the few nobles that sit in small groups, whispering and shooting nervous glances at the other people in the room. Orbs of light flicker over glistening roasted boars, candied root vegetables, and golden rolls of fresh bread. All to be wasted on empty chairs.

I take my usual seat at the royal family's table, noticeably alone. The king is nowhere to be found.

Typically, my father never misses an opportunity to be gazed upon by his court. He sips goblets of wine every evening, under the watch of at least a half-dozen King's Guards while great men admire him, and beautiful women lust after him from afar. I wonder if he has his own spread of wild game and stewed fruits down in the secret dungeon he's hiding in.

Across the room, Hunter stands with his men. Under normal circumstances, I'd try to catch his eye, but the way we left things was so poor, I don't have any right to speak to him again.

There are few things worse than being stared at by anxious

people who don't know what's going on. I gaze into my goblet of blood-red wine, wondering if some fortuneteller could predict my fate by the way it swirls in the golden light.

"Your Highness. I'm sorry to intrude."

I'm startled away from the goblet.

Hunter stands above me, his mouth in a thin line.

"Hunter, I ..."

"I don't enjoy being the one to tell you this, but it seems someone should." His tone is curt, matter-of-fact.

I stand. "Alright. What is going on then? Where is everyone?"

"They're all waiting to see where their future lies." His eyes dart round the dim room. "How their status will change or crumble by the end of the night."

My lips purse. I hate these palace games—speaking in riddles, holding secrets like treasure to be hoarded.

"Speak plainly," I say.

Hunter grabs my arm a little too tightly and directs me toward a corner. For once, I don't think anyone pays any attention to us. No one cares if two lovers hide behind statues to steal kisses. They're all too concerned with their own welfare to care about romance now.

Once we're tucked away in a corner, I wrench my arm out of his grip.

Hunter makes a sound of frustration. "For once, do you think you could be a little more tactful?"

"I don't have anything to hide."

"Secrets keep people alive."

"Secrets get people killed."

His mouth shuts with a snap. He knows I'm referring to Grandmother. All of her secrets, dead along with her ... at least for now. By midnight, I'll be on my way to find the answers. I'll be rid of this place and all of its deceptions and cruelties.

Hunter sighs. "Look, I'm just trying to help you."

I stare him down, my arms crossed at the chest.

"Elena is in labor."

The blood drains from my face. "Now?"

He nods gravely.

Of course, I knew this day would come. I heard her say it herself in the maze this morning. I just thought I'd have more time to prepare. That I'd be long gone by now.

"That's why everyone seems afraid."

He nods again.

Right now, all across the palace, nobles are striking deals and breaking allegiances. Everyone is waiting to see if the new baby is a boy. Or if the king will even care if it's a girl and replace me anyway. I wonder how many bottles of expensive wine are uncorked, at the ready for the announcement.

I swallow, my throat suddenly dry. The scar on my neck burns. My future is just as much in peril as anyone else's. Perhaps even more so.

Hunter puts his hand on my elbow, gently this time. "I don't think anyone else knows about our broken engagement. It would be safer for you if we appear as a united front."

I tilt my head to get a better read on his face. "Why? Why would you care what happens to me? We're not betrothed anymore. It would be better for you if you show that your allegiance lies elsewhere."

"But it doesn't."

I stare at him; not sure I understand.

"My allegiance will never be with an illegitimate prince over the true-born heir of Llwyn."

His loyalty has nothing to do with me personally. Not anymore, at least. I can't blame him for that.

For a moment, I contemplate telling him what I heard in the labyrinth this morning. That the child isn't just illegitimate, but a lie, a deception intended to put his family in the king's favor. But the thought doesn't last long. It's not worth it. I'll be gone soon anyway and I am so, so tired of these palace games.

"I think ..." Hunter pauses.

His hesitation worries me more than anything else. If steady, stalwart Hunter is afraid, maybe I should be too.

"I think you should prepare."

"For what, exactly?"

He looks over my shoulder. "I'm not sure, but I have a bad feeling about all of this. I don't trust him."

My father, the Fox King. His sworn liege.

Behind me, I hear the unmistakable clang of metal on metal that could only mean one thing—the copper guard. I turn to see the King's Guards marching into the feast hall. They spot us and pivot in our direction, Commander Malen at the helm. Dread coats my insides like spilled tar, sticky and thick.

Malen stops before me, his face smug. "Your Highness, you need to come with us."

I stand my ground. "No."

"Then we will have to take you by force," he says. He gives Hunter a challenging look.

"She can walk herself," Hunter says, his voice firm. Threatening.

"I will not." I pull my shoulders back. "I'll do as I see fit. I'm the heir to the throne."

"We'll see about that." Commander Malen reaches out for my arm, but I wrench it away.

He motions to his knights and, in one swift motion, they encircle me, reaching out to grab my arms. No amount of wriggling makes them let go.

"Don't fight, Sienna," Hunter says, an edge of fear in his voice.

"Let me go!" I try to kick and bite, but I'm nothing when up against copper plated armor. They drag me toward the thick wooden doors.

Those who dared come to the dining hall tonight are all staring, openmouthed, as I fight with every ounce of strength I have. No doubt they'll run to their families to report seeing the heir dragged away at supper. They'll hardly believe their luck.

As the knights pull me through the door, Hunter scrambles after us, trying to push them off me. He lands a punch on one guard's face, then tries to wrench me out of his grasp. Two more guards break away from the group to pull him off of me.

"Don't interfere," Malen tells his son, a firm hand on his chest.

"Hunter!" I call.

"Sienna!"

The wooden door of the great hall slams shut as the guards drag me away. They take me down into a servants' hall, then twist and turn through dark corridors beyond. No one has to tell me where we're going. I know it with every fiber of my being.

When they finally throw me into a dark cell, far beneath the palace, I'm bruised and scratched from fighting. I scream profanities at them for several moments before I realize we're not alone. Near the door, a man stands facing away from me, bouncing lightly on his feet. I don't need to see his face to recognize him.

My father turns toward me, slowly. In his arms, he holds a sleeping newborn wrapped in a blanket of spun copper.

"I'd like you to meet my son." Father's voice is calm, odd. He smiles. "My new heir."

From my spot on the floor, I watch him bounce the baby boy like a proud father. Vaguely, I wonder if he ever held me with such love and compassion. I doubt it.

"What's his name?" I ask. My scraped knees sting and my dress is soaked through from the puddle I'm kneeling in.

Father pauses, thinking. "I've decided to name him Fennec, The Pale Fox."

Only then do I notice the tuft of white blond hair on the baby's head. Not a hint of auburn in sight.

At this moment, I finally understand what my almost-wedding truly was: an excuse to get me out of the way. To marry me off to a beloved man with no political machinations. To make room for a new heir.

And I threw it in his face.

There's a long silence between us as I watch my father bounce the sleeping newborn. Then he slowly walks toward the doorway. He pauses to turn back to me.

"It turns out there will be a royal wedding after all," he says.

My brain scrambles to catch up.

Father chuckles lowly. "Oh, no." He shakes his head. "Not yours. That opportunity has passed." He gazes down at the baby boy with a love I've never seen in him before. "It will be mine. To my new bride, the one who gave the kingdom a *true* heir. An heir worthy of the Fox Throne."

My mouth hangs open, stunned.

Father shrugs. "I no longer have a use for you."

The rusty door hinges screech closed as father walks away, cooing and bouncing his baby boy. My screams of rage echo behind them in the dank cell.

"Let me out!" I attack the door, kicking, pounding and scratching until my nails break and bleed.

It's no use. After all, I already saw one of these cells last night. But, unlike Father's hideaway, there's nothing here to keep me company but the scrabbling of rats' feet and the steady drip of condensation from the ceiling. This is unmistakably a forgetting place.

And I am truly, thoroughly, left for dead.

Chapter 20

Too late. I was too late.

Over and over, I play scenes from the last few days in my mind. All the warning signs were there, but I was too foolhardy to recognize them. I should've left with the Wolf when I had the chance. I should've never come back from the borderlands.

The steady drip, drip, drip of putrid water is maddening enough to make me cover my ears like a child afraid of thunder. It's impossible to know how much time has passed. Eventually, my stomach wrenches with hunger. Thirst claws at my throat, suffocating me. But worst of all is the freezing cold and the uncontrollable shivering from my damp dress.

Rats scamper around the edges of the cell, sticking to the shadows. The light I've conjured is barely enough to reflect on their tiny eyeballs as they watch me, waiting. I'm so weak, soon I won't even have enough energy to maintain an orb of light. There's a real possibility that they'll eat me alive in the dark. Bite by tiny bite.

I wonder if the Wolf finally left without me; if he accepted that I won't return to escort him back to Annwyn.

Panic, true panic, is something I've never experienced before, not even when the corpse wolves chased me through the forest at the borderlands. There, at least, I had guards and horses to help me flee. Here, there's no escape and no one to hear me scream into the darkness. Before death takes me, I fear I'll go mad.

I'm lying on the cold, hard ground, clutching Grandmother's knife and waiting for death to take me when I first hear something outside my cell. The footsteps are so light, I hardly notice them above the scuttle of rats fighting in the corner.

"Who's there?" I call out.

My only answer is a jangle of keys as someone struggles with the lock. When the door swings open, I could cry with relief. But the face that appears in the dim light is pale as death. And it's the last face I ever expected to see.

Elena.

Her skin is slick with sweat and her silver-blond hair hangs limply around her shoulders. Her gown is loose over her still-swollen stomach, the skirts heavy with dried blood. We stare at each other for a long moment and I wonder if I've died and we're meeting in the realm of the dead. If my father has killed her before their wedding, only days after she gave him a son.

A man steps behind her. My faint light casts shadows along his tall, bulky frame—Hunter.

I move to get up, but my feet are numb with cold, and I stumble.

Hunter rushes toward me, worry etched across his face. Shivers wrack my body as he pulls me off the wet floor and holds me to his chest.

"You're here." My voice is scratchy from thirst.

He pulls a waterskin from under his cloak and places it in my hands. Warm water has never tasted so sweet. A wave of dizziness nearly makes my knees buckle and I remind myself to breathe between sips.

"Of course, I'm here. Did you really think I'd just leave you?"

Elena watches us silently, pain etched into the corners of her down-turned mouth. I realize now that she's breathing heavily and leaning against the doorframe for support. I wonder if my father even permitted her to hold her newborn son, or if he stole that moment from her like he steals everything else.

"Thank you," I say to her, the mother of my rival to the throne.

The corners of her mouth only turn down further. "You should go. And fast." Her voice is hoarse and bitter. It's as though the trauma of childbirth has stolen everything from her but the air she breathes. And even that is only a tentative grasp, at best.

Hunter looks back toward her. "Thank you, cousin."

She takes a few slow steps toward him and puts her hand on his cheek. "You always were my favorite, you know."

His eyes soften. "I know."

Her hand on his cheek is pale and trembling, but there's something else I've never noticed. My breath hitches before my brain can catch up. On her middle finger, there's a thin, silver ring with one small decoration. A moth.

Elena notices my gaze and removes her hand. A million questions flood my mind, but there's no time. The fates are cruel in that way.

"Go," she says, then turns to leave.

Hunter reaches out for her. "I should escort you back to your rooms. To make sure you get there safely."

She gives him a piteous look over her shoulder. "Whether I live or die is hardly consequential at this point. But thank you for your concern." She disappears into the dark corridor, her footsteps as light as a moth's wing.

Hunter kisses my temple, then frowns. "I'll get you out of here." He stares into my eyes a little longer than is strictly necessary. I hand his empty waterskin back to him. My head still throbs from dehydration, but the relief I feel is stronger.

"Saving me from death-by-a-thousand rats won't make me change my mind, you know," I say, only half in jest.

"What about death by thirst?" he asks with a small grin.

I shake my head. "Nor death from freezing."

"Damp?"

"Can one die of dampness?"

"Most definitely."

I shake my head. "I mean it, Hunter. I haven't changed my mind about marrying you."

"Yet," he says. "You haven't changed your mind, yet."

I don't know what to say to that.

"Sienna," Hunter grabs my trembling hands. They're coated in grime from the dirt-covered floor and rotting cell door where I clawed at it for hours. He doesn't seem to notice, or maybe he just doesn't care. He looks at me with those warm, brown eyes and somewhere inside of me, a spark of warmth ignites.

"I didn't agree to your father's political matchmaking for any sort of personal or political gain," he says. "I thought you knew me better than that. I agreed because I love you. I always have."

"I ..."

He shakes his head. "It's alright. I know you're not some love-sick girl who yearns for a comfortable home and babies. Or chickens and a washerwoman who visits every second Tuesday."

"I do love chickens."

"Well, that's not surprising. Who doesn't love chickens?"

"And I hate washing clothes. I had to do it a lot in the borderlands." To clean off all the blood, I don't say.

Hunter lets out a dry laugh. "My point is, that won't be our life together, Sienna. We can learn to spin yarn and raise sheep near the mountains. Or, we could pirate a ship and sail the seas, beyond the known world. We can have any life you desire." Hunter rubs his hands over my shoulders, trying to warm me. "I only ask that you let me be even a small part of it."

It sounds wonderful. Simple. But I know it isn't. It can't be. I nearly died down here, and a swift death in the near future isn't off the table yet either. It's too much to process.

His eyes travel over my tangled hair, muddy face, and soggy dress.

"You won't last long like this." He pulls a pack from over his shoulder. Inside is a cloak for me and a simple, brown dress, like something a servant might wear.

My fingers reach for the buttons behind my neck, but they're still numb with cold.

"I can't," I say.

Hunter turns me away from him. With quick, practiced movements, he loosens the buttons down my back. I wonder how many dresses he removed while I was away and whether I should be jealous. He helps me pull the sleeves over my shoulders, his thumbs trailing over the goose pimpled skin of my arms. I sense his eyes on the back of my neck. An entirely different shiver runs through my body.

Hunter steps back, turning away to give me privacy. "Quickly," he says. "We don't have much time."

I finish removing the wet dress and shift, then pull on the homespun gown. It's baggy in places, but not too long. It'll do. With warmer clothes on my body, my legs feel more stable. I walk toward the door, throwing the cloak over me. It's red.

I glance up at him, a questioning look.

He shrugs. "It's the warmest cloak I could find in your rooms. You'll need it. I also have blankets to cover with on the road."

"The road?"

He nods. "I'm rescuing you, my darling. Haven't you realized that yet?"

We run through the passageways, then slow once we emerge onto the main level. It's nighttime; late based on the empty halls and low lights along the walls.

"How did you find me?" I whisper to Hunter.

"It took longer than I'd hoped," he whispers back. "But I eventually made a deal with one of the other King's Guards. He owed me a favor."

"Pretty big favor," I say as we pause to peek around a corner. It's abandoned. We rush forward.

"It helps to know people in high places."

"Like your father?"

Hunter just shrugs. It's all the acknowledgement I need. He's learned to use his political favor to the best advantage. I can't blame him for that, seeing as it's my neck he's saving now.

When we reach the stables, we pass darkened stalls with horses snorting with curiosity. Their big brown eyes watch us from the shadows. They're not used to midnight visitors. Hunter leads me to a paddock with two horses already saddled.

I raise an eyebrow at him. "Stealing horseflesh is a crime punishable by death."

He gives me a wicked grin. "What's one more crime against the king?" He pats one horse on her strong neck.

The horses' ears flicker as they listen to us. They have warm blankets and packs strapped to their rears. The gray mare has an additional lumpy pack with copper armor sticking out the side. Hunter isn't just saving me. He's leaving *with* me.

It strikes me now that Hunter intends to abandon the life he's worked so hard for. There's no way the King's Guard will welcome him back after helping a prisoner escape. Especially not me.

"Wait." I catch his arm as he kneels to help me mount the black horse.

"We don't have time," he whispers.

"You can't do this."

"What are you talking about?" He stands straight and glances over the paddock door to make sure we're still alone.

"Your father ..."

"He will call me a disgrace like he always has."

"You can't come with me." I shake my head. "It'll ruin everything. Your entire life."

Hunter steps forward with a fierceness that takes me off guard. He pins me against the wall with his gaze. "Do you know what I thought while you were locked away in that place?"

I just stare into his fierce brown eyes.

"I thought they'd killed you." He steps even closer. There's barely a foot of space between our bodies now. I don't move away.

"I thought my life was over, Sienna. Because I realized all of this," he gestures to the armor strapped to the back of the mare, "was just a way to get back to you. I understand why you don't want to marry me, but that doesn't change *me*. It doesn't change how I feel about you. It doesn't change that *you* are my life."

His chest rises and falls with each truth-fueled breath. I've never seen this side of Hunter before. His boyish charm has vanished, replaced with a man who knows what he wants.

And what he wants is me. That realization is the most intoxicating thing I've ever felt.

I know it's wrong. I know I shouldn't want this, shouldn't want him ... but I do.

I throw my arms around his shoulders and press my mouth to his, fierce and unthinking. His hand tangles in my hair and he moans from deep in his chest, like he's been holding back for far too long. Hunter pulls my hips against his, his mouth trailing heat down my neck. When he pauses at my scar and kisses it slowly, something in me falters. My heart pounds too hard, too fast, and behind my eyelids, everything flashes white-hot.

There's no space for self-consciousness or fear between us. We are two people playing with fire on the edge of a cliff. We may burn. We will probably fall. But what is the promise of death when you've just glimpsed heaven?

Hunter breaks away reluctantly. He runs a thumb over my swollen lips.

"We have to go."

I nod, breathless.

He grabs my waist to help me onto the black horse. My legs are still a little shaky from my imprisonment, or maybe it was the thrill of passion. Either way, I'm glad to be astride. Hunter mounts his mare, then leans forward in his saddle to unlock the gate. Slowly, he leads us forward, out of the stables and onto the dark, mist-covered road.

When we're far enough that pounding hoofbeats won't wake too many people, we accelerate into a gallop.

"Wait," I call out when we hit the first crossroad. "We need to go to the cemetery first."

It will haunt me forever if I never check to see if the Wolf waited for me. After years of unanswered questions, I can't let this opportunity slide away. I don't want to grow old always wondering, always regretting.

"We can't." Hunter's eyes are wild as he glances behind us.

I turn to look, too. No sign of pursuit yet. "Please. It's important."

Hunter huffs, but pulls his reins toward the northeastern side of the palace grounds. "We'd better hurry."

When we speed through the gates of the cemetery, the gravestones greet us with shadow and curling mist. I don't need to see the Wolf to know he's still here. Something in the air makes my skin prickle with knowing, like a message sent from the old gods.

Hunter and I gallop at full speed until we reach the little pond and my mother's mausoleum. We stop, listening as the water laps against the stones along the pond's shore. Wind blows dried leaves across the grass. Then, as silent as the night, the Wolf steps out from behind the mausoleum.

His dark hair hangs over his gray eyes but I can still see the relief in them. Somehow, he's acquired new, black clothes and cleaned himself up. He seems a little further from death's door now, even though he has the rumpled look of a dog who swam in a pond. At least the mud and the crusted blood are gone. He looks more like the wolf I spotted at the engagement ball, though this shirt hangs loose.

But he's alive.

A weight lifts from my chest. "I thought I'd never see you again. Why didn't you leave?"

He shakes his head slowly. "Not without you. A promise is a promise."

We both look at Hunter, whose face is twisted in confusion. I nod toward the Wolf.

"No," Hunter says, his lips set in a firm line.

"Oh, yes," the Wolf replies. He leaps up onto the back of my horse, then wraps his arms around my waist. A thrill travels up my spine at the close contact with someone so dangerous.

"What are we supposed to do with him?" Hunter speaks to me, but his eyes are on the Wolf at my back.

"I promised to get him to the border."

"Why?"

"He owes me a favor."

"Then why are you the one risking your neck?"

In the silence that follows his accusation, a breeze blows the nearby willow branches like a whispered warning.

"It's ... complicated," I say.

Hunter shakes his head. "I only brought provisions for two."

Tristan leans into the conversation. "I'll fend for myself."

Hunter's eyes are dark with emotion, though I'm not sure what kind. Jealousy? Outrage? He turns to me, his eyes begging me to reconsider.

"Please, Hunter, I need you to trust me."

He doesn't look happy about it, but he finally grants me a curt nod, then turns his horse back toward the gate.

"Wait." Tristan's voice is sharp, like he's a man used to giving orders.

Hunter's exasperation is evident. "We can't! We've already wasted too much time."

Behind me, I feel the Wolf shake his head. He points toward the lumpy armor strapped to the back of Hunter's mare. "You can't bring that."

Hunter's eyes narrow. "I really don't think you're in any position to tell me what I can or can't bring."

The Wolf shakes his head again. "No. It's too conspicuous."

"This," Hunter pats the bulk of copper and bronze behind him. "Might just save our lives someday."

"Not if it gets us killed first."

Hunter's face is growing purple.

"Enough!" I yell. The two men look at me.

I shake my head at Hunter. “I’m sorry, but he’s right.”

Hunter’s jaw drops in indignation.

“It’s heavy. It’ll slow us down. And if people see it, they’ll talk. There aren’t any other King’s Guard on the road.”

Hunter gestures to the lumps of gleaming copper. “This armor could get us favors. We don’t have much to travel on.”

“Then we’ll have to ration our supplies. Spend as little as possible until we get to the border.”

Hunter shakes his head slowly. “I can’t just leave it here in the middle of a cemetery. You have no idea what it cost me to earn this copper.”

My heart aches for him, truly. He traded his freedom, his love of books, and his entire identity for swords, copper armor, and the begrudging respect of his father. That armor cost him *everything*. And we’re making him leave it behind.

I scan the crooked trees and pond reeds before I see our solution. “My mother will watch it for you. No one will find it. I’m the only one who ever visits her.”

Hunter’s face falls as he looks forlornly at the mausoleum. “Are you sure about this?”

“Yes.” My stomach clenches at the lie, but there’s no better option.

With a dramatic sigh, Hunter jumps down from his mare and unties his armor. The clanking sets my teeth on edge. I get the sense that he’s biting his tongue to keep from wasting more time on bickering.

While Hunter heaves open the mausoleum door and places his pile of armor lovingly at the foot of my mother’s statue, my eyes scan the rest of the garden. Still no pursuers.

Hunter closes the heavy door and returns to his gray mare. He’s still wearing his gauntlets and has his sword strapped into an ornate copper scabbard. It’s not worth wasting more time to fight about.

I click at my horse to usher him forward. “Let’s go.”

We leave the cemetery and ride true north, toward the wretched borderlands. Toward the Kingdom of Corpses. Toward answers.

Secrets. Theft. Escapes. I've slipped through locked doors, assisted deadly criminals, and told so many lies I've lost count. Foxes are tricksters by nature—sly, silent, always one step ahead. For once, I almost live up to my family's reputation.

Part Three

The Wolf

Chapter 21

Mist covers the ground, swirling around our horse's hooves as we race past the tombstones and ancient trees. The night air has that crisp quality of impending dawn. The dark shadows are tinged with blue in anticipation of the rising sun. Somewhere, a morning bird begins to sing.

We're barely out of the cemetery before I hear another sound that makes my blood curdle in my veins.

I glance back to where Hunter's riding only a few feet behind me. His eyes are wide with fear. He's heard them too.

"And here I thought I'd never have to hear those god-awful creatures again," Tristan mumbles in my ear.

The foxhounds were released from the kennels at last.

We press our horses forward, speeding onto the forest road beyond the northern edge of the palace grounds. We leave trampled field grasses in our wake as we race for the cover of trees. Just as we reach the forest, the first screams ring out behind us. Father didn't waste time warning people that he's released his pets. It sounds as though someone got caught in the crossfires.

Hunter maneuvers his horse so we're racing down the dirt

road, side by side. He glares over at the Wolf on my back. "I blame you for this!"

"They're not after me." His answer is cut short as we duck under a low-hanging branch just in time.

Hunter doesn't let him off that easily. "If we hadn't wasted precious time ..."

"She volunteered to escort me north. I never asked you to come."

"And I never asked you to—"

"We don't have time for this!" I snap. I can't stand the bickering, not when the howls and yips of the foxhounds are growing nearer.

They both snap their mouths closed, but something in the line of Hunter's mouth tells me this argument is far from over ... if we escape the foxhounds, that is.

The trees close in around us, branches reaching out like skeletal fingers. Our horses push themselves harder, somehow understanding the urgency. The sound of the foxhounds grows louder, their howls mingle with the frantic pounding of hoofbeats.

My eye catches a streak of orange racing just beyond the tree line. It's the first foxhound, unbelievably fast for a creature that spends most of its life chained in a dungeon. I squint to get a better look. Its orange-red fur is patchy and crusted with filth. Its jagged, broken teeth are covered in foaming saliva. It's no bigger than a normal fox, but it could never be mistaken for anything other than a rabid creature. It turns its head to look at me through the passing branches and thorny bushes. Its copper eyes gleam with the excitement of a hunt.

Panic rises in my chest. "Faster!" I call out to the horse, but he's already running as fast as he can. He knows we're in danger. He can sense it like the rest of us.

"That thing is not natural," Tristan says behind us. If we were in a normal situation right now, I'd tell him what I think of his queen's corpse army. Undead badgers and bears are not strictly natural either.

Suddenly, a group of foxhounds burst through the trees in front of us, barking and snarling. Our horses scream in terror, nearly toppling over as they dig their hooves into the ground to stop. It takes everything I have to stay astride. Tristan leans forward, pressing our bodies flat onto the horse's back as it leaps and kicks at the foxhounds.

Nearby, Hunter quickly regains control of the gray mare, his years of training with the King's Guard evident in his skill.

The Wolf is not so lucky.

Tristan crashes to the ground, narrowly avoiding our horse's kicking hooves. He's on his feet again in an instant, his stance wide like a fighter's. While the foxhounds' copper eyes are focused on the Wolf, Hunter grabs my reins, turns our horses, and retreats into the forest.

"Stop!" I yell, trying to pull the reins from his hands.

"No, Sienna! We have to keep going." He urges the horses further into the trees.

"We can't leave him!" I jump off the back of the black horse.

Hunter swears behind me as he dismounts. "And why the hell not?!" His anger only fuels mine.

I whirl around to face him. "Because he has something I need!"

Hunter grabs my arm roughly, clearly intending to drag me away from danger against my will. "Whatever it is, it's not worth our lives!"

But he's wrong about that. It's worth mine, even if it's not worth his. With as much strength as I can muster, I shove Hunter off his feet, wrenching one rein from his hands as he falls. He lands with a thump, his face startled, incredulous.

I leap up onto the gray mare's back and we charge through the woods, returning to the fray. The mare's hooves kick up dirt in our haste. I unclip my red cloak and it floats to the ground in our wake.

On the road, Tristan is surrounded. The growling foxhounds encircle him like a well-trained army, their hackles raised. I run the mare directly through the group, trampling at least one creature. The crunch of bone beneath hooves is startlingly satisfying. I've hated these creatures my entire life.

The foxhounds scatter like mice, but it only takes them a moment to refocus. Several leap at my feet in the stirrups as they claw the mare's flesh with their broken, overgrown claws. I pull up my skirts and take out my knife. I slash at their faces as they leap at me again and again. My blade scrapes against flesh, bone, and teeth.

The mare shrieks when a foxhound bites her hindquarters. I turn to stab it in its copper-colored eye. It leaps away with a yelp, but it turns back toward us, its eye-socket dripping blood.

More foxhounds leap at the mare. I can't let her die like this, not like Nell. I jump down to the ground, then smack her rump to send her fleeing into the trees.

The foxhounds are relentless, their teeth bared and copper eyes wild. They limp and skitter around us like injured rats. Part of me pities them for their miserable existence, spending their entire lives locked up in a dark dungeon, starved and tortured by the king.

They should take this opportunity to flee, but they don't. They're too blood-crazed to run. They close in around us in a circle of dark orange and filthy white.

Beside me, Tristan is a whirlwind of motion, his movements precise and deadly. Two foxhounds lie on the ground at his feet, their fur matted crimson with blood. Tristan moves with surprising speed, his fists flying. He lands a solid punch to a foxhound's snout, sending it sprawling. Another leaps at him. He twists, using its momentum to throw it to the ground.

As I watch, several foxhounds suddenly startle away from him, whimpering and limping. One crumbles to the ground, twitching in what appears to be pain. My eyes travel up to Tristan's hands. The smoky mist of shadow power seeps from his palms.

I don't have time to stop and stare for long before another foxhound leaps at me with hungry, feral eyes. I fight with everything I have, using every trick I learned in the borderlands. My knife flashes in the early morning light.

One foxhound knocks me to the ground, its weight pressing me into the dirt. Its breath is hot and foul against my face as it snaps at me, saliva drips nauseatingly onto my cheek. I struggle, my hand scrambling for my fallen knife. I grasp its bronze handle just as a blur of movement knocks the creature off me.

I look up to see Tristan, his eyes fierce with determination. He offers me his hand.

I grasp it, pulling myself to my feet. I grip my knife tightly. Tristan stands beside me, fists clenched, ready for the fight. He's strong, but I can see the strain in his eyes. My knife is slick with blood, and my arm aches. Tristan is panting, his punches becoming more desperate. We're outnumbered, and the foxhounds show no signs of stopping.

Tristan growls as a foxhound latches onto his arm. It sinks its teeth into his bicep. He pries it off, slamming his fist into its head. The foxhound whimpers and falls, but more are closing in.

Another one lunges at him, but I drive my knife into its throat. Hot blood gushes over my hand. A third snaps at Tristan's leg, and he kicks it away with a grunt. We're surrounded, the foxhounds pressing in from all sides.

For a moment, it seems hopeless, but then I catch Tristan's eyes. There's a fire there that steadies me. We can't give up.

"Wrap your arms around me," Tristan says.

I whirl on him, certain I heard wrong. "What?"

"Just do it, Red!"

It's either the Wolf or the hoard of hungry foxhounds, so I choose the Wolf. I grab him around the waist and hold on for gods-knows what's next. His body is firm, and he smells surprisingly like cedar and salt. An unexpected thrill flutters in my chest.

A soundless, purple-tinged shadow explodes out of Tristan's palms. I duck my head into his chest, thinking this isn't the worst way to die, if I had to choose. Everything within a twenty-foot radius of us blows away in a silent burst of power. My eyes are wide as they readjust to the dissipating, misty shadow that follows in its wake.

Not a single surviving foxhound remains.

When all is silent, I slowly release my grip from around the Wolf. He turns to look at me, his gray eyes fierce with emotions I can't read. I feel a thrill of something deep inside me. Admiration? Yes. Curiosity, absolutely. But also something darker. Something akin to jealousy or maybe even desire.

Tristan's knees buckle, and he sinks to the ground. His head hangs low, his dark hair falling over his face.

That's when I notice his blood-soaked sleeve. I kneel to the ground beside him and rip the fabric to reveal the torn flesh beneath. The foxhound ripped muscle from bone.

Tristan looks up at me through his curtain of dark hair. Sweat drips down his face and he's breathing heavily. I wonder if Wolves can succumb to burnout the way we can if we use too much power all at once. This was certainly a large display, but one that saved both of our lives.

"Can you move it?" I ask, touching his shoulder above the wound.

Tristan shakes his head.

"I can help you."

He just nods.

I close my eyes, breathing deep to steady my racing heart. With practiced movements, I coax the power up and out of my sternum. It travels through my body, pooling golden light into my palms. Gently, I place them on the Wolf's wounded arm, healing and easing pain through my fingertips.

The tension in Tristan's face dissolves as he watches me. He's never seen my healing power before, since he was unconscious when I saved his life in the kennels. As the power dissipates, withdrawing back into my depths, Tristan's eyes meet mine. Slowly, he reaches up with his healed arm and cradles my face in his deadly palm.

"You are ..." he hesitates, a look of amazement in his eyes.

The snap of a twig makes us both turn to look. Hunter stares at us, the reins of both horses in his hands. The gray mare snorts, sniffing at his golden hair affectionately. Hunter's eyes are wide as he takes in the foxhound corpses surrounding us.

In Hunter's face, there's a mix of fear and distrust. "You mean to tell me you've had the power to kill all along?"

I know I should be afraid too. Any sane person would be, but all I feel is awe. All my life, I've been told that shadow power is evil, that it's only employed to harm. And I suppose there's truth to that. But just now, it was also used to protect. To save me.

Tristan gets off the ground, wiping dirt from his pants. "No."

"No?" Hunter asks, his face shrouded. "What do you mean, no?"

"I can't just do it on a whim," Tristan snaps. "It has to be life or death. A moment of necessity."

Hunter scoffs. "And here I thought you were a pitiful dog

locked up in the kennels with the others, when all along you've been a cold-blooded killer."

"It's not like that."

"Then what's it like, exactly?" Hunter waves his arms around at the massacre. "Why did you let the King's Guard capture you in the first place? You clearly had the ability to escape. You just let us torture you like that." I see fury in Hunter's eyes. And guilt. No doubt he's remembering how my father made him beat Tristan again and again. "What are you, some kind of masochist?"

Tristan's gray eyes grow dark. "I'm not a killer."

Hunter looks around at the dead foxhounds. "I'd say you are."

Tristan bares his teeth, rage tinting each word. "I don't kill needlessly."

"I'd say you had plenty of 'need'."

"Just because I *can* use my power to kill doesn't mean I *should*."

"We don't have time for this," I say, furious at Hunter. I shoot him a glare and mount the black horse. He's draped my red cloak over its rear like a blanket. I buckle it back over my shoulders with a huff. "Maybe next time the Wolf saves our lives, you could try showing a little gratitude instead of this unveiled contempt."

Tristan raises an eyebrow at me, but Hunter looks crestfallen. He clearly thought I'd side with him. He should know by now that the only side I'm on is my own.

In the distance, the sounds of hoofbeats and more foxhounds reach us.

"We need to keep moving," Tristan says urgently, wiping blood from a shallow cut on his cheek. "It won't take them long to find us again." He kicks a dead foxhound out of the way.

I nod. My heart is pounding, but I'm not entirely sure if it's from the near-death experience or from the Wolf's gray eyes watching me.

Chapter 22

We ride for several hours before Hunter leads us into a small clearing a short distance away from the road. He jumps down from his mare, then turns to me with his hand outstretched, presumably to help me down from the saddle. The Wolf whaps his hand out of the way before jumping down himself. Then he grabs me by the waist and swings me to the ground. The two share a look that makes me roll my eyes.

Hunter stomps back to his mare, where she nibbles on a grassy patch. He whispers into her ear and pats her neck. She snorts in pleasure. My heart clenches when I remember she nearly died because of me. Because I forced her back into the fray of foxhounds. My heart breaks all over again for Nell, the loyal horse who died at the jaws of a corpse wolf.

"What's her name?" I ask.

Both Hunter and the mare look at me. I nod toward the horse. "The mare."

"Oh," Hunter rubs her nose. "Marigold." He turns toward the black horse. "And that's Honor."

I walk up to Marigold and run my hands along her neck.

She whinnies in pleasure. "Thank you, Marigold." I whisper into her ear. "You are a brave horse. I won't forget that."

Hunter unties the saddlebags from her sides then crouches to dig through the provisions he packed. Copper glints in the sun as he sets his gauntlets on the ground next to him, like he's lying a baby down to rest.

"Why did you keep the gauntlets?" I ask.

Hunter spreads his cloak on the ground, gesturing for me to sit on it. "Because people in the villages will ask fewer questions if you travel with one of the king's men. Even without the full set of armor, these are proof that I'm from Caerwen. Copper demands respect."

Behind us, the Wolf scoffs.

Hunter ignores him. "And we're less likely to be attacked by thieves on the road."

"Or," Tristan suggests, "it might make us more of a target."

Hunter lowers his eyes at him, a wheel of wax-covered cheese in his hand. "Only a criminal would think that way."

Tristan shrugs and sits down on a grassy patch of earth, resting his back against the trunk of a tall tree.

I'm not convinced. "Aren't you afraid we'll be recognizable? If Father sent word about our escape ..." I let the implications hang in the air, unsaid.

Hunter continues pulling out provisions: strings of dried sausages, fruit, a squished loaf of bread. "News travels slowly outside of Caerwen. As long as we keep moving, we can stay ahead of the warnings." He turns and hands me an apple.

I reach out to take it, but Hunter grabs my hand. He gives me a meaningful look.

"I hope you know what you're doing," he whispers. He nods toward Tristan. At the fear etched around his eyes, I soften.

"I do," I tell him, even though I'm not entirely sure it's true.

He bends down to pull a knife out of his boot, then slices chunks of cheese from the wheel. I watch with curiosity as he sets the cheese on a plate and removes a small jar of jam from the saddlebag.

"So, what is your plan?" I ask. "Will we wander the forests and valleys of our kingdom, waiting for my new little brother to fall out of favor?"

For the first time since our breakup, Hunter's smile returns.

"Oh, I don't know." He shrugs. "I thought maybe we could become peasants for a little while. Play man and wife—or even just friends—in a land far away from here. No one to make threats or demands upon us anymore." He sighs, like he's imagined this fantasy for a long time.

"That sounds like a beautiful dream."

He nods. "Maybe someday, when we're old and gray, you'll learn to love me again."

My heart clenches in my chest.

He grins, teasing. "I don't want to be off with some other woman with a dozen grandchildren on my knee when that day comes."

"I don't see why not. That sounds like a lovely life." I take a bite of the apple in my hands.

He grows quiet. "Not without you, it doesn't."

Over by the tree, Tristan chuckles.

Hunter glowers in his direction, then leans closer to me so the Wolf can't hear. "How far is it to the borderlands again?"

I give him a chiding look, but smile. Something about the Wolf gets Hunter all out of sorts in a way that I find mildly funny. Usually nothing rattles Hunter like this.

"If we ride quickly and head straight north, we could probably be there in a couple of weeks."

Hunter nods, thinking. "Then we'll need to eat something." He rips off a chunk of bread and uses his knife to spread blackberry jam over it. Then he hands me the first piece.

I'm positively salivating. I shove the entire chunk into my mouth. Hunter passes me a waterskin to wash it down, a worried look in his eyes.

"Better?" he asks.

I nod, then grab more.

"What, nothing for me?" Tristan calls out from where he's dozing in the shade.

Hunter raises an eyebrow. "I thought you were some master hunter who could fend for himself?"

"I am." Tristan crosses his arms over his chest and slumps further against the tree. "I'm just not feeling up to it at the moment."

The look on Hunter's face is enough to make me full belly laugh, in spite of everything.

After I catch my breath again, I take a moment to close my eyes. I drink in the waning sunshine as it trickles through the bare branches on the trees. There's a strong chance that, without Hunter, I'd still be in that cold, damp cell far beneath the palace where no one would ever find me. My heart fills with gratitude alongside a new sense of fear. This ongoing battle between my father and I isn't just a petty family squabble anymore. It's life or death. He absolutely would have left me to die.

When I finally stand, Hunter cleans up the remains of our meager meal. I stoop to grab another apple and throw it to Tristan with a wink. He grins wickedly at Hunter, who chooses to ignore it.

Reluctantly, I walk back toward the horses, but Hunter guides me to the gray mare this time. He helps me up, grumbling. "There's no way in hell I'm letting him ride with you again."

Tristan swings up onto Honor's back, then takes a giant, obnoxious bite of his apple. Juice drips down his jaw as he grins.

We ride well into the night, through forests and past farms with empty fields. The air is cold and an autumn wind rustles the leaves from their branches. Soon, I'm shivering again. I'm so exhausted it's becoming difficult to stay astride my horse, even with Hunter's arms tight around me.

"There's a town up ahead," Tristan calls back to us from atop his horse. "We should stop for the night." He tips his head in my direction.

"I already know that," Hunter says, grumbling.

Tristan lets the attitude slide and leads us toward a wooden bridge that crosses a narrow but deep river. On the other side, there's a small village of thatched roof houses and leaning two-story buildings. Most of the windows are dark for the night, but at the center of the town, a small tavern is still alight with customers. We lead our horses toward a tiny stable and tie them to a hitching post inside the shelter.

When Hunter helps me down from the saddle, my knees buckle beneath me and I struggle to steady myself. I can feel Hunter's eyes as he scans me anxiously. A few paces away, I catch Tristan's glance too, but I don't know him well enough to read his moods.

After we care for the horses, we head toward the tavern. Tristan holds the tavern door open for us as we pass. Inside, there are several long tables with customers who appear to be well into their cups. Their clumsy movements make me suspect they've been drinking for several hours at this point in the night. At the other end of the room, there's a roaring fire in the hearth. I instinctively lean toward it, eager for warmth.

"We'd like a room for the night," Hunter says to the barkeep, who's wiping chipped mugs with a ratty towel.

The barkeep raises an eyebrow at the three of us.

Hunter quickly adds, "Two. Two rooms please." His eyes narrow toward Tristan, no doubt imagining an evening sleeping next to a Wolf. "Three, if you have them."

The man studies us, taking in Hunter's copper gauntlets and my red cloak. Tristan leans against a nearby post, seemingly unconcerned with sharing a room. I wonder if he'd be perfectly happy curling up next to the fireplace like a household pet.

"Can't do that," the barkeep says. Beneath his bushy moustache, his teeth are brown and rotted. "Only got the one."

Hunter visibly cringes. "Alright, she can have it. We'll sleep down here at the tables."

The bartender shakes his head. "Not allowed. It's either the room or the stables with the horses and pigs."

Hunter sputters.

Tristan rolls his eyes and walks forward to join us. "We'll take the room."

Hunter moves to protest, but Tristan holds up a hand. "The lady will be even safer with two of us there to protect her virtue. Don't start on your moral nonsense."

The barkeep shrugs. "I care nothing for morals myself." He holds out a hand.

Before Hunter can dig money from his bag, Tristan drops more than enough coins into the barkeep's hands. "For your discretion," he says, raising an eyebrow.

The barkeep's eyes dart back to Hunter's gauntlets. He nods. "I's always discrete, but I'll not turn down an extra coin or two."

"In that case," Tristan says lightly, "I'll take a mug of your finest ale as well."

Hunter gives Tristan a withering look.

The barkeep joyfully delivers the ale, then points us to a nearby staircase. As we walk up to the room, Hunter leans forward to whisper to Tristan.

"And where did you manage to find so many coins after being imprisoned at the palace for weeks?"

Tristan takes a sip of froth from the top of his mug with noisy relish. "A rich man never divulges his secrets."

"'Rich man'?" Hunter's voice is edged with disgust. "More like 'thief.'"

Tristan takes a large gulp of ale, then shrugs. "Would you like to sleep in the stable with the pigs?"

Hunter glares at Tristan but says nothing.

I sigh. "Could we all just be nice, please?"

The men appraise each other, but quit their bickering.

When Tristan unlocks the door to the room, we all stop and stare. The tiny space has a single, lopsided bed with a ratty pillow and a stained blanket ... and nothing else. Dust covers the narrow sliver of floor in front of the door.

"Is it too late to opt for the pigs?" Tristan asks.

"Not for you," Hunter mumbles.

"I don't care which of you gets the other side of the bed, just don't kick me in the night." I drop onto it and a cloud of dust billows up. I move to cover myself with the blanket, then think better of it. I kick the musty-smelling thing off the bed along with the questionable pillow. Then I pull my cloak over my face to sleep.

From beneath the cover of my cloak, I hear the men wrestle over the pillow and blanket. They argue in hushed tones.

"You're taking the floor," Hunter says.

"Nice try. I think I've slept on enough floors these past weeks to last a lifetime."

"If you don't commit crimes like spying and attempted murder, then you won't have that problem."

I can almost hear the shrug in Tristan's voice. "I'd expect a southerner to understand the necessity of subterfuge and killing one's enemies."

"Stooop!" I groan.

They tussle a little more, but eventually someone jumps onto the mattress next to me. I poke my head out from under my cloak. It's Tristan, smiling ruefully at Hunter, who's clearly contemplating murder from his spot on the floor. He unstraps his bronze sword and lays it lovingly in a corner. Then he uses the filthy blanket to polish the day's grime from his copper-plated gauntlets.

"He's high-maintenance, that one," Tristan mumbles next to me. "Can't even just lie down like a normal person with all that glitter on."

"Swords and armor aren't exactly comfortable to sleep in."

"Then why wear it in the first place?" the Wolf scoffs. "He looks like a prized turkey, chest all puffed out and feathers shining."

"Can't say I've ever seen a prized turkey in armor before."

"No?" Tristan gives me a wicked grin. "And here I thought we just escaped at least a dozen of them."

I swat his arm and Hunter scowls in our direction. He lies down on the ground, bunching the pillow under his head.

"Goodnight," I say into the darkness.

Chapter 23

In the morning, the tavern keeper's wife serves us each a bowl of mushy porridge before we head back out onto the road. Hunter insists I ride with him on Marigold again, which I don't mind.

After a night of lying awake beside Tristan, I need distance. We never touched, but that didn't stop my mind from wandering. Now I can't stop thinking about the rise and fall of his broad chest as he slept beside me. Or the scent of cedar and salt that he left on the bedsheets.

Sunlight makes dappled patterns along the frost-covered forest floor. Everything looks like magic in this light. Our breath mingles, caught in the chill air. The dewy trees drip, and the horses' hooves crunch along the leaf-covered ground. I could almost believe we're just three normal travelers, out on a morning ride.

I pull my heavy red cloak tighter around my shoulders, grateful for its warmth. It's a good thing we escaped Caerwen before the start of winter. Even now, in mid-autumn, the wind is bitter and the night temperatures drop dangerously. But as long as the sun holds out during the day and we keep moving, we should make it to the border before the weather changes for the worse.

Behind me, Hunter sighs. "I'm ready for this whole blasted thing to be over. To find safe harbor somewhere people aren't constantly trying to kill us."

"Or bow to us," I offer.

He nods, thinking. "Maybe a port town along the western coast would be nice. That sounds far enough from Caerwen."

"Maybe." My voice doesn't sound convincing. There's no corner of the realm far enough to escape the Fox King's toxic reach.

His voice is lighthearted again, optimistic. "I could be a fisherman, I think."

"Have you ever fished a day in your life?" I tease.

"Nah," he waves concern away. "But I'll find a friendly old man to teach me. He'll appreciate that I'm so eager to learn. Old people love that."

I smile. I'm glad to see a hint of the old Hunter again. The past few days have been exceptionally difficult. Between breaking off our engagement, rescuing me from certain death, fleeing with the Wolf, and being attacked by a hoard of murderous foxhounds ... I don't blame him for being so grumpy. But I hope the old Hunter is here to stay.

Hunter laughs. "Remember when we were kids and Elena taught us to pick the cellar locks?"

I snort. "Which we then used to steal wine from the cellars."

"See? Old people love to teach young kids new tricks."

"Elena's only one year older than us."

"The rule still applies."

I elbow him in the ribs.

"Gah!" he laughs. "I guess I deserved that."

It's a sweet memory, but the mention of Elena brings back thoughts of Caerwen. Of the damp, rat-infested dungeon and my father's attempt to kill me. My mood sours instantly.

"Why do you think she helped save me?" I ask.

Hunter's tone is more contemplative now. "Because we grew up together. She wouldn't let you die, even if she has become ..." He struggles to find the right word.

"The enemy?" I offer.

"I wouldn't call her that."

"My father's mistress? The future queen of Llwyn? The mother of the new heir?" Behind me, I feel him cringe. But something still doesn't feel right about the whole thing. I can't just chalk it up to our childhood friendship. She wears a silver moth ring. That can't be a coincidence.

"Hunter, there's something you should know about Elena."

Behind me, I can feel his arms stiffen. "Alright. What?"

"I overheard her talking with your father in secret. The baby, the new heir, he's illegitimate."

Hunter is quiet for a long time as Marigold clomps over the leaf-strewn road, snorting happily. "I suspected," he says eventually. "I think most of the nobles do too. But I don't think anyone would dare contradict the Fox King."

I nod. He's right. No one would. "And there's another thing."

He groans. "I'm almost afraid to ask."

"She wears a silver moth ring."

His voice is filled with genuine surprise. "Are you sure?"

"I saw it. When she helped us escape."

"Huh." I can practically hear his mind whirring as it runs through connections and possibilities. None of which we can verify now.

On the horse behind us, Tristan hums a lighthearted tune. A full night's sleep and hot food in his belly made him a little more chipper this morning. Maybe the rest of this trip will be significantly better than the first day.

One can always hope, anyway.

Ahead of us, a man steps casually out of the forest and into the middle of the road. He pauses there, his hands clasped behind his back. The man rocks on his heels and smiles pleasantly as we approach. We pull on our horses' reins a few yards away.

Hunter calls out to the man. "Hello, friend, we don't want any trouble."

"Wonderful!" The man claps his hands and rubs them together. "I don't either."

We stare at the man for a long moment, waiting for him to step aside, but he doesn't.

Tristan clears his throat. "Move."

Hunter shoots him a disapproving glare. Hunter has never been one for rudeness.

The man continues smiling pleasantly. "I don't think so."

Tristan sighs, leaning forward on his horse. "We have places to go. Tell us what you want and let's get this over with."

"Ah," the man says, his smile brightening. "I'm glad you asked."

On either side of the road, several more men step out from behind trees and bushes. They're all dressed in the threadbare clothes of farmers and peasants. They carry pitchforks, kitchen knives, and shovels. One even has a large stick.

Hunter groans. "You can't be serious."

"Oh, but we are," the pleasant man says. "But don't worry, no one need get hurt." He looks pointedly at me. My hackles raise at the insinuation that I need protecting.

"Just hand over your coins and that spectacular pair of gauntlets. Then we'll permit you safe passage."

"How generous of you," Tristan says flatly.

The man points toward me. "And we'll take that fine red cloak too, if you don't mind."

I shoot him my most venomous glare. "I do mind."

"You seem to have plenty of blankets in your packs. You won't be chilly for long."

"No."

Hunter interjects. "How did you know where to find us? Or do you harass everyone on this road?"

The man chuckles. "The boarding man sends you his thanks."

Hunter's eyes grow wide. "That scoundrel! We paid for his silence."

The man nods as if he understands our predicament. "A pretty penny too, I'd wager."

Tristan shakes his head. "And his ale was halfway decent too."

The man raises an eyebrow. "Then you've been drinking some real shit ale, my friend."

Tristan shrugs, agreeing.

"We're not giving you anything," Hunter says, sitting tall in our saddle. "I am a member of the King's Guard, and I demand you let us through."

All around us, the local men shoot each other nervous glances, but the smiling man is not perturbed. "And here I assumed you were a common thief."

"Like you?" Tristan asks, but the man ignores the comment.

He purses his lips, thinking. "If you're a member of the King's Guard, then where is the rest of your famous copper armor?"

Hunter shoots Tristan a murderous glare. "That is irrelevant."

The smiling man just shrugs and gestures toward my cloak. "No matter. We'll take our payment now."

I bristle. "Over my dead body."

"Hold on a minute." Tristan raises his hands placatingly. "How do you know we're even the same customers your overrated bartender mentioned? For all you know, we're a tribe of penniless performers." He points to Hunter. "There you have the hopeless hero and his ingenue."

The man grins. "If they're the main characters, then who, pray tell, are you?"

Tristan grins wickedly. "I'm the villain, of course." His canines are slightly more pointed than seems natural.

For the first time, the man's smile falters. "Hand over your money," he says, all good humor gone. "And that red cloak, sweetheart. Those gauntlets, too. We'll be taking them."

Hunter jumps down from the mare and draws his sword, preventing the men from getting any nearer to me, but I don't need his protection. I jump down from the mare.

"Sienna, no," Hunter says.

I ignore him and fumble under my skirts. Someone whistles. Another farmer makes a lewd gesture, but his face changes when I draw my knife out from the scabbard strapped to my thigh. Maybe it's time I find a more convenient place to keep my weapon.

The jokester lunges first, reaching for my cloak. I sidestep and slash out with my knife, catching his arm. He yelps and stumbles back, clutching his bleeding wound. Hunter takes that moment to charge at another thief, his gauntlet connecting with the man's jaw with a satisfying crunch. The thief drops to the ground, unconscious from a single punch.

Behind us, Tristan intercepts a third thief who's trying to circle around me. He grabs the man's arm and twists, forcing him to drop his pitchfork, while his other fist sends the thief sprawling.

Several more men jump out from hiding spots in the forest, farm tools in hand. None look terribly confident about fighting us, but they want our money more than they fear a whipping.

"Come here, girl." A ruddy man with a great orange beard swipes at me, but I'm faster. I twist out of his grasp just in time.

Unfortunately, I don't notice the tree branch his friend is swinging toward me from the other direction. It catches me in the gut with a dull thump and I fall, sprawled out on the ground. My necklace slips out from its hiding spot beneath my bodice. The ruddy man's eyes grow wide when he sees the silver moth.

"Pretty," he says, grinning at me with brown teeth. "The missus will love that." He reaches for it, but I roll away, swiping my knife at his hand as I go.

"Damn you to the deathless!" he shouts as he clutches his bleeding fingers. Blood drips down his forearm, trickling off his elbow into the dirt.

The thin man holds up his hands. "This ain't worth it." He turns and runs back into the forest.

"Evil wench," the ruddy man yells as he follows him.

Behind me, Hunter and Tristan had similar success with their farmers, most of whom have fled.

When the leader realizes he's the only one remaining, he curses and draws a blade that looks more like a kitchen knife than a dagger. He makes a wild swing at me, but I parry, deflecting his attack. I duck under his next swipe and kick out, catching him in the knee. He goes down with a grunt, and I point my knife at his throat.

"Run while you still can," I hiss. My necklace dangles inches above his nose.

The leader glares up at me, but when I press the knife into the thin skin of his neck, he reconsiders.

"Fine!" he chokes.

I remove my knee and get off him, but I keep my knife

pointed at his throat. He scrambles backward, jumps to his feet, then follows his men back into the forest.

My red cloak catches in a breeze as I watch them retreat.

When I turn around, Tristan is staring at the silver moth on my necklace. He notices I'm watching and points to it. "You'd better put that away, Red. Before anyone else sees."

Something in the way he's looking at it gives me pause. "Why? Because you know this moth?"

He stomps past me to the unconscious thief in the road. "Because the last thing we need is to tempt more thieves with pretty trinkets on display."

I glower at him, but tuck it back inside my bodice anyway.

Hunter nudges the unconscious man with his boot, making sure he's out cold. He crosses his arms in front of his chest, then turns to Tristan.

"Why didn't you use that shadow power of yours?" he asks.

Tristan shrugs, then kneels on the ground. "We had it under control."

I lean in toward Hunter. "The Wolf Code."

"Wolf Code? What the hell is that?"

Tristan looks peeved. "It's not called the 'Wolf Code'. We simply have morals. Honor. Something you southerners could learn a thing or two about."

I roll my eyes. "Let's not start."

Hunter takes the bait. "I don't see anything immoral about saving our asses."

Tristan turns to Hunter. "And would you doom an impoverished family to a life of slow starvation? Because that's what you would've done if I'd killed those men. Poor people do foolish things when their families are suffering." His eyes grow hard. "That's something Annwyn people understand. That's why we don't kill others unless absolutely necessary."

Hunter scoffs, indignant. "Couldn't you just bring him back to life, anyway?"

Tristan whirls around, his face furious. "We do *not* reanimate people."

Hunter pushes back. "No? What about your Dead Queen?"

Tristan shakes his head slowly. "*She* is exactly why we don't do it."

"Only one northerner is allowed immortality then?" Hunter asks. "Sounds selfish to me."

In a flash, Tristan pushes Hunter's back into a nearby tree. For a moment, I fear they're going to fight. But just as quickly, Tristan releases him.

"When we reanimate, the soul is still lost." He says this with an ache in his voice, like he knows from experience what it's like to lose someone he loves. "The creature—or human—is never the same as they were before death claimed them. You can't call people back. Not really. It always causes more pain."

He turns and grabs the unconscious thief by the ankles, then drags him out of the middle of the road. The man's face is a bloody mess, but he'll survive. Though I don't envy the headache he'll have when he wakes.

Tristan takes a coin from the waist of his trousers, then tucks it into the unconscious man's hand before standing to face us. He adds, "When you have the power to reanimate, you learn to respect the sanctity of life. Real life. The sort that has a soul and free thought." He turns from us and walks toward his horse.

Next to me, Hunter digs the toe of his boot into the dirt, appearing somewhat chagrined.

It seems, despite his rough exterior and murderous abilities, Tristan might not be so different from Hunter after all. Both live by a code of honor—the knight sworn to protect the royal family, and the Wolf bound to respect the sanctity of life.

If I'm not mistaken, the look Hunter gives him is a little less hateful. One might even call it "begrudging respect".

Chapter 24

After two more days of travel, icy autumn raindrops begin to fall.

Behind me, Hunter mumbles a curse under his breath. Tristan doesn't bother mumbling. He just says one loud and clear.

The forest comes alive with the sound of dripping leaves. It would be peaceful if we weren't stuck in the middle of it, rain streaming into our eyes and cascading over our mouths. The dirt road turns to a muddy puddle as the horses clomp through it.

I try to stop my teeth from chattering, but it's hopeless. We're all soaked through to the bone. Hunter doesn't complain, but I can feel him shivering behind me. Tristan looks like a wet dog slumped in his horse's saddle. Even Marigold huffs with displeasure.

"I suspect we may drown before we reach the northern border," I say.

Neither man responds.

A rumble of thunder overhead rattles my bones. Before long, our horses struggle with each step, their hooves sinking into the wet earth. I glance up into the sky. Beyond the tree canopy, the downpour shows no sign of letting up.

Up ahead, there's a crossroads. One continues north, the other points toward a small village to the west.

"We need to take shelter," I yell over the pounding rain.

"We have to stay ahead of the King's Guard," Hunter says.

"There's no way they're chasing us in this." I wipe rain water out of my eyes.

I look to Tristan for input, but he's staring down the road toward the village. There's an expression on his face that I can't decipher. It looks like a mix between distrust and resignation. When he sees me watching, he shrugs and turns his horse down the village path. Hunter sighs, then clicks for the mare to follow.

The village isn't what I expected. It's more ruin than town, having been abandoned a long time ago. Despite the pounding rain and rumbling thunder, the street is eerily quiet. The houses, once sturdy with timber and thatch, now stand in various states of decay. Roofs are caved in, walls are covered in creeping vines, and gardens are long-overgrown. Water drips from broken window sills and gutters, adding to the somber atmosphere.

I feel a chill that has little to do with the weather.

We pass through cautiously, looking for a shelter that's still standing. The village is speckled with hints of the past. A wagon lies overturned in the mud, its paint faded and peeling. A shop's sign swings creakily in the wind, the words barely legible under layers of grime.

Eventually, we find a stone hall that could have once been a temple or a town meeting place. Its thick walls have withstood the test of time better than the wooden homes and shops around it. When we approach the door, I jump down from Marigold's back and land on something lumpy. At my feet, there's a soggy rag doll that's so filthy and sun-bleached it matches the road. My heart sinks for the long-ago child who left it behind.

Hunter jumps down after me, and I lead Marigold to the safety of what used to be a stable. One wall has completely collapsed, but the other side is standing and, importantly, dry. Marigold neighs with thanks as I remove the soggy saddle and blanket from her back. But when I drop them to the ground, something catches my eye.

Scorch marks mar the wood beams. This village wasn't just abandoned because of failing crops or poor harvest. Something more sinister happened here.

Tristan walks up behind me and follows my gaze. He squints through the rain at the other buildings. I don't know how I missed the signs before: doors are broken off their hinges, wardrobes block the windows, and weapon gouges pepper the walls. In a nearby garden, piles of blackened, charred remains stick up through the tall grasses like death daisies.

Tristan approaches a broken mace that pokes out from under a pile of decaying debris. His frown deepens. It's oxidized green, the copper long-since tarnished.

"These were your beloved soldiers," he says.

"No." Hunter appears behind us now. "That can't be. That must've belonged to one of the townspeople here."

Rain streams down Tristan's temples as he gives Hunter a long-suffering look. "And how do you suppose a farmer got ahold of advanced weaponry?"

"I ... it's ..." Hunter stumbles, unsure. "We can't know what happened here."

Tristan searches the garden, pushing aside tall, soggy weeds as he goes. He picks up a heavy bronze longsword, half-buried in the dirt. It's old and green with oxidization, but the hilt still bears an unmistakable emblem at the end—a tarnished copper fox.

Tristan raises an eyebrow at Hunter.

"That doesn't make any sense," I reply, shaking my head. "We're already in the south. Why would Llwyn soldiers attack their own people?"

Tristan's expression is grim. "This wasn't always a *southern* town, Red. Territories were drawn and redrawn, again and again."

"That's ridiculous," Hunter says.

But it isn't.

How many times did I move camp along the border? Six? Seven? And how many questions did I ask about those "advancements"? None. Like everyone else, I didn't question the generals who worked for my father. I didn't see maps or documentation laying claim to the land we were squatting on. As far as we knew, it was all a part of Llwyn. Stolen long ago by the Dead Queen's army and recently reclaimed.

My eyes won't break away from the fox on the sword's hilt. The idea that borders could shift so drastically, changing the lives and loyalties of those living within them, is unsettling. It makes me wonder how many other villages suffered similar fates, caught in the crossfire of my father's political games.

Beside me, Hunter's face is devastated. He can see it now too. The lies he's been fed, the manipulation. He turns to me with a ferocity in his eyes that I've never seen before.

"I'll get you your crown someday, Sienna." He walks toward me with determined steps. "Someone must take Llwyn and fix this. All of it." He grabs my hand and holds it to his chest. "You are the true heir to the Fox Throne."

I look around to see if Tristan can help me talk sense into Hunter, but he's gone. Vanished into the rain.

"Hunter," I whisper. "You know I've never—"

"Wanted the crown?" He squeezes my hand. "Yes, I remember. But that's exactly why it *has* to be you. You're the only one who won't use your power to torture, steal, manipulate ..." He lets out a frustrated sigh.

I don't know what to say. He's staring at me with so much love, so much hope. I don't know how I can live under the weight of such expectations.

"Things are different now, Sienna," he says, sensing my hesitation. "I know you. You wouldn't leave your people to suffer at the hands of a monster like your father."

I shake my head. "My new brother will reign someday. My father can't sit on the throne forever." Fear laces through my voice like a needle threaded with dread.

Why have I always been so set against the throne? Why have I always refused to even entertain the possibility of being the Fox Queen someday?

In the pit of my stomach, my power flares, attuned to my emotions. I know why. I've always known.

Fear.

Fear of becoming a corrupt ruler, like my father. Another Fox to be consumed by power and greed.

"Your brother might not rule for *decades*." Hunter shakes his head slowly. "Who knows what sort of monster your father will raise him to be? You, at least, had your grandmother to help you see differently."

I pull my hand out of his grasp. "You can't just *wish* me to be queen, Hunter." My tone is more aggressive than intended. "It's not like I have any say in the matter. I don't have that kind of power." I turn away, nauseous and shaking from emotions I haven't had time to process.

"But you do," Hunter says behind me as I walk away. "You've always had more than you realize."

Deep in my core, my light flares as if in agreement. I squash it down as I stomp through the rain, feeling suddenly unsure about every damn thing in my life. I thought I knew what to do, what I wanted, but maybe I haven't known anything at all.

Inside the stone hall, we're finally out of the rain, but all our gear is soaked through. Hunter strings a line and helps me hang our blankets and spare clothes to dry while Tristan clears the space and uses an axe to break apart old furniture for firewood. Before long, smoke from a small fire rises upward and escapes out the dripping holes in the ceiling. We shiver as we sit as close to the fire as we dare.

The firelight flickers across the stone carvings in the wall. This must have been an important place for these villagers to warrant such craftsmanship. Beautiful women in flowing dresses dance with beasts of the forest, watched over by the phases of the moon. I don't see sun imagery or Fox Kings anywhere, unusual for a place of worship.

"This doesn't look like any temple I've ever seen," I say.

Tristan stares into the flames. "That's because it's dedicated to the old gods of the north."

Behind him, a faded tapestry depicts a tree spirit embracing a woman wearing a sheer white gown. She has a wolf pelt thrown over her shoulders. The imagery is so gorgeously realistic, I can almost hear the lovers' frantic, love-drunk breaths. I blush when I notice the woman's hardened nipples slipping out of her silk dress. Artwork like this would be labeled "obscene" in the traditional south. It makes me wonder what sort of freedom Annwyn women must have that love scenes adorn the walls of their temples.

"Would you tell me about your people?" I ask, feeling the sanctity of the space, even though it was abandoned long ago.

Beside me, Hunter shifts uneasily, but he doesn't protest.

For a minute, I wonder if Tristan heard me, but then he lets out a long sigh. "Places like this are rare in Annwyn these days. It's a hard life, relocating every few years when the soldiers come calling. Art and religion are often the first thing to go when you're a refugee, constantly moving, constantly trying to keep your family alive."

A lump forms in my throat.

The fire crackles while we wait for Tristan to continue. He nods toward the tapestry. "That's the Tree God, the protector of our great northern forests. He wooed the goddess of the moon. Their love was forbidden, since he was a deity of the earth and she of the sky. But she came to him anyway, in the night. She birthed the first fae. And the first wolves." He glances up at me. "That's why wolves howl, you know. They miss their moon mother."

I smile at this until I remember that the last wolf I encountered was of the undead variety. That was not something from a fairytale, as much as I wish it were.

"And what of the corpse wolves?" I ask.

Tristan picks up a stick and pokes the fire. "Those came later, with the first Dead Queen."

Hunter's head shoots up. "There's more than one?"

"There have been several." Tristan grabs another piece of wood from his pile—a table leg, by the look of it—and adds it to the fire. "Whenever one decides to pass on to the spirit realm, another must take her place. The first one is known as the Mother of Corpses because she was the first to exhibit the power of reanimation. She started with the wolves first, because she loved them like children. But there were never many, not then."

"And now?" I ask. The air is thick with tension. Beside me, Hunter's eyes are shadowed as he watches Tristan.

"And now we *need* more of them." Tristan pokes the fire with his stick. "To protect us from the southern invaders."

I expect Hunter to protest, but he doesn't. I search his face for some hint of what he's thinking, but his eyebrows draw together in deep thought. I want to reach out, to smooth away the crease there.

Hunter breaks the silence first. "Tristan, I believe I owe you an apology."

Tristan tilts his head to look up at him, suspicion clear on his face.

I look between the two.

Hunter's expression is grave. "Over the last week, I've not been my true self. I've been cruel, untrusting, and, well ... childish." He clears his throat. "I don't understand you or your kind, but that doesn't give me the right to be so ... ungenerous." His voice is thick with shame, a tone I remember from the thousand tiny failures of our youth. When his father would scold him or beat him for being less than perfect.

I want to reach out, to hold his hand to my chest and tell him it's not his fault.

Hunter catches my eye. "My only defense is that I care for Sienna more than anything else in this world. And, well, I was afraid."

Tristan lifts an eyebrow. "Afraid of the big bad Wolf?"

Hunter smiles slightly. His cheeks grow pink. "I suppose so."

Tristan stands, brushes the dirt off his palms, and holds out a hand.

Hunter shakes it. "Can we start over?"

"We can certainly try not to be at each other's throats constantly." Tristan leans in, as if I won't be able to hear them right next to me. "I think it would make the lady happy."

"Mmm," I agree. "It'd be nice if you'd stop bickering."

Hunter chuckles, chagrined. "I'll try my best."

Chapter 25

I WAKE to the sound of the horses whinnying outside. My head is foggy from deep sleep and for a moment, I forget where I am. The rain has stopped and moonlight streams through the holes in the ceiling, casting a spotlight on the wreckage surrounding us. Across the room, the Tree God and the Moon Goddess are haloed in moonlight, as if the goddess herself is trying to tell me something about lovers in the forest.

Outside, Marigold whinnies again, her tone anxious.

Next to me, Hunter stirs. When he sees me getting to my feet, he scrambles up after me. His still-damp blanket falls to the ground near the smoldering fire embers.

"Sienna," he whispers into the dark. "What are you doing?"

"The horses." I look toward the door.

Tristan mumbles something in his sleep and pulls his blanket over his head.

Outside, something falls over with a crack. I run to the heavy doors and swing them open, expecting to see the King's Guard surrounding us. Instead, there's nothing. Just more moonlight bathing the long-dead city in an ethereal glow. I run over to Marigold and Hunter follows me to help calm Honor.

"Shh ..." I grab her bridle. "Calm, now. It was probably just an animal. Nothing to fret over."

I scan the village as I pet Marigold's gray neck. Her heart beats wildly beneath my palm, but I don't see anything out of the ordinary. The buildings are painted in shades of mist and shadow.

An icy breeze pushes a bundle of leaves down the empty road. I shiver. My clothes are still damp and my fingertips are numb with cold. When we go back, I'll ask Hunter to get the fire going again. If we can't dry out, we'll have bigger problems than the King's Guard to deal with before long. Hypothermia can kill a man as surely as any blade.

Out of the corner of my eye, I see something dark move inside a doorway. I still. Next to me, Marigold stomps her foot. She saw it too.

"Hunter," I whisper.

He turns from whispering into Honor's ear. "What is it?"

I point across the road, toward the half-dilapidated house with no door. "Someone's there."

He squints through the darkness. The only sound around us is the wind and the horses' nervous breathing.

"Are you sure?"

I nod.

"Was it a man, a woman?"

I shake my head. "I don't know. It's too dark."

Hunter moves one hand to the sword at his hip as he steps forward. "I'll investigate."

I put my hand on his arm. "No, not alone."

He pauses, like he'd very much like to force me to stay back, but he knows me better than that. He gives me a curt nod.

The air is cold and still. The skin on the back of my neck prickles as we move cautiously toward the darkened doorway. I can't shake the feeling that we're being watched.

My heart beats wildly in my chest as I lean through the door, expecting to see the king's copper knights waiting for us.

But there's no one there.

The small room has only one exit, and we're standing in it. There's no way anyone could've snuck out in the time it took for us to cross the street. Hunter pushes past me, kicking cobwebbed furniture out of his way and turning over molded bedding. Mice scurry around his feet.

"I don't understand," I say. "I swear, I saw someone."

Hunter looks toward the narrow window.

I shrug. "Maybe? It's a pretty small window."

"Let's look outside."

We walk down the street, listening for any sound that might indicate we're not alone. All I hear is the clatter of dried leaves and our boots on the dirt road.

As we round a bend into what used to be the village square, my heart seizes in my chest.

Standing in the center of the square are three figures cloaked in shadow, their forms shifting and swirling like smoke in the moonlight.

"Please tell me you see them too," I whisper to Hunter.

He answers by grabbing my hand and pulling me back around the corner. We stand up against a wall, frozen in fear.

"What do we do?" I whisper.

Hunter shakes his head. "I don't know."

A small pebble lands at our feet. We both squint into the darkness to look for the source. Across the street, someone crouches in a narrow alley.

Tristan.

He puts a finger over his mouth, telling us to be quiet,

then, quick and silent as a wolf, he flees deeper into the alleyway.

"We should follow him," I whisper.

Hunter shakes his head, then points toward the other direction and mouths, "The horses."

But something in my gut tells me we need to trust the Wolf, that he knows things we don't. I grab Hunter's hand to move toward the alley, but he pulls me back, shaking his head frantically.

Before we can make a decision, the monsters round the corner and turn their hollow, black eyes toward us. For a brief moment, we stare at each other, frozen. Their slick, emaciated bodies are clothed in nothing but swirling shadows. Their terrible over-large mouths gape open, exposing too many teeth. A low, keening wail fills the air and vibrates in my bones.

"Run!" Hunter shouts. Our boots skid against the ground as we race down the alley.

The black, ghost-like creatures glide after us, their movements smooth and unnaturally fast. I glance back and see their skeletal fingers reaching out to grasp us. I force my legs to run faster.

We weave through the narrow alleys and abandoned streets. My heart pounds in my chest. Every corner we turn, every darkened doorway we pass, they are right behind us. Their number multiplies as more of them appear out of the dark corners of the village to join the chase.

We run around the corner and nearly slam into someone.

"Run!" I shout when I see it's Tristan.

He skids to a stop, slipping to the ground. "You don't have to ask me twice."

Hunter helps him up and we sprint through the moonlit streets, trying to lose the terrifying black creatures behind us. Dread fills my chest. It's so heavy, it can't be natural.

"What are those things?" My voice has an edge of terror that I can't mask.

"Wraiths," Tristan says, panting. "Lost souls who died in terrible, unforgivable ways."

"What do they want with us?"

His eyes are worried. "Revenge."

We leap over a forgotten cart blocking the road.

"But we had nothing to do with their deaths!" Hunter yells this behind us, as if he thinks it might help persuade the specters to leave us alone.

"They don't care." Tristan grabs my hand fiercely. "Whatever happens, don't stop, Red. Keep going."

I nod. Fear makes tears prickle at the corners of my eyes.

Suddenly, Tristan stops running. He pushes me forward, then charges back toward the creatures at full speed.

"Tristan, no!" I reach out, but catch nothing but air.

Hunter grabs my shoulders. "You heard him, Sienna. We have to keep going!"

But I can't. Something inside of me pulls, refusing to leave the Wolf. Several yards away, he digs his heels into the ground and thrusts his palms forward. Thick, black mist spews from his hands. The wraiths pause momentarily, as if considering him, but then charge right through his shadow power.

Tristan turns to look back at us. "Go!" he yells. "Go!"

Hunter pulls my arm. "The horses!"

The wraiths gain on Tristan, their long black tongues licking the air in insatiable hunger. I can't let them take him. A panic rises in me, stronger than I can rationally explain. Tristan is sacrificing himself, so I can escape. I won't let him.

I charge forward, wrenching my arm out of Hunter's grasp. Just as the wraiths reach Tristan, he crouches to the ground, ready for the attack.

But it doesn't come.

Instead, I throw every ounce of power I have outward.

There's no controlling it, no channeling it through my palms like I do for healing. An unexpected thrill swells through my veins as my light pulses from my skin in an explosion of power. I don't think, I just surge with energy, like a mighty wave.

A brilliant wall of light blows the wraiths back. They screech in alarm before they dissipate on the spot, turning to ash and leaving the scent of smoke in the air. My light fades along with them and we are once again thrown back into silent midnight.

In the quiet that follows, both Hunter and Tristan stare at me, wide-eyed.

"Sienna," Hunter whispers. "What was that?"

My vision goes black before I hit the ground.

Chapter 26

When I finally wake, it's daylight. Hunter is holding me close to his chest as we ride Marigold through a dusty field, empty of harvest. Marigold's hooves crunch over rocks and dried weeds.

Voices lull me back to awareness.

"I've never seen anything like it," Hunter whispers above my head.

"It's not unheard of for someone to manifest new abilities," Tristan says, his words urgent despite his obvious attempt to keep quiet. "Her ancestors drew the night from the sky and blinded entire armies with light."

A grumble rumbles in Hunter's chest. "Maybe. But those were stories, not proven facts."

"Stories all start somewhere. Look at the Dead Queens. The power to reanimate had to be born first."

When I open my eyes, the late-afternoon sun makes me squint. I groan, startling Hunter.

"You're awake." He calls out to Tristan. "She's awake."

I watch as Tristan pulls the reins to stop his horse.

"How are you feeling?" Hunter asks, propping me

forward on Marigold's saddle. He reaches for a waterskin. "Here, drink some water."

I take it in trembling hands and drink deeply.

"We nearly thought you'd died, Sienna," Hunter says, once I hand the empty skin back to him.

"Burnout." My voice is hoarse, like I've been screaming in my sleep. Exhaustion aches in my bones.

I've only burned out once before, back at the soldier camps. When I started healing the most gruesome cases, I couldn't bear to leave dying men in agony while I rested. I kept pushing myself, kept using my power until it was completely gone. I was unconscious for three entire days after that.

"How long was I out?" I ask.

Hunter looks at Tristan whose expression is grim.

"Almost a full day."

I groan. At least I didn't miss much, just more traveling and numbing cold.

Tristan watches me intently, his eyebrows pinched together.

"What?" I ask.

"You shouldn't have done that."

Hunter shoots him a sharp look. "Don't upset her."

"I'm not upset," I snap, then cough at the strain in my vocal cords. "Are you telling me I shouldn't have saved your life? Again?"

Tristan narrows his eyes and nods once.

I sigh and lean back into Hunter's chest. "Let's go. I've already wasted enough of our time."

Hunter clicks his tongue, and Marigold starts forward. As we pass Tristan, he watches me with one of those looks I can't quite decipher. If I didn't know any better, I'd say it looks a lot like guilt.

If I had more energy, I'd tell him this wasn't his fault. But right now, all I want to do is lean back into Hunter's chest and breathe in the heady scent of him as I drift back to sleep.

Gradually, the land shifts as we travel further north into the vast Korrigan Forest. The trees thicken and stretch taller, their gold and crimson leaves spilling like fire over the hills. It's breathtaking to behold, but Korrigan isn't just a pretty forest, it's deadly too.

At least, that's what all the stories say.

We stop for the night beneath a copse of twisted hawthorns, their thorn-laden branches reaching skyward like gnarled fingers clawing from a grave. The last rays of twilight catch on the golden-yellow leaves still clinging to their boughs. The trees crowd close, trunks hunched and knotted, their bark split like old scars. We set up camp with our backs to them, as if the thorns might serve as a fortress.

Hunter pokes at the campfire with a stick, his copper gauntlets glinting in the firelight.

"I'm not sure we should go this way," he says. "The main road would be safer." His voice is low and worried. He glances up at the dark canopy that blocks all starlight.

"Sure, it would be," Tristan says. "If it weren't crawling with soldiers and King's Guards looking for three fugitives."

For the first time, I realize Tristan has the bronze fox sword that he found in the abandoned village. It's lying on the ground in front of him, glinting in the firelight. While I was unconscious, he must have polished and sharpened it. It's an odd choice for a Wolf, a fox soldier's sword. But it's better than nothing.

"Are you sure you know the way?" Hunter keeps glancing toward me, like he's afraid I'll break again. But I can already feel my power returning, albeit slowly. I won't try using that much all at once again. Next time, I might not be so lucky. Nobles with power have been known to die from burnout when they push themselves too far.

Tristan gives him a lazy look from where he sits cross-legged in the dirt. "How do you think I travelled all the way to Caerwen in the first place?"

Hunter doesn't respond.

The dark forest envelops us like a void. There's no birdsong. No footfalls or snapping branches, only the slow creak of wood and the hush of twilight as it folds around us. This place feels old. Sacred.

I shiver and pull my red cloak tighter around me. The fire does little to chase away the cold sinking into my bones.

Hunter's eyes are fixed on the flames. He's been quiet all evening, more so than usual. There's a tension in his shoulders, a nervous energy that he's trying to hide. But I can see it. And it worries me.

"Hunter," I say softly, drawing his attention. "What's on your mind?"

He looks up, meets my gaze for a moment, then glances away. "Nothing." His tone is unconvincing. His fingers tighten into a fist inside his gauntlets, and for a moment, I think he won't say anything. Then he sighs, heavy and resigned.

"It's this forest. There are stories about it. People say it's cursed." He shakes his head, looking back at the fire. "People disappearing, strange creatures lurking in the shadows, voices that drive men mad. I know it sounds like superstitious nonsense, but I can't shake this feeling ..."

The fire pops loudly, sending a shower of sparks into the night. Tristan digs into the saddlebags, removing rations of dried meat and the last of the cheese wheel.

I put my hand on Hunter's arm. "We'll be careful. We have each other's backs."

Tristan shakes his head and tosses Hunter the cheese. "He's right to be afraid."

I give him a look. "You're not helping."

Tristan's jaw tightens. "It's not helpful to be foolhardy."

"Then what do we need to prepare for? How do we make it through safely?"

Tristan shrugs. "Luck."

I scowl. "Lovely." Still, I draw my knife from its new hiding spot inside the ankle of my boot, then set it next to me.

Tristan takes a bite of stale bread and turns to look up at the dark trees. "The stories say the Heir to the North will return Korrigan Forest to Annwyn." He pauses as we listen to the sounds of the wilderness and the popping fire. "I wonder if that will make the forest happy again. To break the so-called curse. These trees were revered by the Annwyn people for thousands of years. They were our protectors. Until ..." He lets his sentence hang unfinished.

Until my family invaded and pushed his people farther into the frozen north.

Maybe that's why it's cursed. My heart grows heavy, as if I've aged a century in a single moment. It feels as though I understand the plight of this wood. I, too, am haunted by a past that was violently taken from me. A past I can never get back.

"They miss what once was," I say.

Hunter shoots me a curious glance.

Tristan nods. "Maybe so, Red." He tears another hunk of bread with his teeth.

A twig snaps behind us, pulling us out of our thoughts. All three of us jump to our feet, weapons raised.

A woman stands just inside the ring of firelight, trembling and pale. Her filthy hands are raised in front of her in a peaceful gesture. "Please." Her voice shakes with fear. "We mean you no harm."

"We?" Tristan asks with a snarl.

"My children and I. May we approach?"

When we don't respond right away, she continues. "We saw your fire. There's safety in numbers out here. We just wanted to share your warmth for a while." Her eyes travel to the dried meat that Tristan laid out on a rock. "It's been a long time since we dared to light a fire."

I look sideways at Hunter, but I can tell he's wavering. He'd never let a woman or children suffer if he can help it.

"Where are your children?" I ask, my knife raised.

The woman waves at the darkness behind her. Slowly, three filthy children peek out from behind the trees. The oldest boy might be twelve, but the other two children can't be more than six. They look as afraid as their mother does.

"Alright," Hunter says. "We can share our fire."

Behind us, Tristan growls his displeasure, but he doesn't argue. He drops his sword and stomps back to his seat on the ground.

"Thank you," the woman says. She gathers her children around her and they sit huddled together near the fire. The children put their hands as close to the flames as they dare, sniffling and shivering. The woman looks back at Hunter and gives him a small, appreciative smile.

I walk to the other side of the flames, as far away from the seemingly innocuous strangers as I can. "What are you doing in Korrigan with three children?" I ask. "And where are your guides?"

The woman shakes her head. "We don't have any. Not anymore. When we left our home, there were seven of us. We're all that's left."

I look toward Tristan, who still studies them warily. He picks up his fox sword and begins sharpening it with a stone. The eldest boy watches him with awe.

"What are your names?" Hunter asks.

"I'm Gloria." The woman puts a hand on her two smallest children's heads. "The twins are Adabel and Lorens." She nods toward the oldest. "That's Marten Jr. After his father."

"Where is his father?" Hunter asks, but I suspect I already know the answer. The hollow look in the children's eyes tells me everything I need to know.

"The dead wolves," Gloria whispers, a hitch in her voice.

"Corpse wolves?" Tristan leans forward, finally interested. "You're from Annwyn?"

Gloria nods.

"Why are you so far south?"

"The soldiers ..." Gloria swallows. "They took everything. We were simple people, really. My husband was a farmer. His younger brother, too. But the soldiers burned it all to the ground." She closes her eyes, and I can see how much effort it takes for her to hold herself together. I'm sure it's not for our sake, but for the children's.

"It was the third time since we've been married." She shrugs hopelessly. "So, we thought we'd have a better chance living further south, away from the conflict. Away from the encroaching border."

"Away from Annwyn?" Tristan asks, a hint of judgment in his voice.

I shoot him a glare. Who is he to judge a woman for doing what's best for her family's survival?

He notices my gaze and holds up his hands in surrender.

"Where are you going?" Hunter leans forward, a concerned look in his eyes.

"We'd planned to find a farming village where my husband and brother-in-law could start over again. Find some fields no one wants to work." She sighs. "Now? We'll stay anywhere that will have us."

Somewhere out in the distance, wolves howl.

The children's eyes grow wide and they huddle closer to their mother. The twins begin to cry.

"Hush." Gloria runs her fingers through their hair. "These kind people will protect us." Her eyes are pleading as she looks to Hunter, easily the biggest and most soft-hearted of our group.

"We'll do our best tonight," I say. "But in the morning, we'll be travelling back the way you came."

Gloria looks horrified. "No, you can't! It's certain death, I swear it."

Tristan nods. "It is." He sniffs. "For some."

She narrows her eyes at him. "There are corpse wolves near the ruins at Ellyll."

Trisan shrugs. "There are corpse wolves everywhere now."

"At least travel east or west for a day, to give yourself a better chance."

"It would be a waste of time."

She stares at him for a long moment before she turns her attention back to her children, clearly leaving us to whatever fate she thinks we're walking straight into.

Long after the children have fallen asleep by the fire, the wind howls alongside the wolves, their music intertwined. I'm not always sure which is which, making my dreams a confusing, wild mess. But when a creature snarls, just out of sight, I jump up in alarm.

"Don't worry, Red. I won't let them hurt you."

I turn to find Tristan whittling a stick, flicking the shavings into the fire. Flames crackle, illuminating the twisted hawthorn branches behind him. Their shadows dance and reach for us, like spirits trapped beyond the veil.

"Was that a corpse wolf?" I whisper. My voice pitches high, betraying my terror.

He nods, nonplussed.

My heart races in my chest. "I was attacked by one, once."

Tristan raises an eyebrow, but doesn't quit his whittling. "And you lived to tell the tale? Impressive."

His eyes flicker to Hunter, where he snores gently. His breath rises in tiny clouds with each exhale.

"Tristan," I whisper, trying not to wake the others.

His gray eyes meet mine. They glisten in the firelight, full of secrets.

"When we get to the border, you *will* tell me what happened to my grandmother, won't you? You're not just dragging us along for your own benefit?"

His eyes don't flicker away from mine, not even for an instant. "Red, I promise you, once I'm in Annwyn, I will tell you what I know."

Maybe I do believe in the Wolf code of honor, because I trust him. When I finally fall back into a fitful sleep, we're serenaded by a crackling fire and corpse wolves singing to the moon.

Just before dawn, I wake with a start. It takes me a moment to realize why. The fire has burned to little more than embers, and an early morning mist creeps along the ground. A pair of feet in ragged shoes stands inches from my head.

Above me, Gloria and Marten Jr. hold their hands out in offensive stances. Black mist swirls between their palms.

"Give us what remains of your food," Gloria says in a rough whisper. "And we'll go peacefully."

Marten Jr. follows suit. "We have shadow magic, and we *will* hurt you, if we must." His voice trembles, but he stands firm.

Nearby, Hunter startles awake. When he sees we're being robbed, he looks deeply disappointed.

I scan the darkness for the twins and spot them huddled

together by a tree. They're holding onto the bridles of our two horses. Marigold's ears twitch as she watches to see what I'll do.

On the other side of the fire pit, Tristan sits up with an irritated grunt.

"We already knew you'd rob us blind, kid. Just take the saddlebag and be on your way." He tuts. "Honestly, I figured you'd sneak away hours ago." His eyes flicker to the twins with our horses a short distance away. "But you'd better leave those horses. We have a long journey ahead of us." He lifts a lazy hand, holding a sparking ball of blackness that makes their flimsy shadows look like child's play.

Marten Jr's eyes grow wide. His own shadow power dissipates in an instant.

Gloria grabs her son to her chest. "You're a Wolf. You should have told us."

"Why?" Tristan asks, curious. "So you could rob us a different way?"

"Please don't hurt us," Marten Jr. says. His voice cracks.

Tristan sighs, rolling his eyes. "Just go already." He kicks the saddlebag toward them. Marten Jr. scrambles for it, then backs away slowly.

Gloria shoots Hunter an apologetic look. "I'm sorry. I have to take care of my children." She lets out a stifled sob.

At the sound, Hunter looks physically pained. "I know." He briefly glances my way. From the look in his eyes, I know what's coming. Damn Hunter and his overlarge heart.

"Take the horses," he says. "You need them more than we do."

"What?!" Tristan gasps behind us.

Hunter shoots him a look. "I won't have a family of four dying in Korrigan Forest if I can help it."

Tristan groans and flops back on the ground. "Damn knights and their damn guilt complexes ..."

Hunter turns back to Gloria. "And if you come across an abandoned village to the south, stay far away from it."

She nods, then runs back to the twins. She lifts them onto Marigold's back, then helps Marten Jr. climb onto Honor before swinging up behind him. Marigold gives us one mournful look but doesn't protest. She's noble that way. She'll take good care of those children. The family gallops into the forest without a backward glance, the sky lightening around them in a soft, daybreak-blue haze.

Tristan grunts, lying back down on the ground. "Well, I guess we're in for a long walk. And that's the last of the food."

Hunter stares into the forest for a long moment before responding. "We'll have to put that famed Wolf hunting prowess to good use then." There's a challenge in his voice that makes Tristan chuckle.

"I thought you'd never ask."

Chapter 27

Tristan disappears for hours at a time, only to resurface with dead rabbits in tow, like he's simply gone to the market. We roast his catch over whatever measly fire we can manage to make from the damp sticks and logs of the forest.

When we eat, hot juices drip down our chins and all sense of propriety vanishes as if the wilds are turning us into one of their own. As if the storied fae have already claimed us, we just don't know it yet.

"Just stay on the path that heads north," Tristan says, before he vanishes into the trees again. "I'll catch up with you." He seems at ease in this place of mystery, somehow always finding his way back to us.

But I'm not like Tristan, at ease beneath the looming arch of the trees. This forest unsettles me. There's magic here, but I can't understand it, either because it's ancient and we've forgotten the language, or because it was never meant for people at all. It's a magic left behind by the creatures from old stories—the fae who once roamed and ruled these lands thousands of years ago.

The forest feels infinite, the trees endless, the landscape

unbroken. Autumn leaves fall steadily around us, raining down like gentle fire in shades of crimson, gold, and rust. Not for the first time, I wonder if we've wandered into an enchanted wood, the kind that curses its visitors to walk its paths forever.

Up ahead, the sound of trickling water dances through the trees. I pause, listening closely.

Hunter stops too. "I hear it." His face breaks into a wide grin. "We can refill our water stores." He taps his near-empty waterskin where it hangs over one shoulder. "And I wouldn't say no to a bath." He side-eyes me, his face twinkling with mischief.

"I've nearly forgotten what it's like to feel clean."

A fine layer of road dust clings to every inch of me, mingling with the grime of travel. I haven't washed my dress since the palace, but we don't have time to dry clothes on a line—and walking in soaked fabric would surely lead to hypothermia. Still, it would be nice to rinse the parts of me exposed to the elements. I'm suddenly overcome by the urge to scoop water over my face.

"Let's go." I lead the way off the path, toward the sound of water.

Just off the road, we find a break in the trees. A small pool glistens there, ringed with mossy boulders and a pebbled shore. A narrow fountain trickles from a crack between two stones, cascading into the still water below.

Hunter wastes no time. He shrugs off his cloak and jerkin, just like we used to at the river as children. Then his shirt. I try not to stare as he lifts it over his head, the lean muscles of his stomach tightening with the motion.

"What are you doing?" I try not to laugh.

His skin is covered in gooseflesh as he rubs his arms for warmth. "What does it look like?" He grins, hopping on one foot as he pulls off a shoe.

I think he's joking until he drops his breeches. A tiny squeak escapes me as I cover my eyes, laughing outright now.

"Oh, please. It's nothing you haven't seen before." His voice is light with amusement.

"There's a big difference between swimming together as children and you stripping naked as a fully grown man."

I peek between my fingers.

He has a wicked grin on his face. "A big difference, huh?" He winks.

I grab one of his shoes and chuck it at him. He dodges and takes off toward the water, giving me a full view of his—admittedly—gorgeous rear. Then he leaps from the nearest boulder and disappears into the pool.

I'm so surprised I run up to the rocky shore, my mouth hanging open. When he resurfaces and sees my expression, he laughs so hard I worry he might drown.

"It's not funny, Hunter! You'll catch your death!" Even as I say it, an autumn breeze blows open my red cloak, making me shiver.

"The water's warm!" He splashes in the pool like a puppy in a lake. "There must be an underground spring feeding it." Then he dives back under.

I kneel on a flat boulder and reach forward to test the water. He's right, it's not exactly *warm*, but it's certainly not cold. I cup my hands and splash my face. The sigh that escapes me is genuine. I unbuckle my cloak and lay it over a stone, then roll up my sleeves and start scrubbing my skin in earnest.

Hunter paddles over to me, then folds his arms on top of the stone to hold himself in place. "You really should get in here with me, Sienna. It's a once in a lifetime opportunity. When will you ever get the chance to swim in a warm pond in Korrigan Forest again?"

"I think I can live without it." I flick water in his direction.

"I'd rather not freeze to death when I inevitably have to get out again."

Hunter grimaces at the reminder and sinks a little lower into the pool. "You know, I always knew you were smarter than me."

I laugh. "Smarter, no. More cautious, definitely."

He leans toward me and whispers, "Also more stinky." He pushes off the stone and tries to swim away, but I splash water in his face before he gets too far.

"Even without a bath, I'm half as smelly as you!" I yell after him.

He sticks out his tongue and continues paddling in circles around the pool. For one glorious moment, I let myself pretend that we are just two people playing in a forest pond. I forget that we're journeying north with a Wolf. That we're fugitives from the king. That we're being hunted.

Out of the corner of my eye, I catch movement on the far side of the pool. Lily pads sway in the ripples Hunter leaves as he swims in slow circles, the white flowers bobbing with each small wave.

But there's something else.

Farther out, beneath the shifting surface and drifting weeds, something pale flickers just below the waterline. I squint, then rise, stepping carefully from stone to stone as I make my way around the edge of the pool.

There, tangled in the reeds, something moves. For a moment, I think it's silk—just fabric caught among the water lilies. But then I see the curve of a shoulder and the sweep of long hair, fanned out like spilled ink. The rocks keep me from getting closer, but as I lean forward and the light shifts, I see it clearly.

A body floats among the reeds.

"Hunter!" I yell.

He pivots, looking toward me in alarm. "What is it?"

"A woman." I point. "In the lily pads."

She floats face-up. Her pink gown billows around her like she died in the midst of a graceful dance. Her face is peaceful, serene. There's no sign of bloating or decay, so she can't have died long ago. But what was she doing this deep in Korrigan Forest, presumably alone? And how did she drown in such a small pool?

Hunter swims toward us. Within moments, he finds her. He pulls her gently from the reeds, the water lilies tugging at her hair as if reluctant to let her go. He carries her to the shallows, where I splash forward, all thoughts of staying dry forgotten. I kneel in the water, pebbles pressing into my knees.

"Is she alive?" Hunter asks, his brow furrowed in confusion. "She doesn't look dead."

He's right. Her skin still holds a flush, her cheeks frozen in a delicate blush. When I glance at her hands, her fingers aren't blue from death or cold. They're just pale and slender, like crescent moons.

A horrible thought crosses my mind.

"Enchanted?" I ask, like a child lost in one of the library's storybooks.

Thankfully, Hunter doesn't scoff. He spent enough time reading those stories with me when we were young.

"I don't know." The upper half of his body is exposed to the chill air and he shivers. "We can't leave her in here. It's not decent."

He looks over my shoulder, back toward the shore. "Would you ...?"

I look back at his pile of clothes. He's still completely naked under the water.

"Right. Of course." I run back to the large rock and toss Hunter his breeches.

He catches them in one hand, then puts them on under

the surface of the water. They'll be soaked for hours, but there's not much to be done about that.

Partially clothed, he grabs one of the woman's arms. I reach for the other and we start to pull her out of the water. She's heavy with her water-logged dress, heavier than she should be. I look down to see if she's caught on something.

Open eyes stare back at me.

The dead woman is grinning. Only, it's not the grin of a beautiful maiden. Her teeth are far too sharp, and there are far too many of them. As water runs off her skin, her flesh begins to change, turning gray and scaly.

She's a fae. Here, in Llwyn.

I scream and drop her arm. Hunter turns to me in alarm, but it's too late. The creature has fully transformed. The long golden hair and pink dress are gone, replaced by a monstrous body that's not quite human and not quite fish. Her long, scaled tail thrashes the water where her legs used to be, and her once-delicate hands have become webbed fingers tipped with filthy claws.

She grabs Hunter's arm and twists toward the pool with terrifying strength, dragging him toward the deep. He loses his footing and crashes onto the stones. The creature clings to him with an iron grip as he struggles to break free.

"Let him go!" I scream, leaping into the water. "Hunter!"

His words are garbled as the creature pulls him under the water.

I grab the knife from my boot and dive in after them. The pool is much deeper than I expected, its bottom lost in murky green darkness. There's just enough light to make out the creature thrashing as it drags Hunter deeper.

Something hard knocks into my thigh as I swim toward them. My heart lurches and I turn, afraid it's another monster. It isn't, but my relief is short-lived. A human skull drifts past, its mouth gaping in a silent scream. This isn't just an enchanted pool, it's a hidden grave.

I ignore the dead and swim deeper. When I reach the creature, I slash my knife, not caring what part of it I hit. Blood clouds the water in dark swirls. The creature recoils, its wide white eyes flashing with fear. For a moment, it hesitates, looking from Hunter to me and back again. Then it releases him and vanishes into the deep.

It feels too easy, but there's no time to question it. I grab Hunter's arm and kick upward. We break the surface, coughing and gasping, then swim toward the shore. I stumble on the pebbled ground, my dress heavy with water. Hunter pulls me up and together we stumble away from the enchanted pool. I grab my red cloak from where I left it on the stone while Hunter gathers his scattered clothes. Then we run back to the road, barefoot and dripping. We don't stop until it feels my lungs will burst.

When I can go no farther, I collapse onto a pile of leaves and moss, just off the roadside. Hunter wraps his cloak over his bare shoulders. He's shivering so badly he can't put his shoes on. Eventually, he gives up and sinks to the ground beside me.

I sit hunched and soaked, a puddle forming beneath me. Hunter reaches for me and pulls me into his chest.

"Thank you," he whispers into my wet hair. "Thank you."

Water beads on his chest as it rises and falls. He looks mostly unscathed except for a thin cut near his elbow. Blood mingles with water in a slow, red trail down his arm. I must've hurt him during the chaos underwater.

"You're bleeding," I say.

He looks down, surprised, but then shakes his head. "It's nothing."

My teeth start to chatter. He turns me away from him and

fumbles with the ties on my dress. His fingers are visibly stiff from the cold. "We need to get you out of this."

I don't protest. Even though we escaped the creature, the day could still end badly if I can't get my body temperature back up. Hunter helps me peel away my wet clothes, all concern for modesty forgotten. His hands are gentle as they brush over my damp skin, like he's touching something precious. Something forbidden. He averts his eyes when my final layer drops to the ground.

All that remains is the silver moth necklace nestled between my breasts.

He reaches for his pile of dry clothes and pulls his tunic over my head. It's long enough to serve as a chemise, reaching the middle of my thighs. It's warmer than standing before him naked, but not by much.

Hunter pulls me down to the mossy ground. I sit with my back against him, his knees on either side of me. He wraps the red cloak around us, trapping what remains of our body heat as he rubs his hands over my arms. I turn my head and tuck my face into his neck, breathing in the comforting scent of his skin. Slowly, the fear begins to ebb, loosening its grip on the edges of my mind.

Our shivers gradually fade, and our breathing returns to normal. But even once I know we're warm enough to be out of danger, I don't pull away. Instead, I savor the rise and fall of his chest behind me.

Today, I nearly lost him. I sniffle as the tears finally come.

"Shh," Hunter whispers into my hair. "It's okay. We're okay."

But we're not. We're really, truly not okay. And it's my fault for forcing him to escort the Wolf north with me. Because I'm selfish. Because I'm willing to risk other people's lives to get the one thing I want more than anything else—answers.

A shadowy thought crosses my mind: I may not be so different from my father after all.

A sob bursts from my chest. "You were almost eaten by a mermaid!"

Hunter chuckles, his laugh low. "But I wasn't."

"We got lucky."

"There's nothing *lucky* about it. You jumped in after me."

"What if I hadn't?" I whisper. *What if I'm not strong enough to save you next time,* I don't say.

A small grin brightens his face. "I suppose you could've left me to live at the bottom of an enchanted pool with a sometimes-gorgeous water creature." He kisses the tip of my nose. "But no woman, magical or otherwise, could ever compare to a life with you." He smiles and touches my jaw, lifting my gaze to meet his.

My stomach flutters. I wonder if he can feel my rapid heartbeat. Or if he noticed how my breath has become quick and shallow. Suddenly, I realize just how much I want him to feel my beating heart. We escaped death, and now I want to feel really, truly alive.

I sit forward, then turn on my knees to face him. He drops the red cloak and it slides down my back like a gentle waterfall, pooling around our hips. I climb onto his lap, wrapping my legs around his waist.

Hunter's eyes grow wide, but he doesn't stop me. He hardly moves at all as I lift his tunic up. The soft fabric brushes against my breasts and the cool air prickles my skin. My hair, still damp, falls over my chest, barely covering my body from his eager eyes. I toss the tunic onto the moss-covered ground.

"No woman can compare?" I ask, feeling brave. "Not even if our life is spent on the run, gutting fish in port towns and forgoing court life?"

"Even then." His words are deep and slow, like he's had too much wine, but it's me he's drinking in with those big brown eyes. It's me who feels entranced, skin-to-skin out here in a forest with no one around to see us.

Slowly, I trail my hands over his wide shoulders and across his firm chest. I stare meaningfully into his eyes as my fingers explore lower, down his rippled stomach, pausing just above his hip bones. My breath catches somewhere in my throat as I wait for him to accept the invitation.

Finally, he gasps and brings his lips to mine as if he can't hold back any longer. He tastes just like I remember. Sweet, like golden honey, with a touch of earthiness. His fingertips linger on my jawline, then glide down to cradle my neck. He tilts my head, kissing me deeper, so slowly that it feels like a dream. But I need more.

I'm consumed with a sudden hunger to have him. Maybe it's that I almost lost him. Maybe it's because he seems too perfect in this forest filled with darkness. Or maybe it's the way he's looking at me. This is a terrible idea. But right now, I don't care. All I want is *him*.

Hunter trails his mouth down my neck and over my breasts as I arch my back, looking up into the canopy of autumn trees above us. The warmth between my thighs turns hot, insistent. I want to touch every part of him, to trail my fingers over his skin until I've memorized every inch. I want us to get so lost in each other that I no longer care that we're in a dangerous forest, hunted by beasts and men.

Hunter brings his face to mine again and nips at my lower lip. The slight sting makes me gasp. He pulls my body impossibly close. A jolt of desire runs through me at the sound of his shuddering breath along the shell of my ear. I moan, unable to stop the animalistic sound from escaping.

Hunter's hands move down the sides of my breasts, then over my ribs, before he reaches around to grip my ass, hard. I feel the shift in his body as he thickens against my inner thigh.

Without thinking, I reach between us and take him in my hand. He groans, his eyes slipping closed for a moment.

Something hungry unfurls within me. This is what I crave —here at the edge of the world, with darkness pressing in. I need to feel something real, before it all slips away.

"I want you," I say, breathless. I brush my lips down the side of his neck, to kiss the spot where his pulse thrums beneath his skin.

He lets out a guttural noise from deep in his chest. "Sienna, I've wanted you every day since you left."

I push him back onto the damp moss and leaves. Our chests rise and fall as we stare into each other's eyes. My breasts just barely trail over his chest as I lean forward. He grows even harder, pressed against my sex.

"Then take me." I say, slowly, urgently.

He does.

Hunter wraps his arms around my back, flipping me onto the soft ground. Scarlet and gold leaves tangle in my hair. He bites my skin as he trails his mouth down, down, down my body until he's a breath away from the parts of me that ache with need. The parts that hunger for more.

He gives me a very un-Hunter-like grin, one that promises something illicit. Something seductive. He wraps my legs over his shoulders and dips his head, as if in prayer. He tastes me like I'm the sweetest flavor he's ever had, taking his time, making me want to scream out in rising need. I grab his hair like I'm going to fly away and he's the only thing keeping me grounded.

Hunter moves his tongue in gentle circles, exploring every corner of my hidden places. My legs clench involuntarily around his neck as heat travels up my body, toward my flushed face.

Is this what love feels like? The ecstasy of a man's touch? The trust of another person, so complete, that you'll allow them to feel your most vulnerable places? Even as the thought flickers across my mind, I know that I *want* this to be love ... but I'm not convinced I'm capable of that emotion anymore.

What I *do* know, without the shadow of a doubt, is that I need to feel the weight of his body so desperately, I can hardly focus.

"You," I gasp. "I need *you*."

He comes up for air. "Are you sure?" He's breathing heavy now, his chest rising and falling. I sit up and grab his chin, his stubble rough against my fingertips.

"I'm sure." I kiss his mouth, slow and deep, the taste of me still on his lips.

He moans as he gives in. Tension coils deep in my body, begging to be released. Hunter cradles my head in one hand and lowers me back onto the moss. The late afternoon sun haloes around him as he pauses above me, his blond hair catching the golden light.

He holds my gaze as he settles between my thighs. Every nerve pulls tight with anticipation. Hunter leans in, kisses me softly, and sinks deep into me with a breathless reverence. Sparks flash behind my eyes as I finally feel the pressure, the fullness I craved.

"Harder," I beg.

As if that's all the permission he needed, he loses himself in the moment. Hunter forgets about being the sweet, love-struck gentleman. He thrusts into me, hard and needy. I completely unravel as he does it again and again, our bodies growing slick against each other. I am an animal of the deep, dark forest, consumed by need rather than thought. It feels *so good* not to think. Not to worry, or plot, or care. Just to be here together, alive.

"More." My nails scrape across his back in my desperation to pull him closer.

He gives it. All of it. We are gasping, clawing at each other.

Our chests rise and fall as one as he takes me to a place I've never been. To a delicious pain I never knew existed. His breath grows quicker, louder, mixing with mine in a slurry of abandon. Out here in this enchanted forest, the rules and limits of propriety are gone. We lose ourselves in the intoxicating nectar of illicit lust.

The world fractures, the tension inside me shattering in a rush. Light flashes behind my eyes and my limbs tremble as I gasp, helpless against the surge of release. My body tightens around him and he thrusts once, twice, then pulls away just in time. He meets me here, in this place of indescribable bliss.

After, we cling together on the leaf-covered ground, unwilling to let the real world seep back in, like water hovering along the edge of a page. As we lie on the cool forest floor, I know one thing for certain.

I almost lost Hunter today. But now, he's mine forever.

Chapter 28

The forest path is a beautiful sight behind us, made all the more beautiful for having survived it. But the landscape ahead is desolate.

My breath catches in my throat when we finally emerge from the trees. In front of us, as far as the eye can see, is a boneyard. The ground is scarred and uneven, a barren wasteland littered with the remnants of war. Blackened stumps of burned trees jut out from the earth alongside singed banners, torn and tattered, their colors faded to a ghostly memory. Here and there, the bones of unidentifiable beasts lie bleaching in the sun.

The wind howls through the decaying battlefield. It catches a torn banner that's still attached to a post. The fabric flaps wildly in the dusty air. It's faded and splattered with mud, but I can still make out the design: a copper fox on a once-white background.

Next to me, Hunter sees it too. His face is sad, his shoulders heavy with the weight of guilt. But none of this is his fault, of course. It's my father's.

"What's the matter, Red? Haven't you been to the borderlands before?" Tristan asks lightly, his voice a poor attempt at levity. I catch the tension in his jaw, the way his gray eyes turn stormy. He's disturbed too, though he won't admit it.

"Not like this." My voice is a whisper, barely audible over the mournful wind. "The camps ... they're never *on* battlefields."

Tristan just sniffs and starts walking, his boots crushing the brittle earth underfoot. He steps over mounds of turned-up soil and fallen armor, the ground uneven and bone dry.

Hunter steps closer to me. He brushes his fingers over the back of my hand where it hangs limp at my side. His touch is light, hesitant. Like he's not sure how to touch me after the feverish heat of yesterday.

I look up to meet his eyes.

"We'll get through this." He reaches forward and tucks a stray lock of hair away from my face. "All of it."

The intensity of his gaze makes my heart clench. After what happened, he keeps looking at me with barely contained emotion behind his eyes ... And I have no idea how I feel about it. Now that the heat of passion has faded and we're face-to-face with reality again, all I feel is shame and guilt.

I wanted it, yes. I wanted *him*. But it shouldn't have happened.

We're still out here in a battlefield, running for our lives, with no plan beyond reaching the border of Annwyn. How can love possibly blossom under these conditions?

I swallow hard and nod, then turn to follow Tristan across the wasteland. The air is thick with the stench of death, and buzzards call overhead. Their dark shapes float lazily as they wait for fresh carrion.

After nearly an hour of walking, I almost trip over something half-buried in the dirt. At my feet lies a desiccated corpse clad in thick leather armor. A silver insignia is pinned to its chest, so tarnished I can barely make out the shape of a wolf.

The man's eyes, long since eaten by birds, are hollow sockets staring at the sky. His flesh is mummified, stretched tight over bones that look ready to crumble.

Ahead of me, Tristan and Hunter press on.

As we continue to pick our way across the battlefield, I start to notice the world around us is changing. The light is dimmer, as if a storm cloud has passed over the sun. But when I look up, the sky is clear, though hazy. It's as if the sun itself is beginning to fade.

I run to catch up to Hunter. "Wait."

He pauses, half turning back toward me.

"Something isn't right."

"Of course not," Tristan says, turning to see why we've stopped. "We're standing in the middle of a massive graveyard."

I shake my head. "It's not that. The light ..."

All three of us look up. Hunter's face changes, as if he's now realized how dark it's become.

A sense of doom crawls up my spine. "It's much too early for twilight."

In a rush, the air grows colder. It blows my long auburn hair around my face like a windstorm. From the darkened horizon, a thick fog seeps across the ground. It swirls around our feet, then rises steadily until it envelops us completely. In moments, visibility drops to almost nothing.

"Hunter!" I call.

Someone grabs my hand and squeezes it tight. I turn to find him at my side. He's hazy, but visible this close. I let out a breath of relief.

"Sienna, don't let go of my hand." His voice is quiet and cautious.

I nod, even though I'm not sure he can tell.

Tristan emerges from the fog a few feet away. "Stay close," he says. His eyebrows pinch together with concern.

"Is it shadow magic?" I ask.

Tristan stares into the swirling gray. "I don't think so."

He reaches for my free hand. Even now, in these dire circumstances, I hesitate to take it. But we've come this far with the Wolf. It's time to drop the pretense of mistrust.

When I wrap my fingers around his, a warm, tingling sensation climbs up my arm. My power flares to life inside me and I flush with heat, but I ignore it. Now is not the time to lose focus.

Slowly, we inch through the fog, careful not to trip over one another or the desiccated bodies left to rot in this place. When we come upon an overturned cart, Tristan kicks over sun-weathered crates until he finds something useful.

"Here," he says, handing me a long, worn rope. "Tie the middle around your waist. I'll take one end." He looks to Hunter. "You take the other. We'll be able to move faster without getting separated."

For once, Hunter doesn't push back or give Tristan any grief. That's how I know he's as worried as I am. Once the rope is secure around us, Tristan takes a few tentative steps ahead. All too soon, his body vanishes into the gray, the rope slithering across the ground behind him.

"It's alright, Red." Tristan calls out, his voice muffled. "I'll lead the way. We just have to keep moving."

Despite the rope, Hunter grabs my hand again. "I'd feel better with you by my side."

I nod and, together, we follow the rope in Tristan's direction. The ground crunches beneath our boots, grit and brittle bone indistinguishable from each other.

The fog is suffocating, a heavy blanket that muffles sound and distorts shapes. Every rustle, every whisper of movement is amplified, feeding the growing unease that grips my chest. I can't shake the feeling that there are eyes on us, watching our every move despite the impenetrable gray.

Suddenly, the rope jerks forward, catching me off guard. I stumble, letting go of Hunter's hand. I land hard on my knees, but no worse for wear.

"I'm alright," I say as I stand, brushing the dirt from my hands. I turn back.

Hunter is gone.

At my feet, the rope tied between us is slack, leading into the dense fog. I reach to pick it up, but it slithers forward an inch out of my grasp. I freeze, my hand outstretched.

"Hunter?"

The rope moves forward another inch.

"Hunter?" I call out again, louder this time.

Nothing.

I bend forward, reaching for the rope again, but it suddenly begins to slither away, faster this time. I try to hold on, but the rope burns my palms, forcing me to let go. It pulls taut, pinning me between the two men lost in the fog in opposite directions.

The rope pauses, suspended in the air.

"Hunter!" I shout, my voice sharp with panic. "Tristan!" I call the other way.

No answer.

Then both ends of the rope yank tight, jerking me back and forth by the section knotted around my waist. The pressure digs into my stomach, pulling harder and harder until I'm afraid it will slice into my skin—or worse, tear me in half.

I scream and scramble for the knife hidden in the ankle of my boot. Half-blinded by fear, I saw at one end of the rope. Tears spring to my eyes as the fibers resist the blade.

It snaps. At the same moment, the other end goes limp. I collapse to the ground, gasping. The knot around my waist is too tight to undo with my fingers. My hands shake as I use my knife to saw through it. A sob of relief escapes me when it finally snaps off, the frayed ends falling to the dirt. I gasp on my hands and knees, trying to get ahold of myself.

All is silent.

Then, footsteps. Someone is running toward me. I brace myself, but Hunter emerges from the fog, his face full of panic. He gasps in relief when he sees me on the ground. He falls to his knees, pulling me into his arms.

"Sienna! Why didn't you answer me when I called?" He lifts my face, brushing my wild hair from my eyes.

"I was yelling for *you*," I say, alarmed.

He shakes his head. "That's not possible. I've been calling your name ever since you disappeared."

"No, *you* disappeared. I tripped, and you were gone!"

Understanding washes over his face. "It's the fog."

There's no point in asking how that's even possible.

I bolt upright, horrified. "Tristan."

Hunter and I scramble to our feet. Hunter grips my hand tightly.

"Tristan!" I call.

"Tristan!" Hunter follows.

Silence.

Then, "Red?"

Relief washes over me. "Tristan, we're here! Follow my voice!"

A figure emerges from the fog, crouched low, one arm stretched out to feel his way forward.

"Thank the old gods," he says when he sees us. His gray eyes are wide, and his dark hair is a mess, like he's been running his hands through it. He grabs my shoulders and pulls me into his chest, taking me by surprise.

Hunter doesn't let go of my hand.

Tristan's voice is breathless with relief. "I thought I'd lost you."

This place has stripped away his usual icy manner. I've

never seen him this shaken, not even when he was tied up in the kennels. Not even when the foxhounds attacked us on the road.

His eyes move to Hunter. "I thought I'd lost you both."

Hunter's voice has an edge to it. "Not yet, I'm afraid."

"What happened?" I ask, but he just shakes his head.

"I don't know, but the sooner we get out of there, the better." He grabs my hand again. "So, no ropes then." He leads us forward a second time.

We walk through the fog. It snakes over the cracked earth, pooling in the hollows between scattered bones and rusted weapons. My eyes ache from straining against the gray. Then, something catches my attention. A flicker of movement, like a shadow, but it's gone before I can focus on it.

"Did you see that?" I whisper, my voice unsteady. Another glimpse flashes at the edge of my vision, a shadowy figure that vanishes as I turn my head.

Tristan tightens his grip on my hand. "Keep moving."

We walk in silence. The only sounds are the soft crunch of our boots on the brittle ground and the occasional flutter of wings from the carrion birds above. We press on in a desperate, blind march through the fog. Each step takes us farther north, though I have no idea how Tristan knows the way. I start to wonder if he doesn't, if he's just moving forward because there's nothing else to do.

Time loses all meaning in this endless gray. We've been walking for minutes or hours, it's impossible to tell. All that matters is putting one foot in front of the other. We hold onto each other's hands and try to ignore the shadows that follow us and the sense that we're not alone.

I glance at Tristan. His face is pale and drawn in the dim light. He meets my eyes briefly, then looks ahead again. His gaze sharpens, and I turn to see what he's staring at.

Ghostly figures begin to appear in the fog, their forms flickering like candle flames in a breeze.

My heart pounds as one moves closer, materializing into a man. At first, I think he's just another soldier, lost like us. But when he comes within five feet, I finally see him clearly. His arm hangs limp, dislocated at the shoulder. His ankle is twisted at an unnatural angle. He's wearing tarnished bronze armor that's smeared with blood. At the center of his chest plate, a copper fox snarls.

But most startling are the man's eyes. They're wide and black with fear.

"Did you see them?" he whispers hysterically. Spittle flies from his mouth. His eyes dart around the fog. "The wolves. They brought the wolves!" He reaches for Tristan's shoulders, shaking him.

"Get off of me!" Tristan breaks the man's hold.

The soldier tumbles to the ground in a rattling heap of armor. He digs his heels into the dirt, scooting backward into the blanket of gray.

"What the—" But before Hunter can finish his sentence, another figure stumbles into view. He's just as panicked as the first man, but he's practically a boy still. His clothes are dark with mud or blood, I can't tell which. Maybe both.

"I want to go home," he sobs.

There's a gaping wound at his chest, as if something took a bite out of him and left him to die slowly. I can see his lungs moving behind cracked ribs with each ragged breath. There's no way this boy could be standing, let alone walking through the fog.

I'm too stunned to speak.

Hunter steps closer, one arm outstretched as if to block the boy from getting any nearer.

"Where am I?" the boy asks, his voice breaking. Tears, dark

with blood, ooze around his black eyes and down his sallow cheeks. "I want to go home."

Then he turns and runs back into the fog.

"Tristan, what are they?" My voice is barely more than a whisper.

Tristan doesn't answer immediately. When he does, his voice is grim. "Just keep your eyes on the ground ahead and don't stop moving."

He tugs my hand forward, Hunter taking up the rear. He quickens his pace, and I stumble to keep up. Panic shoots through my mind like flashes of lightning. What sort of nightmare place is this?

Every few seconds, a low growl reaches our ears, making me jump and look around wildly. The fog seems alive with men and creatures alike, most of them just out of sight.

"They're ghosts," Tristan says as we walk. "Wraiths of dead soldiers, trapped in the fog. It's a magic only the queen can wield. Only she can manipulate the dead."

"How?" Hunter asks, his eyes darting wildly around us.

Tristan shrugs. "She's the Dead Queen. The living can't possibly understand her power."

A sudden realization shoots through me. "She was here? At the borderlands?"

He nods, his mouth a grim line. "At some point in the past. No one else could do something like this."

"This is torture." Anger flares to life within me. "Why punish them beyond death when winning the battle would suffice?"

"Because the Dead Queen is *evil*, Sienna." Hunter says behind me. His voice has an uncharacteristic edge to it. "Haven't you known that your whole life?" His eyes dart to Tristan with suspicion. "This whole scheme to bring the Wolf back to Annwyn was a mistake."

Tristan doesn't contradict him. For a man who's gone

through so much pain in the name of Annwyn—capture, torture, foxhounds, thieves—this strikes me as odd.

"What? No defense?" I ask, piqued.

Tristan's voice is a low growl. "I'm a Wolf, Red. I serve my queen, but I don't have to like her."

We pass the remnants of a man, curled up on the ground. His clothes are torn and his rib cage is a bloody mess of bruises and broken bones. It looks like he was trampled. He buries his face in his hands as he weeps.

Somewhere, a corpse wolf howls, long and low. The shadowy wraiths around us freeze as one.

Nearest to us, the weeping man slowly straightens. He turns and stares directly at me with black eyes. I stifle a shriek at the sight of him. His face is mangled beyond recognition, his features completely obliterated, turned into a mess of pulp. His skull is crushed on one side and phantom fluids still drip onto his shoulders.

All around us, the wraiths stare in our direction, their dark eyes boring through the fog.

"We need to move," Tristan says.

We run. The dead follow us, their numbers growing with every step. A copper-clad knight lumbers after us, an empty void where his head should be. From the mist, a wraith horse emerges, galloping on broken legs. Its rider is slumped forward, a spear jutting from his chest.

None of the wraiths speak. They only watch, eyes black and unblinking as they track our every move.

"What do we do?" Hunter yells.

"Nothing!" Tristan says, panting. "I can't fight this!"

We won't make it. We're surrounded with nowhere to go. More and more dead seem to appear through the fog.

Desperation fuels me as I reach deep within myself, calling upon my power. It ripples and grows inside me like a building storm. I pull away from Hunter and Tristan and thrust my palms forward. With a burst of energy, light sizzles in front of us, burning off the fog. In its place is a small clearing. The wraiths in its path disappear into thin air, dissolving like smoke.

"They need the fog to exist," Tristan says, a wide grin on his face. "Do it again!"

Already, the fog is closing back in.

"No!" Hunter shouts.

I look back to find his eyes, wide with fear for me.

"Sienna don't," he pleads. "You can't keep doing that, you'll burn out again."

"She can do this!" Tristan yells.

"No, she can't!" Hunter insists. "She's not some weapon for you to use."

Tristan points wildly at me. "She's stronger than you think!"

"I'm not calling her weak! I'm just trying to protect—"

"Stop it!" I scream. "I can do this!"

Even as I say it, my pulse is pounding too fast. My skin feels flushed with heat, my bones hollow. I have no idea if I can do this, but I'm going to try my damn hardest to get us out of here. We can not become wraiths too, lost in this mist for all eternity.

I blast more fog away. As we run, Tristan beams at me. Something in his eyes almost looks like pride. Hunter stops protesting, but his eyebrows draw together in concern. He tries to help, calling his own light power, but the most he can do is create a measly orb of light. It does nothing against the fog, or the wraiths that chase us.

We push forward, understanding that we cannot stop again, not even for a moment.

The wraiths wail, unable to reach us. For now, we have some semblance of safety—if I can keep this up long enough to escape this cursed place. But it's getting harder. Shadows flicker at the edges of my vision. Each blast takes more effort than the last and the power doesn't rise so easily anymore. Exhaustion nips at my bones. I grit my teeth with determination to stay focused.

We keep running. I break another opening in the fog, but my light sputters like a candle flame caught in the wind. I pretend not to notice. I pretend I'm fine.

Finally, after what feels like an eternity, the fog begins to thin. The wraiths grow distant and we stumble out of the battlefield, breathless, but alive.

My knees threaten to buckle by the time we find a spot to camp for the night. We huddle near the safety of a patch of innocent-looking trees. Nothing cursed or haunted here, as far as we can tell.

As he builds a fire, Hunter shoots me worried glances. Tristan, on the other hand, seems unconcerned as he stretches out on the leaf-covered ground to stare up at the darkening sky. It's as if he never doubted me for a second. His faith in my power sends an unexpected thrill through me, but it doesn't stop the dread that's pooling in my stomach. I've pushed my power too far, too soon after recovering from burnout. My core feels hollow. Empty.

And it's terrifying.

"Are you sure you're alright, Sienna?" Hunter asks. The worried creases around his eyes are amplified by the firelight.

I tuck my arms under my red cloak to hide the shaking. He doesn't need to know that my chest aches and my core feels scraped clean. The light is gone. Nothing rises when I call it. There's only emptiness.

We made it out of the fog just in time.

"You burned out, didn't you?" Hunter asks, his voice quiet.

I bite my tongue, refusing to admit he was right. "We didn't have a choice."

Hunter nods. "I know. You were remarkable out there. Truly." He heaves a shaky breath. "We would have died without you. Thank you."

Tears threaten my eyes, but I'm not sure if they're from relief or fear. I don't know how long this burnout will last. And I'm afraid of what could happen to us without it.

Hunter sits next to me and reaches for my hand, but I pull away.

"Don't," I say a little too sharply.

Hurt flashes across his face, but he nods. "I get it. Just …" He pauses, searching for the right words. "When you need me, I'm here." He hesitates, then stands and walks away.

The night is quiet, but for the crackling fire and the hoot of a distant owl. We sit in silence, each lost in our own thoughts. The horrors of the battlefield slowly fade into the recent past. Above us, the skies are gorgeously clear. I've never been so thankful to see stars in all my life.

Along the darkened horizon, the Spires stand haloed in moonlight. Their icy peaks are a clear mark of Annwyn territory. We'll reach the base of those mountains by tomorrow evening. Then, Tristan will finally tell me what happened to my grandmother, our deal complete. After that, Hunter and I will have to find a safe harbor somewhere my father can't reach us.

A pit forms in my stomach. Tomorrow, I'll have my answers. I should be filled with excitement. Years of searching will finally come to an end. So why am I inexplicably filled with sorrow? A twinge in my heart tells me exactly why.

My eyes dart to where Tristan sits, staring up at the stars.

Chapter 29

When we head out at dawn, the world is quiet. The Spires loom in the distance, a morning haze covering its peaks in a white shroud.

We don't speak much as we head north over hills and through valleys filled with dried grasses and purple fall flowers. They catch on my dress and tug me back, like they want to keep me from reaching the mountains. Scattered here and there are patches of trees and large piles of boulders left behind by some ancient land movement—or a giant of old, depending on who you ask.

By late afternoon, the mountains take up most of the horizon ahead of us. Jagged peaks stand tall against the sky, their rocky faces reflecting the golden sun.

Hunter keeps trying to catch my eye, but I avoid him. I can't help pulling away. Shame nips at my heels like a foxhound. It tells me I'm a terrible human being. That I'm too much like my father, withholding affection to manipulate people. But I know it's more complicated than that. My mind is a jumbled mess of emotions that logically should be so simple.

Hunter loves me. I *should* love him too.

"What will you do once you reach Annwyn?" I ask Tristan. I reach down to pluck a fluffy stem of grass, then pick the seeds off one by one.

"Go home to his Dead Queen like a good boy, I expect," Hunter mumbles, under his breath.

Tristan ignores the jibe. "I'll return to Gwyllion Castle. To answer to my queen." He doesn't sound excited.

"And then?" I ask, disentangling my red cape from a patch of particularly aggressive grasses.

Tristan looks sidelong at me. "And then, I'll see what else I can do to stop your father from taking more of my people's territory."

Hunter rubs the bridge of his nose, like listening to the Wolf talk of insurgence is enough to give him a headache.

I look up at the Spires and a rush of triumph surges through me, pushing away every ounce of exhaustion. We're so close. Maybe two hours away. Three at most. There's an almost physical weight lifting from my shoulders, like all the unanswered questions around Grandmother's death have held me down, kept me from soaring.

We walk past some oddly shaped boulders. They're square and piled on top of each other. But then we pass several more and it makes me pause. I lean closer. These are not normal boulders. If I didn't know any better, I'd say they were cut with tools. A bracket sticks out of one, more rust than metal.

I run to catch up to Tristan and Hunter. "Are these ..." my words disappear before I can say them. We've paused at the crest of a hill. Down below, an enormous, crumbled city spreads out before us.

"Wow," Hunter whispers.

The final miles leading to the base of the Spires are a tangled stretch of weathered ruins and half-swallowed paths. A crumbling battlement wall sags under the weight of time.

Arches and towers tilt dangerously, ready to collapse with the next strong gust of wind. Ornate gardens have long since overgrown, their designs lost beneath a snarl of thorns and brambles.

At the heart of the city, the shadow of a grand stone castle looms, still clinging to life. Beyond that, the last of the valley rests beneath the looming presence of the Spires.

"What is this place?" I ask.

"Ellyll," Tristan says, reverence in his voice. "It was the center of Annwyn, our royal seat, until ..."

"Until we tore it to the ground."

To my surprise, he shakes his head. "For once, I can't blame your ancestors for this. This destruction is much older. It dates back to the first Dead Queen, five hundred years ago." His expression darkens, his mouth tightening. "This is where the human kings and queens of old Annwyn ruled. Long before the Llwyn Wars started. When the first Dead Queen usurped the northern throne and took Annwyn."

Hunter tilts his head. "This castle belongs to the Heir to the North?"

Tristan nods. "What's left of it, anyway."

"Where do the fae land in this tale?" I ask.

Tristan stares out over the ruins. "The old fae were our cousins, in a sense. The fae rulers had intermarried, interbred, giving the human nobility powers no other people possessed. Unfortunately, humans used that power to oppress the lesser fae. And then they bound the fae kings and queens into eternal slumber, taking their courts for themselves."

Hunter snorts.

Tristan's eyes dart toward him, darkly. "Or so the stories say. It *was* two thousand years ago. No one knows for sure how they did it."

"Or if it's even true," Hunter mumbles under his breath.

Tristan shrugs. His eyes scan the crumbling towers and

still-standing archways. "Ellyll was once the most beautiful city in the world. Lovingly created by expert fae craftsmen, until the first Dead Queen destroyed it to punish the humans who lived here."

Ellyll must have been a massive city. Ruins stretch out to the left and right of us, running parallel to the Spires as far as the eye can see. The roots of massive trees hold some structures partially in place, but most buildings deteriorated completely.

"If the first Dead Queen was so monstrous, why do you serve the reigning one?" Hunter eyes Tristan with suspicion.

Tristan ignores the question. "Come on," he says, marching forward. "The trees at the foot of the Spires mark the start of Annwyn. We're nearly there." He nods toward the distance where the mountain forest meets the valley on the other side of Ellyll.

We weave through the skeletal remains of the once-great city, finding most pathways blocked by trees or piles of stone. I can almost see it, the bustling life that once existed here. People living without the constant threat of war. Living with fae magic that no one alive can comprehend.

We pass by a carved, stone temple with columns almost completely covered in vines. This time, I recognize the moon goddess and her wolves, carved into the old stone. Even pockmarked and faded, the wild abandon of the old goddess sends a thrill through me.

Tristan leads us as straight north as he can with all the obstacles in our path. When we finally reach the crumbled wall at the edge of the city, we climb over a section that's reduced to piles of pebbles. Before us, at the foot of the mountain, is a narrow valley speckled with more giant boulders. Beyond that, the tree line marks the border into Annwyn.

It's so close, I can almost smell the northern wilds carried on the breeze.

"We've made it," Hunter says, almost as if he was afraid we wouldn't.

"Not yet." Tristan trudges forward, heading across the valley. "I need to touch Annwyn soil." He gives me a pointed look.

I roll my eyes and scramble over the last of the city's ruins.

Somewhere ahead, a long, shrill whistle pierces the air. We stop in our tracks, freezing like mice at the cry of a hawk. Dread floods my veins, thick and cold.

One by one, copper-clad knights step out from behind the boulders scattered across the valley, blocking our path to the forest at the foot of the mountains. Blocking our way to Annwyn. Archers climb up nearby boulders and draw arrows, ready to shoot us if we attempt to escape.

We've walked straight into a trap.

A towering figure in gleaming armor rides out from behind a stone outcropping. Even without the decorations on his horse's saddle, I'd recognize him anywhere. The haughty sneer, the upturned chin, the disapproving glare—Commander Malen. Hunter's father.

He whistles again, sharp and high. Then he turns to watch as more soldiers pour out from behind the far end of the ruined city walls. My father isn't taking any chances this time.

I glance at Hunter. His jaw is tight, his teeth grinding. One hand hovers near the sword at his hip.

Malen sighs theatrically at us. "How disappointing."

Hunter steps forward, placing me a few feet behind him. "One would think you'd be used to disappointment when looking at me, Father." His voice is strong, confident. But I can see the way his fingers tremble at his side. Nothing can scare a grown man like his angry father.

Malen scowls. "Surrender now, and perhaps the king will show mercy."

Tristan scoffs beside us, his voice low and bitter. "Sounds

highly unlikely." He turns to Commander Malen. "How did you even find us? There are hundreds of miles of borderland."

Malen nods, considering. "We were lucky enough to happen upon a woman with three, filthy brats on the main road. Riding some rather familiar-looking horses from the royal stable."

Tristan groans, shooting Hunter a murderous glare.

"Once we told them the crime for stealing royal horses was punishable by death, they were more than happy to tell us about the three fugitives they met off-trail in Korrigan Forest. The Wolf, the knight, and the maiden were heading straight for Ellyll. So, we took the main roads to get here before you did."

"You'd stoop so low as to threaten to execute children?" Hunter's voice is venomous.

Malen's eyebrows raise. "Actually execute?" he pauses, considering. "Possibly. If I believed the crime were truly committed. There's no use in permitting child thieves to grow up and become adult thieves."

"They weren't thieves," Hunter says.

Tristan waggles his head noncommittally.

Hunter narrows his eyes at him. "At least, they didn't steal from the king."

"No, they didn't," Malen says lightly. "You did." The silence that followed is thick with threats. He continues, "But I'm not concerned with the petty theft of horseflesh. I'm here to see justice served for crimes against the king."

I laugh. "And what crimes were those? Refusing to be murdered by a tyrant?"

Malen shrugs. "It hardly matters what I think."

I glance at Hunter, his grip on his sword tightens. His voice is firm. "I won't let you take them."

"*Let* me?" His father tilts his head, like it was a curious thing to say. "I doubt there's much you can do about it." He raises an eyebrow. "You've always been the poorest student in the classroom. Barely scraping by. Dragging our good name through the mud." He shakes his head. "You are no son of mine." He spits at the ground.

Even now, Hunter flinches.

I step forward and put a hand on Hunter's arm. "You've always been a better man than him. He's a fool if he can't see it."

Hunter doesn't say anything in response.

"Still listening to the Little Fox, I see." His father leans forward on his horse. "She's always been a bad influence."

"You'd better watch your tongue," I hiss. "Speaking about the heir to Llwyn like that."

He just laughs. "*Former*, my girl. Former heir to Llwyn. And a thorn in the king's side since the day you were born."

"At least I was a true-born heir," I snap. "Unlike the boy your people are passing off as my brother."

This gets a reaction out of him. His cool-headed mask falls. Doubtless he thought his ruse was still a secret. He sits up, his face growing dark. "What do you know of anything beyond storybooks and borderland camps?"

I smile the most sinister grin I can manage. "A lot more than you'd like, I'd wager."

Next to me Hunter grabs my wrist. "Don't, Sienna. He lashes out when he's angry."

Tristan leans into the huddle. "He's already angry."

"Well goading him never helps," Hunter snaps.

"I'm waiting," his father calls. "Come quietly, or we will have to use force."

All around us, archers draw their bowstrings and soldiers unsheathe bronze swords.

Tristan's eyes meet mine, urgency blazing. Hunter's lips tighten into a thin line. He nods, a silent understanding forming between them. Then he draws his sword and steps forward, facing his father with a stance I'm sure he's practiced a thousand times in the training yard.

"We will not."

"Wonderful," Malen says flatly. "We've travelled too far from the palace to go back without a little fun." He nods to his men and they begin inching toward us.

"Run," Hunter says to me, bracing himself for the fight.

"Not without you." Panic rises in my chest.

He doesn't take his eyes off the approaching enemy. "I love you, Sienna. Let me do this for you."

Tristan grabs my hand, pulling, but I can't leave my only friend.

"Hunter, no. Come with us!"

"You *will* have a crown someday." Hunter's eyes burn with intensity. "And I'll do my part to get it for you." He turns and charges toward the oncoming soldiers.

In a flash, our world turns black with shadow. I blink several times before I realize Tristan blanketed us in darkness. I can't see Hunter anymore. I can barely see a foot in front of me. Beyond the shadows, I hear the clang of swords and the whoosh of arrows as archers shoot toward us.

"Let's go," Tristan says urgently.

"No!" I turn and push him full in the chest, but he doesn't budge. An arrow pierces the ground, barely a foot away from my boot.

"This shadow won't last forever, Red. We leave, now!" He grabs my arm and I wrench it free in my attempt to run toward Hunter, to help him.

With unrestrained strength, the Wolf picks me up and throws me over his broad shoulder.

"Put me down!" I pound on his back with my fists.

He only holds me tighter as he runs in the wrong direction.

Over the clash of metal and pounding footsteps, I hear Hunter's voice. "Take care of her, Tristan!"

Tristan sprints toward the city ruins with me kicking and screaming. True to his word, the further we run from the fight, the more the shadow dissipates. At the crumbling wall, he skids to a halt and drops me to my feet.

"I need you to run, Red. You understand?"

My eyes keep searching for Hunter in the chaos behind us.

Tristan grabs my chin roughly, forcing me to look at him. "If you can't focus, they'll kill you."

"But Hunter—"

"Will die for nothing if you don't escape."

Tears prick my eyes, but I know he's right. I nod.

As we scramble up the city wall, I can't help but glance back one last time. My heart sinks. The shadow is little more than whisps of smoke now. Hunter is surrounded, fighting the knights who used to be his brothers. It's a losing battle and we all know it. But that's not the point. Hunter, with his noble sensibilities and courageous heart, is sacrificing himself so that Tristan and I have a chance to escape.

"Focus!" Tristan yells. His hand clamps around my wrist.

"But we can't leave him!"

"Yes, we can." His eyes bore into mine. "And we *will*."

A soldier catches up to us and Tristan swings his bronze sword. The man falls over the side of the wall and his armor makes a sickening crunch on the rubble below. The sound of battle fades behind us as we plunge deeper into the ruinous labyrinth of Ellyll.

"In here." Tristan practically pushes me through a narrow alley hidden by tree roots and overgrown bushes. We crouch low, trying to catch our breath. The sound of clanking armor grows louder, then fainter as soldiers run past.

Now that I have a moment to think, to breathe, a sudden fury ignites in me. We were so close! I can't give up now. I draw my knife from the ankle of my boot. In the span of a breath, I whirl on Tristan, pushing him into the stone wall, my silver blade at his chest.

After the momentary shock, he lets out a low laugh. "Here we are again, Red. Isn't this how we met?"

"Tell me," I demand, pressing my blade higher, up toward his throat. "I held up my end of the bargain. I got you to the border." I nod toward the mountain. "You saw it with your own eyes."

"Saw," he repeats. "I have not stepped on Annwyn soil yet, as you recall."

"Tell me!" Tears of desperation prickle at the corners of my eyes.

The Wolf stares at me for a long moment. "No."

My face twists in rage. "You promised you'd tell me what happened to my grandmother if I helped you escape. You promised!" I bang on his chest with my fist.

"I promised I'd tell you what I know." Tristan says. He leans in toward my ear. "All I know is she's dead and the queen knows who killed her."

Numbness crystalizes over me like ice. "So, it *was* murder." My voice is frail. I knew it was true. Deep in my core, I *knew* Grandmother's death wasn't an accident. Fury blazes anew in my chest. I was right all along.

My gaze travels back up to the Wolf's cold, gray eyes.

"Come with me," he says.

The bluntness of his request catches me off guard. "What?"

He grabs my hand on his chest. "Come with me, Red. If you stop now, here, at the edge of the border, you'll never know the truth. Someone out there does."

I scoff. "In Annwyn."

His eyes don't flicker away from mine for even an instant. "Yes, in Annwyn."

"I can't." Even as I say it, I'm not exactly sure why. It's foolhardy. It's forbidden. It's walking straight into enemy territory with nothing but a single Wolf to protect me.

And yet. I've already destroyed my entire life here in Llwyn. My father tried to murder me, then made a false son his new heir. I have no one left. Even as the thought crosses my mind, Hunter's face flickers to the front. I've ruined his life too.

"You've wanted this for years." Tristan whispers. "You won't stop now. Not when you're so close."

He's right, and I hate that he is. I can't give up now. The Wolf has only known me a little over a month, and somehow, he already sees straight through me.

My mouth forms a thin, determined line. I nod only once, but it's enough.

He pushes my knife away from his chest, satisfied. "We need to keep moving."

We step out of the shadows, our footsteps quiet against the broken stone. Tristan moves west through the ruins, past collapsed fountains and ivy-choked courtyards. Some inner walls, still sheltered from sun and rain, hold faint traces of old paint. Faded frescoes depict once-great men and women locked in scenes from centuries past. Their faces watch us, like ghosts of families and lives long forgotten.

Someone blocks the path ahead. Two soldiers step out, swords raised. Tristan moves back, lifting his own blade in defense. They strike first. Metal clashes as he parries, blocks, then parries again.

I've never seen him fight like this before. He's graceful and deeply intimidating, pushing forward with the relentless energy and skill of a trained swordsman. The Dead Queen's Wolves must train with more than just their dark shadow powers.

One soldier lunges for me. I twist out of his reach and

flash my knife, knowing it won't do much against full armor, but I slash anyway. I won't be dragged back to my father's palace of horrors. I'm going to find out who murdered Grandmother. I'm too close to fail now.

The soldier grabs the fabric of my red hood and yanks, knocking me backward. I hit the ground hard, my knife skidding out of reach. Before I can recover, he's on top of me, pinning my arms down with his knees. He fumbles for a rope, trying to bind my wrists as I twist and buck, but he's too heavy. I try to reach inside for my power—a spark, a flicker, anything—but all I find is emptiness.

Suddenly, he drops the rope with a cry of pain. His body curls inward, and he lets out a gut-wrenching groan. I shove him off of me, and this time he doesn't resist. He collapses to the side, clutching his head. I scramble to my feet and grab my knife in one swift motion.

I turn to see Tristan, eyes blazing with hatred, black power crackling in his hands. His soldier is writhing on the ground too.

"We have to keep moving!" I hiss. More soldiers will find us any second. We can't waste time torturing these two. A beat passes before Tristan releases the soldiers from his power. We keep running.

The ruins twist into a maze of obstacles. We weave around collapsed walls and leap over gnarled roots, our movements driven by instinct. My lungs burn, but I don't slow down.

Tristan's voice cuts through the chaos. "Don't stop, Red!"

I risk a glance back. Half a dozen soldiers are gaining on us, Commander Malen at the front, his eyes burning with fury. The knights move in unison, their heavy footfalls pounding the earth behind us.

We vault over the crumbling remains of Ellyll's ancient wall and burst back into the open valley, exposed and vulnerable. Overhead, the sky is darkening into twilight, the sky aflame with orange and pink. Dozens of soldiers clamor behind us, but I don't look back again.

I stumble. Gravel bites into my knees and scrapes my palms bloody. The Wolf turns back and reaches for my hand. The moment his skin touches mine, our eyes lock. Where I expected to see fear, I find a storm instead. His eyes are the fierce, roiling gray of a tempest.

My heart leaps into my throat as an undeniable heat rises within me. Here, on the edge of death, time seems to hold its breath. I was a fool for not seeing this sooner. The Wolf isn't fighting for me because I saved him in Caerwen. His protection has nothing to do with some Wolf code of honor. And he isn't risking his life for mine because his queen expects him to.

He's protecting me because he *cares* about me.

Suddenly, Tristan pulls me to my feet and shoves me ahead of him. "Keep going, Red. Find the queen."

With his eyes still locked on mine, a thick, black mist engulfs him. Like a surging shadow, it surrounds the soldiers. They cry out in alarm and confusion.

Before I can turn to run, rough hands grab me from behind.

Then, the world goes black.

Chapter 30

I COME BACK to consciousness slowly. My arms are pinned behind my back, tied with rough rope that bites into my wrists. A flickering light hurts my eyes and I squint until they adjust.

Night has fallen. An enormous bonfire blazes a few yards away, its sparks rising like fireflies. Scattered throughout the field, orbs of light glow around the knights with noble blood, those who inherited light power.

We're in the shadow of the Spires, less than half a mile from the Annwyn border. The sight makes my chest ache. *So close.* We're so close, I want to scream at the injustice of it all. All around me, soldiers stand at attention, listening intently to Commander Malen.

I do a quick assessment, moving my body slowly, limb by limb. No broken bones or severe lacerations. I can breathe without pain in my ribs and I'm fully clothed. But one thing is horribly wrong.

My moth necklace is gone.

I scan my surroundings, searching for Tristan, but he's nowhere to be found. Some small part of me is relieved, but it's short-lived. Hunter sits, tied up a few feet away. His face is a mass of bruises, pulverized by his father's men. His copper gauntlets are missing, and there's a look of despair in his eyes when they meet mine.

"Sienna ..." he whispers through bloody lips. A soldier silences him with a rough shove.

The rope scrapes my wrists as I struggle to sit up.

"Ah," Hunter's father turns toward us, his orb of light illuminating his face. "The false heir awakens."

"Where's Tristan?" I demand, as if I still have any power here whatsoever.

"Who?" Commander Malen scrunches his face in disgust. "Oh, you mean the Wolf. He probably ran off to his den in the wilderness by now. It hardly matters." He stands before me. "*You* are who we came here for." He flicks his head toward his son. "Hunter was just a bonus."

"What a doting father," I say, trying to unnerve him.

"You know, I don't think I am." He pauses. "I was once. Before he turned out to be such a disgrace. Always holed up in that musty old library, filling his head with fantasies instead of playing with swords like real men do. I practically begged the king to make him one of his Guards." He winces in disgust, like the memory still hurts him.

Hunter's shoulders slump.

My blood roars in my ears. It infuriates me to see him like this. "Any man would be proud to have a son like him."

"He's no longer my son." Malen snaps. "And you," he lowers his eyes at me. "Are no longer the heir to the Fox Throne. Your father sent us to fetch you, to make sure you face proper punishment."

"I think you mean 'execution'," I say. "He doesn't want two potential heirs floating around, muddying the succession."

Malen shrugs. "Call it what you wish." He walks to one of

his men and holds out his hand expectantly. The soldier passes Hunter's copper gauntlets and sword.

Beside me, I feel Hunter still.

"These are soiled," Malen says, inspecting them in the flickering firelight. "Ruined at the hands of an unloyal King's Guard." He walks up to Hunter and holds them out for him to see. "You thought you could have the best of both worlds. A knight's respect and none of the responsibility."

He tuts. Then, quick as a striking adder, he turns and hurls the sword and gauntlets into the fire.

"No!" Hunter tries to lunge forward, but his father shoves him back down. He lands hard in the dirt, his hands still bound behind him. Firelight dances in his wide, disbelieving eyes.

As the bonfire blazes, the dented copper begins to glisten, then melt, dripping into the coals.

"You play a good knight, but you've always been unworthy," Commander Malen says. "And now you're a criminal."

For one brief moment, I think I see genuine grief in his eyes. It's gone before I can be sure, replaced by the stoicism of a man ruled by ambition and greed. He shakes his head, as if clearing it from bittersweet memories. Then he pulls something out from where it's tucked into the waist of his armor. A moth dangles from a thin, silvery chain.

Grandmother's necklace.

"Did you think I wouldn't recognize this?" he asks, voice low. "She wore it around the palace every day, chin high, like she thought she was better than the rest of us. Like she was some kind of queen." He spits. "She wasn't even noble born. She was a traitor."

The silver moth swings from the chain in his hand. For several long moments, the only sound is the crackle of the fire.

Then, a roar echoes throughout the valley.

Every soldier looks up in alarm. As one, we stare toward the forest at the edge of the valley, where trees are shrouded in shadows cast by the mountains beyond.

At first, what moves between the trees appears to be an illusion. Mist seeps out from the forest, curling around tree trunks and cascading over rocks. White, luminescent eyes blaze in the dark.

"No ..." a soldier behind me whispers, his voice thick with dread.

A silent army of corpse beasts emerges from the forest, illuminated by the light of the full moon.

An enormous bear with jagged, yellow teeth steps out first. Its ribs protrude through its matted fur making it appear malformed, as if drawn by a severely disturbed child. Wolverines follow. Their long claws drag on the ground and festering wounds cover their bodies. A giant elk appears in the mist with an unnaturally large number of points on his antlers. It walks on broken limbs that bow with each step, bone piercing through blackened flesh.

Then, the wolves arrive. Dozens of them.

The great beasts slather and twitch as if held back by some invisible power. Their glowing, white eyes lock onto us, eager to rip us to shreds. I wonder if this all-consuming fear is what grandmother felt in her final moments.

I just hope the dead kill quickly.

Trailing behind them, almost invisible in the shadows, are two figures. One is unmistakably Tristan. Relief makes my limbs weak. But then, I notice the other figure and a chill runs down my spine. She is tall and unnaturally thin. She wears a midnight-black gown, her face obscured by a dark hood. Tristan stands several steps behind her in deference and I know, deep in my gut, who that woman is.

The Dead Queen.

The beasts wait at the edge of the forest, mist swirling at their feet. Every living thing in the valley has stilled. We hold our breath, waiting to see what will happen. The dread is so thick it glues us in place, like mud around an open grave.

Beside me, one soldier begins to hyperventilate. "They won't come here," he says. "This is Llwyn territory. They wouldn't dare."

But they would. I've seen it before.

The hooded figure raises a black-gloved hand in front of her obscured face and exhales a short puff of air. Smoke, as thick and black as midnight, billows out from her breath. The undead beasts charge toward us at impossible speeds.

I steel my spine for what's to come.

The smoke reaches us a heartbeat before the beasts do, swallowing every orb of light, even the roaring bonfire. The knights at the front of the line scream first. Their terror is all the more awful in the dark. I'm afraid that horrible noise will be the last thing I hear before I die.

The smoke doesn't linger. It slowly dissolves to expose chaos illuminated by the bright, full moon. Corpse wolves tear at the bodies of men as they try to crawl away. Wolverines slice through metal armor with their unnaturally long claws as maggots wiggle through their dead flesh, falling to the ground at their feet.

To my left, I hear pounding hooves. I turn my head to see the elk charging right at me, its many points sharp as knives. I roll away just in time, my hands still tied behind my back. The elk tilts its enormous, decaying head down and impales a knight. Blood spurts over the beast's antlers, but it keeps running, the knight still screaming.

I shut my eyes, trying to forget the look of pain and terror on the man's face. Straining backward, I reach for the moth knife still tucked inside my boot. My fingertips brush the cool silver as the rope bites into my wrists. Slowly, I ease it free. It slips from my boot and falls to the ground. Twisting to the side, I grab it behind my back. Sweat beads on my skin as I try to ignore the carnage and screams echoing around me. I can barely hold the knife behind me, but I drag the blade back and forth in small, scraping movements. It's agonizingly slow, but finally, I feel the fibers give way.

"Sienna!"

My head snaps up. Hunter is a few feet away, his wrists still bound. I crawl to him and start sawing through his bindings. As soon as he's free, he grabs a fallen spear from the ground.

We run, weaving between men locked in battle with beasts. Bronze swords flash, but they're no match for teeth and claws. On top of a boulder, an archer aims at us—until a corpse wolf crashes into him, sending his arrow harmlessly into the sky.

We sprint toward the safety of Ellyll, but a figure leaps into our path, sword swinging. Hunter ducks just in time to avoid a killing blow, then whirls around, spear raised.

It's Commander Malen. He's lost his helmet, but his copper-plated armor still gleams in the firelight. My grandmother's silver moth swings from a chain around his neck. His breath comes in ragged bursts through clenched teeth.

"This ends now!" he shouts, leveling his silver-and-copper sword at his son. The blade glints in the shifting light.

Hunter doesn't move. He stands his ground, spear still aimed at his father.

Commander Malen takes slow steps in our direction. "You let that whore ruin everything I've built!" Spit flies from his mouth as he shouts at Hunter. Whatever control he once held has shattered. I've never seen a man so completely unhinged.

"Don't ever call her that!" Hunter's eyes are dark with fury.

"If you hadn't been born—if you hadn't been so besotted

with her—none of this would have happened!" Malen snarls. His eyes are wild. Not afraid, but enraged.

"If you weren't so blinded by greed and ambition, you'd see that none of this is our fault," Hunter fires back. "The king is corrupt. You're a smart man. You must know that."

Malen lets out a dry laugh. "And what does that matter?" He gives Hunter a condescending look, like he's scolding a child. "As long as we come out on top, what happens to the rest of them is irrelevant. This is war, Hunter, not some child's storybook about rescuing damsels. There's no right and wrong. Only survival of the smartest, the strongest, the most powerful." His sword trembles in his hand. "You're blinded by a pretty face." He spits at Hunter's feet.

Hunter doesn't flinch. He holds his spear steady, his eyes locked on his father. "I love her."

Malen barks a bitter laugh and gives a mocking bow. "Spoken like a true hero." He turns slowly, shifting the tip of his sword from Hunter to me.

Hunter stiffens. "Don't."

"Or what?" Malen asks, his voice sharp with challenge. "You'll stab me?" He sneers. "I've known you your entire life, son. You have no spine. You're weak." Malen shakes his head slowly. "And I am done with both of you."

Malen charges toward me just as Hunter raises his spear, ready to throw—but he doesn't get the chance.

The corpse bear barrels between us.

I leap aside a heartbeat before it would have trampled me.

Commander Malen is not so lucky. The corpse bear slams into him with its massive head—more skull than muzzle—knocking him flat. He lets out a startled sound, his eyes going wide as he stares up at the towering beast. But he doesn't have time to fight back.

The bear swipes, its claws slicing clean through his armor.

Blood spills from the gashes in his chest. It pools beneath him like a mountain spring. As he gasps for air, more blood bubbles out of his mouth. For the briefest moment, his gaze flickers to Hunter. I almost think I see regret there, words left unsaid.

Then the corpse bear crushes his skull in a single bite.

Hunter stands frozen, eyes wide, as a dead creature eats his father alive. But we can't stay here. We can't wait for the bear to turn on us.

I grab Commander Malen's fallen sword from the ground and a flash of silver catches my eye. Grandmother's moth necklace glimmers in the trampled grass. I snatch that up too, then seize Hunter's arm.

"Hunter."

He turns to me, still in shock.

"I'm sorry, but we can't ..." I press his father's sword into his hands.

He takes it with trembling fingers. It's more ornate than his melted King's Guard blade. The pommel is shaped like a copper fox's face, its eyes set with rubies. The crossguard curves into the fox's tail, its tip dipped in silver. It's the sword of a man who did everything to claw his way into the king's good graces. It's the sword of a man who is now dead because of it.

Hunter's grip tightens. His eyes burn with new resolve.

Together, we run.

Around us, the battle has turned into a twisted dance of shadow and blood. The bonfire has spilled over and a blaze rapidly consumes the dried autumn grasses of the valley. Smoke billows up into the sky, the fire greedy in its hunger to burn. The fire illuminates the carnage that surrounds us. Men, gaping, bleeding, dead. Corpse wolves with gore on their maws search for their next target. One spots me. Its white eyes reflect the inferno around us.

"Keep running!" Hunter yells, snapping back into survival mode. He stands with his father's sword at the ready.

"No, Hunter!"

The corpse wolf snarls in a low, haunting rumble. As if it delights in drawing out the torture. As if it enjoys the taste of mounting fear.

"I love you, Sienna." Hunter steels his gaze on the corpse wolf. "This is not how you die." He runs toward the creature.

"Hunter!" My voice is high, hysterical with fear.

The corpse wolf sprints—faster than anything with broken legs and rotting sinew should be able to. Hunter slides to the ground just as the corpse wolf lunges toward me. He swings his sword upward, the blade slicing, spraying blackened, fetid blood across the grass.

Then, from behind a wall of fire, another wolf emerges, its milky eyes locking onto mine. I turn and run.

The creature charges after me. I can't fight it with just a knife. My power is still empty, burned out by the wraiths. I search wildly through the chaos for any escape. Up ahead, a narrow gap between two boulders is my only shot.

With barely a second to spare, I dive for it, squeezing through the tight crevice. The wolf snaps at my heels, its teeth tearing through the hem of my red cloak. I shove myself deeper into the rocks, panting, as the wolf snarls and lunges. Its hot, putrid breath washes over my face as it tries to reach me.

Suddenly, there's a loud thwack and the creature falls to the ground. For several seconds, I stare at its white eyes and unmoving jaws before I realize someone is yelling for me.

"Red! Red, hurry!"

A familiar hand reaches into the crack to help me out. I grab it, stepping on the corpse wolf's head as I crawl out from between the rocks. When I emerge, I see Tristan. Sweat drips down his temples and there's blood smeared across his cheek.

"Tristan?"

"Are you alright?" The blazing fire reflects in his eyes. He's lost his fox sword, but he's clearly improvised. At his feet lies the corpse wolf, its head severed cleanly from its body by an axe still buried in its neck.

I nod. "I'm fine." Several yards behind him, a wolverine feasts on a man's internal organs. "How did you ...?" I can't stop staring at the beheaded wolf. "Can you kill what's already dead?"

"It's their one weakness," Tristan says. "Severing the spine."

I nod, like that makes any sense at all. In a world where the dead can rise, what's a little severing of the spine?

Tristan's expression turns grave. "It's now or never."

Annwyn. This is our one chance to reach the trees at the base of the Spires and cross into enemy territory. I hesitate, scanning the chaos for any sign of Hunter. When I turn back to Tristan, he shakes his head slowly. We can't wait. I know this in my bones, but it doesn't make it less painful.

I follow him, weaving through boulders and rubble. We pass the chaos of dying men and undead creatures, all illuminated by uncontrollable fire. Finally, we make it to the edge of the valley. The shadowed trees are just ahead when a voice cuts through the air, calling my name.

I freeze. Tristan notices and turns back, urgently waving me forward.

"Red! What are you doing? We're nearly there!"

That's when we both see him.

Hunter.

Gone is the clean-cut boy in gleaming copper armor. He's limping after us, pain etched into every line of his bruised face. He's filthy, caked in dirt and blood, some of it likely not his. More drips from a gash at his temple. He looks nothing like the boy I grew up with. The boy I loved before the world ruined me.

And yet—he's never looked more beautiful.

"What are you doing?!" he yells.

It takes me a moment to realize he isn't talking to me.

"I told you to protect her, not kidnap her!" His face is lit with a rage I've never seen before. He steps nose to nose with Tristan, who stands there coolly, as if Hunter had simply asked whether he takes sugar in his tea.

"He isn't *taking* me." I wedge myself between them. "I'm going by my own free will."

"Into Annwyn territory? Have you lost your mind?" He gestures wildly toward the blood-drenched battlefield behind us, where the dead still feast and fires burn.

That's when I realize—the Dead Queen is gone. She sent her monsters after us and then vanished, slipping back into the veil of shadow and mist.

Hunter points toward the valley, where flames have reached the last of the city walls and screams echo through the smoke. "They have more of those monsters in there!"

Tristan cuts in calmly. "There are monsters everywhere."

"Shut up, Wolf!" Hunter snaps.

For a moment, it looks like Tristan might argue, but one glance at my expression and he shuts his mouth.

"Hunter," I say, trying to reason with him. "That's a risk I have to take."

His shoulders slump. "You were just going to leave me? Again?"

"I have to."

He shakes his head slow and disbelieving. "No, Sienna. You really don't." His voice shifts. "I can take care of you! We can make a life together, without Foxes and Wolves and everything that's in-between." He reaches for my hand, but I take a step back.

"I can't," I whisper. "Deep down, you must know that."

He scrubs his hands over his face in frustration. Then he takes a breath and looks at me, voice tight with anguish. "Is this about what I did?"

"No, Hunter. I—"

"How long are you going to punish me for one, stupid mistake?"

"Mistake?" A hot coal of anger sparks in my chest. "It wasn't a simple *mistake*." I stare at him, wide-eyed. "You betrayed me. To *my father*."

Out of the corner of my eye, I notice Tristan wince.

Hunter's face crumples. "I didn't know, Sienna. How could I have known what he would do?" His voice is pleading, but I'm not ready—or perhaps not willing—to forgive.

"You know my father as well as I do. And you chose *him*."

"I didn't mean to."

"So, you *didn't* tell my father that I was searching for information about Grandmother? After he explicitly told me not to?"

"I ... yes, but ..." Hunter shakes his head. "It wasn't like that."

Tristan watches in silence, but I see the tension in his stance. His eyes keep darting toward the burning valley behind us and what remains of the battle.

"No? What was it like then?" I fold my arms. "What was it like to watch him burn every last scrap of Grandmother's letters. All of her portraits. All of her books and gowns and gifts. *Everything* turned to ash." My voice cracks. "Everything, except the knife I hid under my skirts." A sob claws its way up my throat, but I swallow it down.

Tristan tries to grab my attention. "We *really* need to leave."

"I was afraid." Hunter's voice is almost pleading now. "I saw you sneaking out at night, alone ..."

"When I left you behind, you mean?"

Hunter flinches and I know I've hit the bone. He was jealous that I stopped spending every waking moment with him, that I was preoccupied with something—someone—other than him. He's always wanted to have all of my attention, all of my time. When I left him behind, he just couldn't bear it. So, he tried to claw me back to him, any way he could.

The tragic thing is, he knows me better than anyone. I've never been the kind of person you can tie down. He should've known clinging too hard just pushes me farther away. And he certainly should've known better than to use my father against me.

"Please, Sienna. You can't trust him." His eyes dart to Tristan.

Tristan steps in, his voice calm but firm. "She knows full well what she's doing." He nods toward the trees, his eyes locking on mine.

Hunter wheels around to face him. "I wasn't talking to you, Wolf!"

Tristan's nostrils flare "She doesn't need your permission."

Hunter pulls back and punches Tristan in the jaw. Even without his gauntlets, the crack if impact is startling. Tristan stumbles back, and falls to the ground, his eyes wide in genuine shock.

"YOU!" Hunter yells. "I *never* should have helped you. We should have left you there in the cemetery to rot!"

Tristan rises calmly, brushing dust from his breeches. "You can come with us."

"To Annwyn?" Hunter lets out a disbelieving laugh. "You're our *enemy*, Wolf. Annwyn killed her grandmother!"

I push between them again, holding my ground. "They know what happened to her, Hunter." I lift my chin, defiant.

"This is *my* choice. I'm not some ignorant girl running away without reason."

He glares at Tristan, then turns back to me.

"Grandmother," I say softly, my voice pleading. "She's the reason I'm going."

He shakes his head slowly, in disbelief. "You can't bring her back, Sienna."

His words hit me harder than a crack to the jaw ever could. "I know that," I whisper.

Hunter reaches for my hand. His voice is low, gentle. "When will this searching ever end? When will you be able to live your own life again?"

"I don't know." I shake my head, banishing the grief that threatens to consume me, even after all these years.

"Is she truly worth sacrificing your own life for?"

And there it is, the ever-haunting question. I've lived my entire life in the shadow of death—Grandmother's, the borderland soldiers', even my mother's. The truth is, I don't know how to live without them. Without the grief that's molded to my bones like a second skin. Without the dead, I am alone.

"Please," he whispers. "Stay."

Behind his eyes, I see all those years of pain and sadness. Of never truly belonging. We both know the feeling of isolation. Maybe that's why we ended up here, at the edge of the world. Adrift. Lost.

Hunter's face crumbles. "Is everything my fault?" he asks, barely audible.

The pain in his voice extinguishes my anger like water sizzling on hot coals. I put one of my filthy hands on his blood-smeared cheek. "Hunter, this isn't because of you."

His shoulders sag. "But everything is still in shambles."

I lean in, pressing my forehead to his. We close our eyes and breathe each other in—the closeness, the intimacy we've shared. He will forever be a part of me. I know this as surely as I know my own name.

I stand on tiptoe and kiss him. He winces from the pain, but doesn't pull away. His tears mix with mine, salty and devastating. When I draw back, he doesn't stop me. He keeps his eyes closed, as if he can't bear to watch me go.

"I'm sorry," I whisper, the memory of his lips still lingering on mine.

Then I turn and run into the mountain forest, with the sound of heartbreak and carnage at my heels.

CHAPTER 31

THE WEEKS SPENT TRAVELING through Llwyn did nothing to prepare me for the brutal climb through the Spires. Trees twist up rocky paths slick with rain. In some places, the slopes are stripped bare by punishing winds. Most of the leaves have fallen now, and the bitter cold chafes at my exposed skin. Even the mud puddles are coated in a thin layer of ice. Autumn is truly gone now.

Tristan remains a mostly silent companion, like a dark shadow leading me through this miserable landscape. He spends his days scouting ahead and his nights squinting up at the moon through the branches.

The searing pain in my legs and chest has faded, though the first few days of climbing were agony. Now, over a week into our mountain crossing, I may not move with the Wolf's grace, but at least I'm not slowing us down. Not much, anyway.

I reach for a branch to pull myself up a steep stretch of the path. It snaps in my hand, and I stumble—forward or upward, I can't quite tell at this angle.

Thunder rumbles off the mountain's face, and a sharp gust of wind makes me brace myself for the cold. As much as I detest this red cloak, I'm grateful for its warmth. Without it, I'd likely be dead by now.

Like Hunter probably is.

The thought feels like a stab to the gut, but it's nothing compared to the ache in my chest over losing my best friend. No, not losing. Abandoning. I left him on the edge of a mountain surrounded by unnatural beasts and a blazing inferno. And I did it after he saved me from certain death and helped me travel hundreds of miles with a fugitive.

I feel like the worst person alive. My father being a notable exception. I'm not sure I'm worthy of my grandmother's good name or her reputation. Maybe it's a mercy that she's dead, so she doesn't have to see me stoop so low.

"Do you need to stop?" Tristan asks, a few yards ahead of me.

I'm straining every single muscle in my body to climb this damnable mountain. Meanwhile, the Wolf prances ahead like we're on a relaxing stroll in the garden.

"No," I snap, regretting it the instant it's out of my mouth. I grab onto another branch to help pull me upward and onward. Even in the growing darkness, I can see the corners of his mouth turn up slightly. My foot slips on a patch of gravel and I fall onto my knees. I wince.

"You alright?" he calls, his tone clearly unworried.

I nod.

"There's something up here I want you to see."

All I can do is clench my jaw and nod at him from my spot in the mud. I can do this. I've already crossed an entire country, battled thieves and foxhounds and corpse wolves. I can handle a measly mountain range.

A white owl soars ahead of us, disappearing into the trees

beyond. These woods are quiet. In Korrigan Forest, the trees felt alive with creatures scuttling, crying out, and watching us constantly. Here, there's nothing but the wind in the branches above us. Somehow, nothing has harassed us on our journey through the mountains. But, then again, maybe no human or creature is foolish enough to make the crossing so late in the season.

Just when I think I can't take another step, I notice Tristan standing ahead, silhouetted against the stars. He's waiting for me at a clearing on top of a rocky outcropping.

My legs are wobbly underneath me when I step out onto the flat rock. He's right at the edge, clearly unafraid of falling. The wind howls a song I've never heard before, warning of the dangers of mountain peaks and a winter that's bound to start any day now. My hair blows wildly around my head and the red cloak flies out behind me. I inch closer to him at the edge of the cliff.

Tristan's face is pale in the moonlight. His eyes are closed as if savoring the icy wind on his skin. He looks ... calm. Even after everything we've been through. When I look away from his face and out beyond the cliff, I gasp.

We are standing at the edge of the world.

Spires, as far as the eye can see, are aglow in moonlight and shadow. Beyond them, stars. Billions of them. More stars than I ever knew existed. It's as if Annwyn isn't even under the same sky as Llwyn.

"It's ..." I'm at a loss for the correct word.

"Terrifying? Treacherous?" Tristan asks without looking at me.

I shake my head slowly, not wanting to blink and miss even a second of this view. It's as if the world has suddenly opened its soul wide before me, a vulnerable heart in a horrifying time.

"Majestic," I whisper, my word lost in the wind.

Tristan must hear me because he opens one eye to look at me curiously, then he lifts his hand to point toward the east. "There, look."

I squint against the darkness until I see what he's pointing at. In the distance is a dark slice of sea. And there, nestled upon a cliff, is a castle. It stands black against the silver moonlight. Even from this distance, I can see it's ancient, with leaning towers and sagging defense walls. It's little more than a shadowed ruin. But it's still magnificent.

"Gwyllion," Tristan says. "That's where we're headed. It's the current seat of the Dead Queen."

"It's crumbling."

"Everything is this far north. But it's not as ruinous as Ellyll."

"Yet."

Tristan nods, deep in thought.

A cloud slips across the moon, casting the castle in shadow, like a shroud pulled over the eyes of the dead.

"This is what he wants to take next," Tristan says quietly, beside me.

He doesn't have to tell me who *he* is.

The Wolf's mouth hardens into a grim line. "He'll destroy this place. Destroy everything in his path to get the queen."

I draw in a steady breath, then turn to him. "Then we won't let him."

Tristan looks unsure. His lips part like he wants to tell me something but can't.

Beneath my heel, the cliff's edge begins to crumble. Tristan reaches out to grab me, catching me before I slip. He pulls me against him, and for one breathless instant, we're chest to chest, his arm locked around my waist. It lasts only a second, and yet it stretches—an endless, suspended heartbeat.

In the hush that follows, the first snowflakes of winter

begin to fall. One lands on his cheek, and my gaze lifts to meet his. Our eyes lock. In this moment, I finally see what I've done to my life. I gave up everything—everyone—for the promises made by a steely-eyed Wolf. I am standing on a true precipice, and there is no turning back now.

He steps away, dropping his hands like they're on fire. It leaves me momentarily dizzy. Behind him, something catches my eye. A shadow moves against the gently falling snow.

"Tristan!" I gasp in shock.

Tristan turns around slowly, his eyes lingering on mine longer than they should. From beneath a twisted, ancient tree on the edge of the cliff, steps a tall, thin woman. She's wearing a black gown, her hood pulled low over her face. This close, I can see more of her than I wish to. Her lips are black with rot and dead skin peels away from the bone along her jaw, exposing some of her lower teeth.

Next to me, Tristan kneels in deference to his queen.

The dead woman speaks. "Have you found that which we seek?" Her voice rattles like dying breath.

My skin crawls as if it knows to be deeply afraid.

Tristan gives the Dead Queen a curt nod.

Her shrouded face turns toward me. While I can't see her eyes beneath her hood, I can feel them linger at the scar across my throat.

"She saved me from the Fox King," Tristan sounds almost defensive.

The woman tilts her head, her spine cracking with the movement. "How curious."

"She's the—" Tristan starts, but the queen interjects.

"The *true* heir to the Fox Throne, I know." She steps closer to me and I steel myself against the instinct to flee. "A fox is a curious creature. Solitary, not like wolves who live in packs. Foxes look out for themselves."

A large white moth emerges from the gloom beneath the

trees. It flutters against the wind and gently falling snow, straining to reach its target.

It shouldn't be alive in this cold. The realization strikes low and hard in my gut. No, of course it shouldn't be. And it isn't. My eyes follow the moth as it flutters around the Dead Queen, then lands on her shoulder. Its tattered wings open and close as it fights against the gale.

It's a sign. I square my shoulders, steeling myself for the battle ahead. I cannot lose. My entire life has led up to this moment.

"I require payment." I steady my voice. "Answers about a woman who died on the border many years ago."

The Dead Queen laughs ominously. "But there have been so many of those. I couldn't possibly know every dead woman in the borderlands."

"I think you knew her. Her name was Áine." My voice is iron, immovable. Uncompromising.

The Dead Queen pauses as if studying me from underneath her black hood. She shouldn't be able to see me from under there, but, then again, I don't know how dead eyes work.

"I think you're right," she says, finally. Her black-gloved hands reach up to pull back her hood, to look me directly in the eyes for the first time.

I've seen much horror in my life, from cruel kings to undead creatures made of nightmares. I've watched men die gruesome deaths and felt the breath of monsters on my neck.

But no horror has ever been as awful a sight as the Dead Queen's face.

It's not her white, opalescent eyes or the claw marks across her flesh that disturb me so. It's not the oozing wounds or the putrefied skin that send me reeling on hands and knees, sick and dizzy. No, her dead flesh doesn't frighten me. It's what's underneath.

I will recognize that woman until my dying day.

The Dead Queen takes off one black, silken glove and reaches toward me with a skeletal hand.

"I hear you've been searching for me, Granddaughter."

Also by Briar Knightly

Want to read more of the *Thrones of Ruin* series?

The Dead Queen

A reluctant heir. A deadly secret. A wolf who prowls the shadows of the Fox King's court.

In this dark fairytale retelling of Little Red Riding Hood, the line between predator and protector is as thin as a knife's blade.

(Thrones of Ruin, Book One)

The Fox Heir

A fae ruin. A dangerous wolf. An heir who must kill what's already dead.

Sienna escaped the Fox King, but there's more to fear than the Dead Queen in a kingdom haunted by curses that never die.

(Thrones of Ruin, Book 2)

Available now

Please consider leaving a review on Amazon or Goodreads

About the Author

Briar Knightly writes fantasy and romance. She is an award-winning author under a different pen name. When she's not working as a librarian, she spends her days writing, drinking tea, and pampering her giant cat. She lives in the Midwest.

Let's keep in touch!

You can find me on:

Instagram @Briar.Knightly
TikTok @BriarKnightly
BriarKnightly.com

Would you like to be the first to learn about new books, bonus content, and more?
Sign up for my newsletter!

Acknowledgments

To my family, thank you for being so patient with me every time I snuck away to work in my writing closet in the wee hours of the morning. And after bedtime. And on weekends when there were a million other things I should've been doing. You supported me through all of my harebrained schemes and fantastical ideas. I don't take that for granted.

Thank you so much to my beta readers! You all helped make The Dead Queen sizzle and shine: Chista Ghanaatgar, Holly Baker, Irina Thompson, Corinne Hoag, Terin Larkin, and the writers' group at my local public library.

Lastly, thank you to all the librarians and library workers out there. Preserving the right to read can be a thankless job. You are appreciated.

www.ingramcontent.com/pod-product-compliance
Lightning Source LLC
Chambersburg PA
CBHW050015120726
47903CB00006B/1777

* 9 7 9 8 9 9 9 7 8 5 7 1 8 *